Sins of
the Fathers

A.J. McCarthy

ISBN: 978-1-61296-966-4
PUBLISHED BY BLACK ROSE WRITING
www.blackrosewriting.com

Printed in the United States of America
Suggested Retail Price (SRP) $19.95

Sins of the Fathers is printed in Plantagenet Cherokee

I would like to dedicate my novel to my late father, Glen, who had no discernible sins, but who would have been very proud to read this story.

SINS OF THE FATHERS

Chapter 1:

Charlie took a fortifying breath and stared at the ceiling. She knew it would be finished soon, but it was never soon enough. She didn't understand why she hated it so much. A lot of people didn't seem to mind at all, many even claimed to enjoy it.

She heard a couple of grunts and a snort, and knew it was almost time. He was so predictable, like clockwork. They had been together for almost six years, and he wasn't very complicated. It was no surprise she found it so easy to interpret the signs.

The room was cramped and stuffy. A sliver of sunlight crept in through the window, fighting its way through the dust, and past a high stack of storage boxes. It wasn't a great space, but it was all she had.

When he whimpered and licked her foot, she knew he was ready.

'It's okay, Harley. I'm almost done,' she said. A pair of brown eyes focused on her hopefully.

She would open one more envelope, enter the bill into her computer, and put everything away for the day. Unfortunately, running a business called for days when she did her bookkeeping and paid bills, but she hated it all the same. She would rather be doing physical chores.

Under the beat-up desk, a slightly overweight pug turned in circles a couple of times and plopped back onto Charlie's feet. She knew he would be patient for only a few more minutes, until he would again hint it was time for their walk.

She picked up the next envelope, but before ripping it open, she gave it a second glance. It didn't look like her usual business mail, the paper being an expensive velum. The name Charlene Butler and her address were scrawled almost illegibly across the front.

Intrigued, she slid a handwritten, one-page sheet out of the envelope. Unable to help herself, she glanced to the bottom of the page, but there was no sign-off.

Shrugging, she read the short note.

Dear Charlene,

My name is Vincent. That name most likely means nothing to you. I wouldn't expect it to. You're a very busy woman and meet a lot of people in the course of a day. One more person wouldn't be noticed.

I've been watching you and I'm very impressed. You seem to be able to do many things at the same time. You must have had an interesting childhood. Did your parents raise you to be so independent and capable? Have you ever considered the concept of nature versus nurture? I would love to get together with you so we could discuss it, among other things.

You probably wouldn't be interested in spending time with a guy like me. You probably think you're above that.

Let's wait and see.

Charlie shivered despite the warmth of the office, glancing around the room as if expecting to see someone peeking from behind a box. This was beyond weird. Who was this guy? Did she have a stalker? First of all, who wrote real, handwritten letters these days? The art of letter-writing had been lost long ago, drowned by technology. Not that this was an artful letter by any stretch of the imagination, but it certainly wasn't in keeping with the e-mails and texts of today's generation.

Secondly, what was all that crap about being independent and capable? And nature versus nurture? He wanted to get together with her to have an existential conversation? Two strangers discussing the deeper meaning of life?

Charlie shook her head and set the letter aside. She knew she should toss it in the recycling bin, but she wanted to show it to Frank. Maybe he could shed light on the mystery.

Papers fluttered as she packed up her things and lowered the screen of her laptop. Grabbing the letter, she folded it and tucked it into the back pocket of her worn jeans. When Charlie stepped away from her chair, Harley roused himself and padded behind her to the door of the office, taking a few seconds to stretch his little beige body. She didn't tell him to stay behind. It was two o'clock in the afternoon. It was his time.

Behind the bar, Frank wiped the counter with a well-used rag. Charlie was certain she had the cleanest establishment in the entire city of Montreal. Frank always had a rag in his back pocket, and she swore he could catch a drop off someone's glass before it hit the dark mahogany counter.

'Hey, Frank. Not too busy, is it?'

He lifted a big shoulder in a shrug.

'About as busy as it'll get this time of day. What's up? You tired of paying bills?' he said with a teasing grin. She gave him a wry smile. Everyone knew she hated to sit behind a desk for hours on end, alone in an office. She was a people person and much preferred the company of her staff and customers.

'Yeah. I needed to stretch my legs.'

Contrary to what she said, Charlie settled onto one of the heavy, wooden bar stools as Harley took his usual position on the floor next to her.

'You know anyone by the name of Vincent?'

The smooth, ebony skin of Frank's forehead creased.

'Vincent? I went to high school with a guy named Vincent, but that's it. Nobody recently.'

Charlie gazed absentmindedly at the line of bottles on the wall behind Frank and caught a glimpse of herself in the mirror, her face almost as pale as the reflection of the white walls behind her. She looked younger than her thirty-two years. Her dark brown hair was tied back in a haphazard ponytail, and her face was free of make-up. She never bothered fixing herself up until later in the afternoon, when people came in for after-work drinks.

'Why're you asking? Somebody hassling you?'

Ever since he started working for Charlie five years earlier, Frank took it upon himself to be her protector. Despite Charlie's efforts to convince him otherwise, he was sure she needed someone to watch over her. Her gaze slid over the deep scar on his bicep, half-hidden by the sleeve of his t-shirt. It was a physical reminder of what he had suffered trying to defend his little sister when he was fifteen and she was twelve. The instinct to protect was ingrained in him from an early age, and Charlie admitted it came in handy to have a six-foot-four man with perfectly-toned muscles standing behind her when some guy decided to get overly friendly.

She smiled in an effort to put Frank at ease.

'I got a letter in the mail from a guy named Vincent. He sounds harmless enough.'

He laid his hand, palm up, on his treasured counter.

'Let's see it.'

The folded paper looked inoffensive as she set it in his hand, and she wondered if she should have kept it to herself. She didn't like upsetting Frank, but she appreciated his input. His instincts were sharp for his relatively young age of twenty-five.

His face remained expressionless as he read the letter, but when he handed it back to her his lips turned up in a small smile.

'You're right. He sounds harmless. Weird, but harmless. I'll keep a lookout for a dweeb following you around.'

He leaned over the counter and looked toward the floor.

'Eh, Harley, you and me, we'll take care of her, won't we?'

The dog looked up at Frank and his mistress with a worried expression. Charlie laughed.

'Thanks. I knew I could count on you guys.'

Frank Hill had worked for Charlie at the bar part-time while he studied at Concordia University. Right out of the gate, their personalities had meshed. He was as hard-working, dependable, and fiercely loyal as Charlie. A year ago, he graduated with a degree in Communications. As far as Charlie knew, Frank hadn't looked for a job in his chosen field of study. Truth be told, she was afraid to ask him about it because of what the answer may be. If she lost Frank, she would lose her right arm.

Charlie slid off the stool and went behind the bar to grab a leash and a roll of doggie poop bags, and as she squeezed by, she gave Frank's arm an affectionate pat. Harley showed his customary enthusiasm at the idea of a walk, and within a few moments, they were out on the street.

Frank's laid-back attitude to the letter eased Charlie's mind. It could be a college guy responding to a dare. There were a lot of McGill and Concordia students who came into the pub on a regular basis, often trying to show off in front of each other and flirting with Charlie. Even though she was at least ten years older than most of them, they found her attractive enough to give it a try. She could generally head them off with a few well-chosen words. If not, an elbow often did the trick.

The breeze felt cool on her exposed neck, and Harley lifted his flat, black nose, breathing in the scent of the fresh spring air. Charlie put the letter out of her mind for now. They walked along Drummond Street to René-Lévesque, leading them to a park on the other side of Peel. Charlie gazed at the many monuments and the stately Sun Life Building overlooking the park as Harley sniffed and snorted, diligently searching for the perfect spot to do his business. When it was over, Charlie tugged on his leash, and the two set off for a walk around the block.

What could have been a brisk walk was hampered by the many shopkeepers and other regulars who stepped outside to take advantage of the sunny day. Harley, always a sucker for attention, stopped to be petted, and in many cases, given a special treat. Since Charlie took the dog to work with her every day, and they routinely walked the same route, he was a well-known and popular sight in this area of downtown Montreal.

Charlie had been born and raised in the neighborhood, and she loved it. Most of all, she loved the diversity of Montreal. Conversation switched freely between French and English, often being a mix of the two. The variety of cultures, races, beliefs, and traditions contributed to the vibrancy of the city. And, like most big cities, the neighborhoods segued smoothly from one distinct personality to another.

Woman and dog made it back to Butler's Pub in time to get ready for the first of the late-afternoon customers. Even on Tuesdays, they drew a steady crowd, something Charlie credited partly to the combination of an Irish pub with a sports bar. It had the warmth of mahogany furnishings for the traditionalists, and the TV screens to satisfy the sports junkies. The walls were decorated with prints of Irish scenery and local professional athletes. But she believed her biggest asset was her staff. Frank had an infectious, welcoming smile, and her full-time servers, Melissa and Nathalie, were outgoing and charming.

Charlie settled Harley into the back room and took her place behind the bar with Frank. She'd work there unless there was a need to help with the service to the tables. As the customers came in, she greeted many by name. Those she didn't know, she made it her business to get to know them. The evening progressed as usual, and the letter was all but forgotten.

CHAPTER 2:

Three days later, it was remembered anew when Charlie found another envelope in the mail. She expected it to be from the mysterious Vincent again, but she was in for another surprise.

Dear Charlene,

You probably don't know me, but my name is Amy. We're about the same age. I always wanted to work as a bartender, but I guess it wasn't meant to be. You're certainly a very fortunate person to be where you are today at such a young age. I hope you appreciate everything you have.

I've been watching you, and I can't help but be impressed. You seem to have a lot going on. You have good friends and a great business. It must be nice to feel so productive and appreciated. I wish I had a life like yours.

Maybe someday we could get together and compare lives. I would enjoy that.

It didn't make sense to Charlie. The first letter had seemed like a come-on, but this one wasn't. It was apparently written by a woman, yet the handwriting looked very similar to that of the previous letter.

The bottom, right-hand drawer of her desk squeaked noisily as Charlie looked for the slightly crumpled letter she had received a few days earlier. She laid the two papers side-by-side on her desktop. She was right; the handwriting was precisely the same. The two envelopes were also made of the same paper, with no return address on either of them.

A ball of anxiety grew in her chest. It was easy enough to write off the first letter as a prank, but things were more bizarre than she had thought. Charlie grabbed the most recent letter and charged from the room, Harley scampering to keep up with her.

This time, Frank didn't brush it off.

'This has me worried. You should go to the cops,' he said.

'You think so? What can they do about it? They're just letters.'

'I don't know. Maybe nothing, but what if this guy's dangerous? What if you're not the only one? What if this is happening to other women, and maybe they can catch the guy? I think it's worth a try.'

'But this one is from a woman.'

'Or a guy posing as a woman. It's the same handwriting, remember?'

'You could be right,' she said, chewing on her lip. 'Damn, I don't have time for this. I've got a business to run. It's Friday, and we'll have a full house tonight. I'll go tomorrow morning.'

'That's fine, but, don't go off by yourself anywhere tonight. I'll walk you home.'

'You don't have to do that. It's out of your way.'

Frank gave her a look that discouraged any arguments. She wasn't sure she even wanted to argue. The letters bothered her more than she wanted to admit.

The following morning, Charlie knocked on her neighbor's door at precisely eight thirty. It was opened by a woman with a small, wrinkled face, squinting through the crack. When she recognized Charlie and her little pug, she flung the door open widely.

'Bonjour!'

'Bonjour, Madame Lafrance. I wondered if I could ask a favor of you.'

'Of course. You want me to keep Harley for a while?' the woman asked hopefully, with a slight French accent.

'Yes, please. I shouldn't be too long, and he's already done his business, so you don't have to take him out in this weather.'

Harley, for his part, was quite happy to visit the octogenarian, certain to be hopelessly spoiled.

14

Within minutes, Charlie ducked her head and skipped over puddles in her rush to reach the subway, the two letters tucked securely into her bag. She suspected she might be on a fool's errand, but she had to see it through, if only to reassure Frank. She asked herself how long she could put up with his constant hovering. One night was more than enough.

The previous evening, the pub had been full to the seams. She had hired a popular local band, and the small dance floor was almost worn thin from all the shuffling and jumping feet. Normally, Charlie would have helped with the table orders, but Frank insisted she stay behind the bar with him where he could keep an eye on her. Charlie complained about his demands, but she didn't put up much of a fight. Her first love had always been to work behind the bar, mixing drinks and gabbing with the customers.

It was also Frank's specialty. He could talk sports and cars with the guys and come off as a man's man, while his charming smile and his good looks attracted the women. Charlie suspected many of the female regulars had a crush on Frank, and he had a way of making each of them feel special. Charlie smiled as she thought how they didn't stand a chance. The bartender's heart was already taken.

At three o'clock in the morning, Frank delivered Charlie safely to her door, but it was four o'clock before she eventually fell asleep. Wide awake by seven thirty, she prepared to go to the police station and get it over with. It may be an exercise in futility, but at least she could say she tried.

Inside the police station, the silence was almost eerie. It may have been the damp weather. Or it could have been the dullness of the walls and furniture, but it was as if a pall of dreariness was cast over the building.

Charlie told her story to the officer at the front desk and was directed to a small waiting room until someone could see her. What she was told would be a few minutes turned in to an hour. She was about to give up and go home when a young woman came to her, speaking in rapid French and gesturing to an adjacent hallway.

The police officer to whom Charlie was led was an older man with a heavy beer-gut hanging over his belt. His head was a shiny dome full of dents, like a metal ball that had been kicked around a few too many

15

times.

Officer Martel's smile reeked of insincerity as he waved his hand vaguely at a dingy chair facing his gray metal desk, his eyes bored and distant. Charlie knew she had wasted her time by coming here, but, nevertheless, she removed the papers from her bag and got to the point.

'I've received two letters this week. I don't know who they're from, but they seem to be written by the same person, even though he or she uses different names.'

The man took the letters, unfolded them, and laid them beside each other on his desk. After less than a minute, he looked at her, his eyes still bored and expressionless.

'Which one did you get first?'

'The one from Vincent.'

He nodded as if the information made a difference, but Charlie sensed he truly didn't care.

'They don't sound threatening.'

'No, I know that, but they're creepy.'

'Uh huh.'

'I wondered if you've had anything else like this come in recently.'

'Not that I know of.'

Charlie gestured to the computer on his desk.

'Is there any way of checking?'

He looked at her as if considering the idea, then glanced at the computer with a puzzled expression.

'Maybe.'

He spent a few minutes typing on the keyboard and staring at the screen with the same flat expression. Finally, he shrugged.

'Don't see anything.'

Charlie glared at him, thinking the city of Montreal was in trouble if this attitude was typical of all its police officers. She reached over, gathered the letters, carefully folded them, and put them in her bag.

'Thank you for your time,' she said stiffly, standing to leave.

'If there's anything else, let us know, but I don't see anything there for you to worry about. If you really want, I can open a case file.'

'No, don't bother. You're clearly very busy.'

Chapter 3:

Monday's mail brought another letter. This time, Frank was lounging in a chair, his long legs settled on the corner of her desk, when Charlie found it among her pile of bills.

'Here we go again,' she said shakily. The floor vibrated as Frank's feet came off her desk. He stood and leaned over, peering across at the envelope.

'Maybe you should wear gloves or something, in case we need to have it tested for fingerprints,' he suggested.

'First of all, God knows how many hands have touched it by now, and, second of all, the police won't be bothered testing for fingerprints.'

'I think you just landed on a lazy cop. You should go back.'

'Yes, I agree, and no, I disagree.'

'I'll go with you. I'll get them to listen.'

His tone suggested he would be only too happy to make them listen.

'How about we look at this one first?'

Dear Charlene,

Hello, my name is Ben. I always wanted to live in Montreal. It seems like a great city, with a lot of exciting events. I know it can be cold in the wintertime, but I think I would have gotten used to it. Your bar looks like a nice place to hang out. I would have loved to have the chance to spend more time there.

Maybe some time we can get together and discuss it. I think we would have a lot in common.

'It's someone who came to the pub.'

Frank's voice was strained and angry. Charlie looked up from the letter to see his fists clenched and his jaw set.

'It's okay, Frank. It's just a prank,' she said, not believing her own words, but wanting to say something to deflect his anger.

'Bullshit! Don't try to pretend you're not worried about this.'

He was right. She was worried, and getting more worried with the arrival of each letter. She felt watched, and she had no clue how sane the watcher was. But, she didn't want Frank to get involved in an incident with some nutcase. She reached across the desk and put her hand on his arm, her pale skin a sharp contrast to his.

'Frank, we won't get our boxers in a twist. I can handle it. He'll eventually get bored with the whole thing and move on.'

'How can you be sure of that?'

'It's a feeling I have.'

He snorted, shaking his head.

'What if you went back to the police?' he asked, circling back to the same subject.

'They blew me off last time. And this letter is no more threatening than the other ones. It's just creepy.'

'We have to get help to catch this guy. I have a friend whose father hired a private investigator once. I could get his name, and you could hire him.'

'I don't know. What could he do? How would he ever find the guy?'

'They have ways. If he can't do it, he'll tell you.'

Within seconds, his cell phone appeared in his hand, and he was sending off a text.

'It won't be long. Joe'll get back to me, and we can call the guy.'

'Frank, I don't want you to get involved in this. I can handle it.'

'Stop it. We're in this together. Do you really think I'd turn around, walk out of here, and leave you to handle this on your own?'

Charlie glanced at the floor before returning her gaze to Frank. This was the guy who had been her best friend and her rock for the last five years, as she had been for him. Instinctively, he would be the first person she would call if she was in trouble, but she also worked hard to maintain her independence. It went against the grain for her to ask for help.

'No, of course not. It's just…I worry about you.'

'That was a long time ago. I was a teenager. I can handle myself now. Physically, I think I'm better equipped than you, no matter how tough you are.'

'Of course,' she said, glancing at his muscular arms. 'But all the same, I'm a big girl. I want to handle this.'

Chapter 4:

Charlie was doing an inventory count when the door banged open behind her. Her heart pumped madly as she spun around and saw Frank coming toward her, an excited look on his face. She forced a smile, not wanting him to notice how jumpy she was. Fortunately, he was distracted by Harley's greeting, which customarily involved a full-body wiggle and a few happy whimpers.

'He's coming here this afternoon,' he announced proudly.

'Who?'

'The private detective guy.'

'Really? Frank, I thought you would have discussed it with me first. I've got a lot to do today. It's not good timing.'

'When will it be good timing? When you're in the hospital because you've been attacked by some creep?'

'Come on. It won't come to that.'

'Of course not,' he said, rolling his eyes. 'Look, all you have to do is talk to this guy. Tell him what's going on and ask him if he can help.'

Charlie replaced the bottles under the bar with a little more force than necessary. The clanging echoed through the empty barroom.

'All right. I'll see him. What time?' she asked brusquely.

Frank looked at his watch.

'Pretty soon, I think.'

Charlie groaned. There were two things she hated. One was having her routine disrupted, and the other was having people prying into her personal life. Now she would have to suffer through both.

On the heels of that thought, the door to the pub opened. His head cleared the door frame by about four inches. He wore an old, Montreal Expos ball cap and a t-shirt that had seen better days. His jeans were clean but well-worn, and the whole distinguished outfit was completed with a pair of work boots.

Charlie released her breath. It wasn't the detective, so she had additional time to check her inventory while Frank took care of this guy. She gave the stranger a nod and a welcoming smile, turned her back to him, and continued her work.

Harley's nails clicked on the hardwood floor as he trotted over to the man to do a sniff check.

'Hey there, little guy. You're a cute one, aren't you?'

Charlie smiled to herself. General opinion was divided between pugs being really cute, or just ugly-cute. She considered them genuinely cute, and invariably appreciated someone who fell along the same lines.

She heard the scrape of a stool as it was pulled away from the bar.

'What can I serve you?' Frank asked.

'Are you Charlie?'

'Why are you looking for Charlie?'

Charlie winced. Frank was in full protective mode. She turned to get a good look at the stranger. He was in his mid to late thirties, lean, and good-looking in a rough kind of way. This couldn't be the private eye, could it?

'I have business with Charlie. If you're not him, where can I find him?'

'I'm Charlie.'

There was a split-second of hesitation when he focused on her. The man stood up, stretched over the bar, and reached out his arm. As his hand closed around hers, she could sense Frank's tension beside her, and she gave her friend a quick look to say, 'Hey, you asked him to come here'.

'You're the private detective?' she asked, directing her attention to the stranger.

'I am. My name is Simmons. Everybody calls me Simm.'

'Your name is Simm Simmons?'

'No,' he said. 'My last name is Simmons, but everyone calls me Simm.'

'What's your first name?'

'It doesn't matter.'

'It does if I decide to hire you. I'd have to know what name to write on the check.'

'You'd just write it out to my company name.'

'You don't look like a private detective.'

'Don't worry, I am. I'm working undercover right now.'

Charlie's eyes narrowed. She couldn't tell if he was pulling her leg or not.

The man pulled a business card out of the back pocket of his jeans and set it on the spotless counter. She glanced at it, noting its plainness. It had the name Simmons Investigations written on it with a phone number underneath. No logo, no fancy graphics, no address, and no full name.

Chapter 5:

'Got any ideas?'

'About who it could be? No, none,' Charlie said.

'Fallen out with anyone lately? Friends? Acquaintances? Relatives?' Simm asked.

'None of the above.'

'Boyfriends, current or past? Wives of boyfriends, current or past?'

Charlie gave him a look that could have curdled milk. She didn't find him amusing.

'No. How long is this going to go on? I have work to do.'

'Look, you hired me to find out what's happening with these letters. I need information. I can't work in the dark.'

'I didn't hire you. Frank did. As a matter of fact, he could answer all your questions.'

'You're the one who seems to be the target,' he said flatly.

Charlie winced. She didn't like the sound of the word 'target'. This man's attitude rubbed her the wrong way, for some reason. It seemed as if he had taken an instant dislike to her, a reaction that was foreign to her. She regretted agreeing to Frank's decision to hire a private detective, although she recalled she hadn't been given much chance to decline. She stood, intending to head out to the main room.

'What are you hiding?'

'I'm not hiding anything,' she answered, her eyes flashing.

He looked at his notepad.

'Your name is Charlene Butler, a.k.a. Charlie, you've owned this pub for eight years, you have no family, and Frank is your full-time employee. You're a fountain of information.'

'That's all there is to tell.'

'How about your parents' names?'

'They're both dead. They have nothing to do with this.'

He pulled off his ball cap, ran his fingers roughly through his hair, and yanked it back on.

'All right. Have it your way. It'll take me a lot longer, but I'll start with what I have. I'll end up knowing everything anyway.'

The chair scraped noisily on the ceramic floor as he stood. Charlie felt petty. She hated talking about herself, and she hadn't been mentally prepared for this inquisition.

'Okay, sit. I'll tell you more.'

'Gee, thanks.'

He made a show of poising his pen over his notepad. He certainly had his fair share of sarcasm, Charlie thought.

'My parents were Pat and Patricia Butler, and...'

'Pat and Patricia? You're kidding, right?'

'No, I'm not, Mr. Simm Simmons,' she responded, her eyebrows raised.

'Okay, fair enough. Was this your father's place?'

'No, he was a dentist.'

After a couple of strokes of his pen, he looked at her expectantly. She shrugged.

'My mother worked as a school secretary. That's it.'

'No siblings?'

'None.'

'You grew up in Montreal?'

'Yep. About five blocks over. I never lived anywhere else.'

'Okay, you already told me you studied business at Concordia. Then you bought the pub, right?'

'Uh huh.'

'Business is good?'

'Pretty good. Steady.'

'How many employees do you have?

'Seven, apart from me. Some are full-time, some part-time. We have a lot of shifts.'

'How long have your parents been dead?'

'My father passed away ten years ago from cancer. My mother was killed in a car accident six years ago.'

He grimaced.

'Sorry to hear that. It must have been tough.'

'Yep.'

'Slow down. I'm having trouble taking this all in. Are you always so talkative?'

She didn't smile, but she enjoyed making him work for his money. She may have to give up the information, but she didn't have to make it overly easy for him.

'You know what?' he said. 'I'm going to start with this mountain of data. It'll probably take me days to sift through it all and organize my notes, but I'll get back to you when I'm done.'

'Enjoy.'

'If you happen to get any more letters, or worse yet, physically threatened, let me know. Or Frank can let me know, since you could be either in the hospital or the morgue.'

He gave her a cynical little smile and a nod before he headed out the door, letting it slam a little harder than necessary.

Charlie sighed. She had been a bit of an ass. Her hard, Irish head tended to make her a little impulsive and obstinate, but at least she could recognize those characteristics in herself. That was always a good start.

CHAPTER 6:

Simm was pissed. Why did some people have to be such hard-asses? They hire him to do a job, and then throw marbles in front of him, just so they can watch him slip and slide. He didn't enjoy being a source of amusement for people.

Simm went through some files and made a few follow-up calls. He worked from a rented, two-room office on Murray Street in a not very classy building. In one room, he had a small filing cabinet and his desk, bare of papers but home to a laptop computer. The other room housed a combination photocopy machine and scanner. A neat stack of paper and office supplies occupied a small corner. It was large enough for another desk if he ever needed an assistant/receptionist, but he didn't expect to need one at any point in the foreseeable future. As it was, he barely made enough to pay the bills.

Recently, people hadn't been knocking down his door trying to get him to take their case. Unfortunately, the Butler case was the biggest he had to work on at this time, and it was typical of his usual work load. People often had problems they felt weren't being taken seriously by the authorities, and, in most cases, they were right. The police didn't have time for all the little things. Random, unthreatening letters were considered very small stuff by law enforcement when there were so many more demanding and urgent cases to worry about.

For Simm, the case was frustrating on a couple of fronts. First of all, he had very little to go on to move it ahead. This was mostly because of the lack of cooperation on the part of Ms. Butler, leading him neatly into the second cause of his frustration, Charlie. Simply put, she bothered him.

Staring out the window, he admitted her appearance disturbed him, and it may even be the major source of his irritation. When he first saw her in the bar, a jolt coursed through him like someone had stuck a pin in his back. Her brown hair pulled back into a silky ponytail brought back so many memories he was momentarily rendered speechless.

He thought he handled himself professionally when 'Charlie the man' turned out to be 'Charlie the woman', but facing her full-on was almost too much for him. She had the same girl-next-door look as Helen, fresh-faced with wide blue eyes, and an engaging smile. She was slim and pretty, but not in a delicate, don't-ask-me-to-take-out-the-garbage kind of way. Helen had been the same.

Of course, the engaging smile disappeared when she realized he was a private investigator and not a customer. That's when the wall of China landed in a downtown Montreal pub.

He knew he would have to start off cold on this one.

Simm wouldn't be put off by the attitude of his newest client. He'd experienced similar problems with others. Obviously, Charlie Butler didn't want him on the case. Her friend Frank had made the arrangements, and for some reason, she wasn't open to the idea. Maybe discovering that reason would bring him closer to finding out who had sent her the letters.

He wondered about the relationship between her and the bartender. The vibes they gave off implied they were close, but how close? Could Frank be a suspect, even though he was the one to contact a private detective? It wouldn't be the first time someone tried that trick to throw off an investigation.

A loud buzz shook him out of his reverie. He glanced at the door with a frown, as if it was the door's fault for sending an unexpected visitor to his office.

Out of habit, he analysed the sound of the footsteps climbing the stairs. It was a woman in a tight-fitting dress and high heels. She was around his age of thirty-five, blond, well-built, and broken-hearted after the recent death of her husband. She wanted answers, and of course, the comfort of another man, perhaps a currently-single private investigator.

When she walked into his office, his fantasy dissipated like a drop of water on a hot stove. The woman filled the physical attributes he had imagined, right down to the sequined, high-heeled sandals, but he knew her heart was whole, and she wasn't coming to him looking for comfort.

'Susan? What are you doing here?'

'What a greeting. You really need to practice your social skills, Simm,' the woman said, approaching him and giving him a hug and a kiss on the cheek. He returned the gesture with little enthusiasm.

'Okay, I will. Why are you here?' he said.

'I expected at least a, 'how have you been?', or maybe a question about Jim and the kids.'

'How have you been? How are Jim and the kids? And to what do I owe the pleasure?'

'He's dying,' the woman said, her smile disappearing.

Simm felt a small twinge and promptly dismissed it. He didn't care, and he refused to be affected by it.

'Thanks for letting me know. I'm busy now, but I'll be in touch someday.' After he's dead, he thought, shuffling aimlessly through some papers on his desk.

'Don't be like this. Why do you have to be such a tough guy?'

'I have my reasons and you know it.'

'A lot of time has passed, and a lot of water has flowed under the bridge.'

'Not enough, as far as I'm concerned.'

Chapter 7:

Charlie's apartment was on Bishop Street, within walking distance of the pub. It was one of six apartments in a red brick, three-storied building, circa 1920. Charlie had lived on the middle floor for the past six years. The location was perfect, being close to work and having everything else she needed within walking distance. The inside had been renovated to include a bright open-concept living area, kitchen, two bedrooms, and a bathroom. Her furniture was contemporary and basic, keeping the space uncluttered, in sharp contrast to the crowded atmosphere of the pub.

Most of the time, woman and dog walked between work and home. Now, Frank wouldn't hear of it. He insisted on walking her home and looking around her apartment before he left her for the night. Charlie made a token protest, but deep down she was glad to have his company. It was nice to have someone to chat with on the way home, and the safe feeling she had with him by her side was a bonus.

Charlie and Harley had their nightly ritual. First, she made a snack for them both. Then, she showered and slipped into her pyjamas. When they were both settled into bed, her under the covers and Harley on top of the bedspread beside her, she caught up on the news using her tablet, checked her social media sites, read a few pages of a novel, and switched off the light. No matter how late she got home from the bar, it was the only way for her to relax before falling asleep.

Charlie knew some people thought she led a lonely life because it was years since she'd had a romantic relationship. Her last one hadn't ended well, but she didn't blame her ex for leaving. Having to compete with Butler's Pub for her attention would discourage the most devoted of lovers. After all, she spent most of her time at her place of business, and she didn't plan to change that for anyone.

The fact that her parents divorced when she was fifteen may have something to do with her distaste for a relationship. Her mother had been so bitter and disillusioned about her father Charlie thought she was probably better off remaining single. The pub was a much more loyal and solid companion.

However, at a time like this, she would like to have a guy in her life, someone she could curl up next to and with whom she could feel secure. Just the presence of another living, breathing person would go a long way to making her feel at ease in her own home.

She fell asleep as usual, with Harley's warmth radiating through the blankets to her legs. It seemed like mere minutes later she was startled awake by his bark near her ear. He stood next to her head, his eyes trained on the bedroom door, a low growl rumbling in his throat.

Every once in a while, the pug was spooked by a noise. She could always soothe him with a pat and a few soft words, but this time Charlie was also on full alert. She lay for a few moments with the blankets clutched to her throat before glancing at her night table.

'Damn,' she whispered. Harley focused his big eyes on her as if to say, 'What now?'

'I left the phone in the other room.'

Charlie wanted to kick herself for being so irresponsible. She had no means of communication.

The good news was Harley was no longer reacting to any perceived intruder. As a matter of fact, he seemed to have forgotten the incident altogether, concentrating on scratching an itch rather than protecting his mistress.

Charlie, however, wasn't so relaxed. She soundlessly slid out of bed and inched toward the door in the darkness. She winced when the door squeaked as she gingerly pulled it open. She stopped, waiting and listening for any sign of another human being in her apartment. All she heard were Harley's paws hitting the floor. She realized his intent a moment too late. He squeezed through the open space before she could stop him. The last thing she wanted was for him to come face-to-face with a dangerous felon.

'Harley!' she said in a loud whisper. 'Come back here!'

The little dog ignored her and continued to the kitchen. Charlie had no choice but to follow him. His calmness was reassuring, but she didn't know if they would both find a surprise when they entered the room.

Luckily, the hallway and the kitchen were clear. Charlie fumbled in a drawer to find a large carving knife. Armed, she snagged a portable phone, punched in 9-1-1, and held her finger over the 'dial' button, as she cautiously made her way through the rest of the apartment. There was nothing unusual. No one was there, and no doors or windows showed signs of tampering. Her heart rate returned to normal.

'Really, Harley? Did you just want to scare me?'

The dog looked suitably chastised for a split second and trotted back to the bedroom, his head held high.

Charlie decided to add another aspect to her nightly ritual, sliding the knife under her pillow.

Chapter 8:

Simm's cell phone rang, and he frowned at the screen when he spotted the name on the call display. He didn't feel up to this right now. He sighed as he hit the answer button.

'Hey, Walt. How's it going?'

'I'm surprised you answered.'

Simm was relieved his grimace wasn't visible to the caller. Walt didn't have to know how close to the mark he was.

'I always answer when I can. You know that.'

'Haven't seen you in a while.'

'I've been busy,' Simm said.

'Oh yeah, how's this private investigator stuff going?'

Simm's hackles rose.

'It's a great hobby,' he responded, not bothering to mask his sarcasm.

'There's no need to get angry. I was just asking. It interests me.'

'I'm sure it does.'

'I was hoping we could get together sometime soon.'

'Really? A reunion? Just you and me, or were you planning to invite others.'

'Just you and me. We should talk.'

Simm sighed again and ran his hand through his hair. He took a deep breath before filling the silence between them. He was sure Walt had heard it.

'Listen, if I thought you wanted to get together just to talk and catch up on old times, I'd be there like a dog at dinnertime. But I know that's not the case. I'm not getting drawn back into all of it. I think I've made it clear to everyone. I already had a visit from Susan.'

'She told me, and yes, you were very clear. But people change. I'm sure you've changed. We all have. Sooner or later, it'll be time to bury the hatchet.'

'Walt, you know my hatchet isn't aimed at you. If you ever need me to help you out of a jam, I'm there. But as for all the rest…I can't.'

'Some day, you'll have no choice.'

'I doubt it, but if the day ever comes, I'll make my decision then. Right now, my life is good, and I plan to keep it that way.'

The call ended, and Simm stood for several moments clutching the cell phone in his hand, tempted to throw it across the room. Instead, he took a deep breath and tossed it as gently as possible onto the couch.

Chapter 9:

'He probably won't come back.'

Charlie laughed at the sulkiness on Frank's face. She had never seen him pout.

'Are you serious? You sound like you've got a crush on him.'

He threw his precious rag onto the bar.

'I went to the trouble of finding him for you, and you hardly gave him two minutes of your time. Do you want to find this guy or not?'

'I'm sorry. I know you meant well, and I appreciate what you did. To be honest, I was prepared to cooperate, but that devil we know so well hopped onto my shoulder and there was nothing I could do.'

'Why don't you call him and see if he's discovered anything?'

'I doubt he's even working on it.'

'I repeat, why don't you call?'

'I will. When I'm ready.'

She ignored the rolling of Frank's eyes and got back to work. She told herself she would call Mr. Simm Simmons when she had two minutes. She knew very well finding two available minutes could take days.

At two o'clock that afternoon, she and Harley took their afternoon walk, starting with the park. Afterward, Harley led the way to meet and greet his faithful fans, knowing there would be at least a few tasty handouts on such a beautiful sunny day.

They had turned the corner on to a quieter street and walked a few steps when Charlie's arms were forcibly grabbed from behind. Her shriek of surprise was swiftly muffled as a hand covered her mouth, and the assailant's other arm circled her waist and arms, pulling her back against a big, hard body.

'You're coming with me,' a voice growled in her ear.

Charlie saw Harley ahead of her, yipping and whimpering. Her first thought was to protect him. She let go of the leash and hoped he would run to safety. Her next thought was to find a way to break the man's hold. As she lifted her leg to give him a backward kick to the shin, her suddenly-free body staggered forward. She would have fallen face-first on the sidewalk if someone hadn't latched on to her shirt from behind.

'Come here, Harley. There's nothing to worry about.'

Stunned, she watched her dog wag his curly, little tail energetically and scamper over to the tall man leaning over to pet him. She was about to slam her arm down on the back of his neck when she recognized the Expos logo on the back of his cap and the slightly long, dark hair sticking out from underneath.

'What the hell! What are you doing?'

Simm straightened up and regarded her sternly.

'Proving a point.'

'What point would that be? That you can scare the wits out of people? That you're crazy?'

'That you're vulnerable even in broad daylight. That you have a dyed-in-the-wool routine, one that everyone is aware of and can be used to their advantage.'

'I do not!'

'Every day at two o'clock you take Harley for a walk. You go to the park first, then you walk around the block in the same direction every time, you visit the same people, and you arrive back at the pub at two thirty. Harley naps while you do other things until the after-work crowd shows up.'

'Who told you that? Were you talking to Frank?'

'I watched you, and I did a bit of detective work because, believe it or not, that's what I do.'

'You're a pain in the ass.'

'You're just mad because I'm right. You're also the perfect victim. Whoever wants to get at you can do so just by following your clockwork schedule.'

Charlie grumbled. She wanted to argue with him, but she knew he had a point. She was a creature of habit. Everyone in the neighborhood knew so. That's why the shopkeepers and restaurant workers always kept an eye out for Harley at the same time every day. With no rebuttal to offer, she snatched Harley's leash, turned on her heel, and headed back to the pub. She came to an abrupt stop when Harley dug in his paws.

'Come on, boy. We're going back,' she said.

The little dog refused to budge, and Charlie knew why. They weren't going in the right direction. He had people who were waiting for him, and he knew it. Charlie's cheeks flushed pink when she heard a snicker beside her.

'I guess that kinda confirms it, doesn't it?'

Charlie marched over, picked up Harley, and despite the wriggling and whimpers, carried him back to Butler's. She knew Simm was behind her, but she stared silently ahead. She hated to be proven wrong, and she was more than a little annoyed that her pet had corroborated Simm's point.

Frank had his back to them, dusting the back of the bar, when they walked into the pub. Looking over his shoulder, he smiled and opened his mouth to speak, but quickly slammed it shut. Charlie knew her expression was the reason for his silence, but she didn't care. The bartender simply nodded as they walked past him on their way to the office.

'Did you have another purpose today, Mr. Simm Simmons?' Charlie asked as she watched him lower his long frame into a not-too-solid chair.

'I was hoping you would answer more questions for me, but it doesn't look like you're in the mood.'

'No, I'm not in the mood, but if it'll give you a purpose in life, I'd be willing to do it.'

'How generous of you.'

Charlie rolled her eyes. 'Could we start please? I have other things to do.'

'All right. How about we start with Frank?'

'Why?'

'Because I have to start somewhere. Is that a good enough reason?'

Charlie sighed. She had to get over her irritation with this guy. If she cooperated he would be out of her hair all the sooner, and maybe as a bonus they would find out what was going on with the mysterious letters.

'Frank started working here five years ago as a part-time student. Now he works here full-time. What else can I say? He's a great guy, a good worker, dependable, loyal, and a good friend.'

'Is that it? You're just friends, nothing else?'

'Nothing else.'

'Is he single?'

'He's not married, but he has a significant other.'

'Does she live with him?'

'He.'

'What?'

'It's a he, and yes, he lives with him.'

'Okay, what's the name of his partner?'

'Paul.'

'Can you give me any more information about him?'

'What else do you need to know? He's tall; he has blond hair, a straight nose, all his own teeth.'

'What does he do for a living?'

'He works in the warehouse at a transport company, a lot of shift work. He's a nice guy. What possible impact can this have on your investigation, Mr. Simm Simmons?'

'I don't know at this point, but anything can be significant, and it's Simm, please.'

'All right, Mr. Simm Please, you can continue with your I'm-going-nowhere-with-this questioning.'

Charlie watched as the detective stared at his notes, his jaw flexing. She grudgingly admitted he was good. She had pushed a lot of buttons, and he was still in control of his temper. Barely in control, but he was doing better than she would have under the same circumstances.

'Okay, so Frank is the greatest guy in the world, you're the most popular woman in Montreal, and there's no one on this earth who would want to bother you. So why are you getting the letters?'

'I don't know. That's what you're supposed to find out for me.'

'Exactly. With absolutely no help from you.'

He snapped his notebook shut and stood up.

'I'll be in touch.'

Charlie winced as the door slammed shut behind him.

CHAPTER 10:

'I should give it up. I don't need the money that badly, and I absolutely don't need the aggravation.'

He jabbed the computer keys harder than necessary, typing with his index fingers.

'Why do I have to get clients like this? What the hell did I do to deserve her?' Simm glared around the empty room as if looking for someone to answer his questions.

A few additional hard jabs, and he shook his head in frustration. He sucked in some air and let it out deliberately. He had to refocus, but it wasn't easy. Not only was he annoyed by the roadblocks in his investigation, which were primarily caused by his client, but said client still bothered him on a personal front. Too many memories resurfaced when he saw her, and it added to his level of irritation.

'I'm getting nowhere. I'm outta here.'

Simm shut off the computer, grabbed his jacket, and locked up the office for the night.

As he drove out of the parking lot, intending to go home, something made him turn in the opposite direction. He went a few streets over and was glad to discover a little luck was with him when he found a precious parking spot near his destination.

There was merely a small sign above the door to prove the place existed, and in the dark, it wasn't very visible. It was also faded from years of rough weather, but the words 'Ye Old Irish Pub' could still be seen if you squinted hard enough.

The interior was as dark as the exterior, but not quite as dreary. It wasn't crowded, which was to be expected for a weeknight, but Simm knew they did a decent business on weekends. As he looked around, he recognized most of the people in the room. He didn't know whether that was a good sign or not.

'Well, if it isn't Simm himself,' boomed a loud voice with a halfway decent Irish accent for someone who had never set foot on the Emerald Isle. He also had red hair and a beard, giving him a somewhat leprechaunish look, a dash of authenticity.

'Hey, Danny Boy, how's it going?'

'Grand, Simm, just grand. Set your arse down on that stool, and I'll pour you a cool one.'

The man's real name was Daniel Bergeron, and he was of French Canadian descent, but he insisted on being called Danny Boy. As a reminder to the customers, the song of the same name played several times a day over the bar's speakers.

'It's been a while since you've graced us with your presence,' the man said as he poured a glass of Guinness and set it in front of Simm. 'To what do I owe the pleasure?'

'Would you believe I was lonely?'

'Ye missed me old mug, did ya now?'

'How could I not?' Simm answered with a grin.

Simm made small talk with the pub owner for a few minutes, catching up on the news, which was actually just more of the same.

'Have you ever heard of Butler's Pub?' Simm asked.

'Over on Drummond?'

'That's the one.'

'Yeah, I know it. It used to be O'Reilly's way back when.'

'Until it was bought by Charlene Butler.'

'Yeah, something like that.'

'What do you mean by 'something like that'?'

Daniel shrugged his shoulders.

'I don't know. There was some connection there. She was tied to O'Reilly somehow.' He glanced to each side before leaning over to speak to Simm in a low voice. 'Actually, Jim O'Reilly was tied to a lot of things in Montreal, and most of it wasn't legal.'

This was an interesting development, Simm thought. He was disappointed in himself for not looking further into the background of the pub. But, at least he had the forethought to talk to his contacts. All was not lost.

'Is Charlie also tied to things that are not quite legal?'

'Hmm, I can't say. I haven't heard anything, but that doesn't mean she walks the straight and narrow. From what I hear, she has a good business going.'

'Yeah, she does.'

'You doin' a job that involves her?'

'Something like that. See you around, Danny Boy. Thanks for the info.'

The older man nodded and moved along the bar to serve another customer, a regular by the look of him, as Simm made his way to the door.

Outside, he zipped up his jacket against the cool Montreal night. He had some interesting information to think about, and he wanted to get online.

CHAPTER 11:

Charlie stepped onto the walkway in front of her apartment building. She was later than usual today and in a hurry. She stopped, wondering if she had remembered to bring the form for the renewal of her permit. She had worked on it at home, and planned to finish it today.

As she dug around in her tote bag, trying to control an unusually energetic Harley, who was straining on his leash, she heard a familiar voice.

'Hey, big guy, how's it goin'?'

Charlie scowled at the big man bent over petting her dog.

'Why are you here?'

'Good morning to you too,' Simm said, straightening. Charlie was forced to look up and squint against the sunlight beaming at her from behind his head.

'Good morning. Why are you here?'

'You live here. I wanted to talk to you. I came here. It's pretty simple.'

'I'm on my way to work.'

'Fine. I'll give you a lift and we can talk on the way.'

'I like to walk. Harley likes to walk.'

'Harley, you want to go in the car?'

The little dog cocked his head to the side and wagged his tail furiously, his squat little body shivering with excitement.

'I think he wants to go in the car.'

Charlie was impressed by Simm's keen power of observation.

'He does that anytime anyone asks him a question,' she explained patiently.

'Harley, let's go in the car,' Simm said, turning and heading to a beige, older-model Toyota Corolla sedan.

Harley ran after him, pulling Charlie along with surprising strength for a small dog. As soon as the passenger-side door opened, Harley jumped in and sat on the seat, his tongue lolling happily out of his mouth. Charlie tugged on his leash, but the dog dug his paws in stubbornly and jumped on Simm's lap almost before the man had a chance to settle into the driver's seat. Laughing, Simm gestured to the now-empty passenger seat.

'Hop in. I don't think Harley wants to walk.'

Charlie sent her supposedly loyal pet a dirty look as she lowered herself into the car and pulled the door shut. Again, she tugged on his leash to pull the dog onto her lap. He was reluctant, but quickly realized the advantage he would have by putting his front paws on the dash, giving him an unrestricted view during this rare, joyous event.

'So, what did you want to talk to me about?' Charlie asked, as Simm eased the car into traffic.

'I just wanted a little more history about you and the bar.'

'There's not much more to give you. I've owned it for eight years, and it keeps me busy. What else is there to know?'

'Are the mortgage payments tough to make?'

'What does that have to do with anything?'

'It could be pertinent.'

'I don't see how.'

'What bank holds the mortgage?'

'That's personal information.'

Charlie braced herself to keep from falling against Simm, caught off-guard by the rapid swerving of the car. Harley slid off her knee and scrambled to regain his foothold. They jolted to a stop in a parking lot, and there was a moment of stunned silence after the engine was shut off.

'What the hell?' Charlie exclaimed, regaining her senses.

'Yeah, exactly, what the hell?'

The composed person Charlie thought she was dealing with turned in his seat to glare at her, his expression angry.

'You don't have a mortgage, do you, Charlie?'

'I…'

'You never did. Why? Because the business was given to you, wasn't it? You inherited it from a man old enough to be your father. So why don't you tell me about your relationship with Jim O'Reilly?'

'Oh no you don't!' she shouted. 'Don't you dare go where you're trying to go. That is unacceptable. Jim was like a second father to me, and I won't allow you to besmirch his memory with your dirty innuendos. He was a good man, and I loved him.'

Charlie was furious. What business did he have snooping into her life? And then to insinuate that her relationship with Jim O'Reilly was anything other than what it was, she wanted to hit him. Several times. Instead, she tried to gather a whimpering Harley in her arms, grab her purse, and open the door at the same time. When she heard the locks snap shut on all the doors, she whirled to face him.

'Stop being an ass. I don't give a shit what you think about me, but just so you know, you're fired.'

'What's your problem? You must be hiding something if you don't want to talk about it.'

'I'm not hiding anything. I just don't like talking about my personal life. It's none of your business.'

'Someone has made it his business. And if you want to find out who it is, you're going to have to share a bit of it with me. I can't keep working blind.'

Charlie took a few deep breaths, trying to calm herself. On one level, she knew he was right, but on another level, it irked to have someone snooping into her private business. Yet Simm was a professional snoop. She would learn to cope with it. She gritted her teeth and rolled her shoulders.

'Okay. I inherited the pub from Jim O'Reilly. He was my father's friend, and I worked at the bar part-time while I was a student. When I finished school, I started full-time. I loved it, and I had a knack for it. Jim taught me everything he knew. When he was diagnosed with cancer, I took over running the place for him, and he left it to me when he died. That's all there is.'

'What about his son? Do you think he resented the fact that the business was left to someone else besides him?'

'Terry? No, of course not. He was already a little too familiar with bars. Now he can't go near them. Too much temptation.'

'It doesn't matter. He could've hired someone to run it for him. He could've hired you. At least he would be earning some money.'

'He has a job. You don't have to worry about Terry. His dad didn't leave him destitute. He's doing all right for himself, and he's perfectly happy.'

'So, let's say, financially, he's healthy. It's still gotta hurt when your dad hands the family business over to someone else, especially someone who's not even related.'

'I may not be a blood relative, but like I said, Jim was like a second father to me. Ergo, I was like a daughter to him. Terry and I get along fine. He doesn't resent me in the least.'

Simm merely looked at her and nodded. He seemed to be either holding back judgement, or preparing for another attack.

'What about the West End Gang?'

Attack, it was. Charlie fumed. This was why she didn't discuss her private life with anyone. It continually led to stupid misinterpretations.

'You were having fun with your research, weren't you?'

'Since you weren't sharing, I had to do research. You could've saved me a lot of time and trouble, but it's your dime, and you want to pay it.'

'Jim's involvement with the West End Gang ended many years before he died. I was a young child at the time. He was clean.'

'After he served time?'

'Yes.'

'Do you believe that? It's usually pretty hard to dissociate yourself from those organizations.'

'The Irish Mafia isn't the same as the Italian Mafia. They don't have the same structure. Anyway, Jim was a small player for them. He did his time and didn't want to go back. He had a son and a future to think of.'

'Do you think anyone within the Gang would still have hard feelings against Jim?'

'No, of course not. Why would they? It's been years. If there were any hard feelings, they would have dealt with them long ago. And why me? I had nothing to do with it.'

'I'm exploring possibilities. And there seems to be a lot of them.'

'None among the ones you've presented to me so far.'

'That's what you think. With a bit of extra digging, I may come up with something else.'

Chapter 12:

Charlie put the scene behind her. She should have known Simm would discover the truth about Jim and the pub, but she was convinced it was a dead end. At least now it was in the open, and they could move on to something else.

Besides, a day had passed, and it was difficult to be bad-tempered when the scent of lilac blossoms was heavy in the air. People she met on the street smiled and enjoyed the season after a long, cold winter. Even Harley, who was happy year-round, had an extra little bounce in his step.

They showed up at the pub late morning. As she tossed her purse onto her desk, she spotted the pile of mail on her desk. One of the items was a conspicuously large brown envelope, something she didn't commonly receive.

Hesitantly, Charlie removed the package from the pile. It was heavy and thick, obviously lined with bubble wrap. Her name and address was typed on a sticker, but there was no return address. Her skin chilled.

She circled her desk and fumbled with the drawer, trying to find a pair of scissors. Getting a grip on them, she picked up the envelope again, and noticed the writing on the back.

Dear Charlene,

My name is Mike. You don't know me. I could have grown up next to you. Maybe you would have been kind to me, smiled at me, given me candy on Halloween. Maybe we would have been friends. But, we'll never know, will we?

47

Charlie stared at the note, puzzled, for several moments. What the hell was in here? What was it about? She thought about asking Frank to open it for her, but that seemed like a wimpy thing to do. It was only a package, after all. It wasn't as if something living would jump out at her.

She picked up the scissors and carefully cut open the end of the envelope. Cautiously peeking in, she saw what appeared to be a plastic bag, but it wasn't obvious what was inside. She upended the envelope and let the bag slide out onto the desk.

And screamed.

Chapter 13:

Simm drove as fast as he could in the mid-day traffic. He had hardly understood a word as Charlie had shouted into the phone, but he got the message that it was urgent. When he turned on to Drummond, he saw the authorities had made it there before him, the emergency lights reflecting in the pub's front windows. Even though Simm was relatively sure Charlie was unharmed, the sight of the police cars spiked his fear level up a notch.

He didn't worry about searching for a parking spot. He pulled up behind one of the cop cars and jabbed the button for his four-way flashers before jumping out of the car. He was inside the building within seconds of arriving.

Charlie's office door was ajar and as Simm stepped inside, his first impression was that the space was much too crowded. But, then again, four burly policemen took up a lot of space. Add to that the six-foot-four mass of Frank, and a tiny old man –whoever he was– and we had an overpopulation problem. Simm couldn't even see Charlie.

His second step into the room was blocked by a police officer.

'Vous ne pouvez pas entrer ici, monsieur.'

'She called me,' Simm said, to explain why he could indeed come into the room.

The officer looked over his shoulder toward a far corner just as Frank stepped to the left, and Simm spotted Charlie sitting on the chair in front of her desk. Her eyes were red and swollen, and when she looked at him, he saw those eyes were also glazed with shock. The source of that shock was, as yet, unknown to him.

He made his way over, stepping around the little old man who was arguing with one of the police officers, who was in turn trying to politely hustle him out of the room.

Simm wedged into a spot beside Charlie.

'What happened?'

'It was awful.'

'What was?'

'It was in an envelope, for God's sake!'

'What was in an envelope?'

'It was gross.'

'What?'

'Body parts.'

Simm looked at Frank, hoping for another explanation, something that didn't revive memories of old news. It had been only a handful of years since Luka Magnotta had killed and dismembered Lin Jun and mailed his limbs to schools and political party offices. It wasn't something people, including the Montreal police force, would forget anytime soon.

'They look like organs,' Frank explained grimly.

'Human organs?'

Frank lifted his shoulders and spread his arms in the age-old gesture of, 'I have no idea'.

'Where did you find them?' Simm asked Charlie.

'They were in the mail.'

'Jesus,' Simm muttered.

'That's what I said. Can you imagine how horrible that is? Someone sent me body parts by the mail.'

'Organs,' Frank interjected.

'Frank, stop it,' Charlie said in a voice that allowed no argument. The message was clear; to Charlie they were body parts, there was no point in trying to qualify it.

The next picture that flashed through Simm's mind was the classic image from The Godfather when Marlon Brando woke up to a severed horse's head in his bed. He thought Mafia, moving his theory one step closer in that direction.

He left Charlie and Frank to settle their difference of opinion and went to talk to the cops.

He chose the sole female, thinking she may be more receptive to his charm.

'Excuse me, my name is Simm. I'm working for Ms. Butler. I wonder if I could have a look at the package she received.'

'What do you mean by working?' she asked, her gaze sharp and defensive.

'She hired me as a private detective because of the anonymous letters she was receiving.'

He didn't add that the cops had been no help to Charlie and now the situation had escalated. He thought that particular approach may not work with this group.

'She won't need your services anymore. It's a police matter now.'

'I disagree. I think I can still work on this in conjunction with the police.'

'We don't do conjunction with private detectives.'

'Then, as a concerned friend of the victim, could I please see the envelope?'

Simm had almost run out of patience and politeness with this cop, and now he wished he had tucked his charm away and simply dealt with someone who would cut him some slack. Luckily for him, a slack-cutter had overheard their conversation.

'There's no harm in letting him look at it. If he's already done some investigating, we could maybe use what he's got.'

Thank God for the voice of reason.

His saviour, a cop almost as tall as Simm and much broader, received a scowl from his partner for his trouble, but Simm didn't care. At least he would get a look at whatever had been deposited into Charlie's mailbox.

He wasn't quite prepared for the sight. It was much more disgusting than he had expected, a bloody mess in a plastic bag. He wasn't sure who had determined they were organs, and how they had gone about doing so, but he could see how Charlie would be traumatized by this. He tore his gaze away from it and looked at the more cooperative cop.

'So, what's the next step?'

'We'll send it to the lab to be analysed, find out what it actually is, and we'll get back to Ms. Butler about it. We'll check for fingerprints, and we're going to look more closely at the other letters she received. What can you tell us about your discoveries so far?'

'To tell you the truth, I haven't been on the case very long. I've looked in to background information, family history, that type of thing, but there isn't anything that's jumped out at me so far.'

'Maybe you can come to the station and fill us in on what you have, and it'll save us some time.'

The cop handed Simm his card, and Simm returned the favor. As he turned and walked back to Charlie, he asked himself what had made him hold back the information he had about Jim O'Reilly and his Irish Mafia connection. And the fact that the man had a son who was essentially snubbed in his will.

Chapter 14:

Charlie and her two shadows, a man and a pug, arrived at Butler's early the following day. Simm had insisted on picking her up and escorting her to work. For a reason that she didn't want to explore too deeply, she didn't argue. She installed Harley in the office so he could get his beauty sleep and released Simm from his duties. Frank was present to take over as her bodyguard. Then, she vigorously attacked some spring cleaning in the bar section. She needed good physical work to take her mind off her troubles.

The late afternoon rush was underway, and Charlie was taking orders from a young couple when the two police officers entered the pub. A hush came over the crowd. Her blood chilled when she recognized them from the day before. She immediately finished up with the couple, handed over her duties to another employee, and motioned to Frank to join her.

Knowing their topic of conversation wouldn't be appropriate to be dealt with in public, Charlie invited everyone to the office in the back of the building. As they left the bar area, she heard the conversation pick up again, presumably much of it speculation about why the police were here.

The four of them crowded into Charlie's office, getting seated as Harley made the rounds and greeted everyone individually before heading back to his cushion to resume his nap.

'What do you have to tell me?' Charlie asked, addressing the male detective, who had introduced himself as Detective Alain Ranfort.

'We sent the specimen to the lab for testing, and fortunately they were not human.'

'They weren't? What were they?'

'Sheep.'

'Sheep?' Charlie felt a flash of relief, but it was instantly replaced by chagrin on behalf of the sheep. 'How would someone get sheep parts?'

'That's what we're trying to find out. There were six of them in the bag.'

Charlie was stunned. It was hard to imagine how someone could get hold of half a dozen sheep organs in downtown Montreal. But it would be even stranger to have six human parts in the bag. No matter what, they were dealing with a very sick person.

'What kind?' she asked.

'Excuse me?'

'What kind of organs were they?'

The detective looked at his partner.

'Heart, kidney, liver, two of each,' the woman said.

Charlie shivered.

'So, what's the next move?' she said.

'We keep looking,' he continued. 'We've contacted the people at MacDonald College. It's an agricultural campus. Maybe they'll have leads for us, or maybe they'll discover some organs have gone missing. It's a start. Meanwhile, I suggest you remain vigilant and avoid going out alone.'

'Don't worry. We're making sure of that,' Frank said. The detective looked at Frank and nodded approvingly.

The officers stood to go. There was nothing else to add, and Charlie was still too baffled to know what questions she should ask.

When she was alone in her office, she picked up the phone to call Simm. He answered on the first ring.

'Where are you?' she asked.

'I had a few things to finish up for another case. What's up?'

'The police just left. The organs came from sheep.'

There were a few moments of silence on the other end of the line.

'Boy, I wasn't expecting that one.'

'Neither was I. But, on the other hand, at least they weren't human.'

'Yeah, I get that. Look, I'll be over a little later.'

'No rush. I'm not going anywhere. I'll be here until late tonight.'

Charlie tried to shake off the feeling of weirdness that blanketed her. She served tables, worked the bar, and cleaned up between shifts. It was late in the evening when she noticed Simm sitting at the bar, drinking a beer. She had no idea how long he had been there, and glancing at her watch, she realized she had already been at work for fourteen hours and had merely stopped to take Harley for his walks, with Frank close by her side. Exhaustion seeped through her body.

She propped herself on the stool next to Simm and noticed her reflection in the mirror behind the bar. She grimaced when she saw she looked even worse than she felt.

'I'll get Harley and we'll head home,' Simm said.

Charlie nodded her head in response, too tired to come up with an alternative.

Within a few minutes, Charlie and Harley were tucked into Simm's car and heading along the damp streets of Montreal. Fog swirled eerily around her apartment building, dampening Charlie's spirits even further. It struck her that it wasn't a cheerful-looking building, and she should think about finding another place.

'It's starting to rain a little harder. I'll drop you off at the door, and I'll park the car.'

'You don't have to come in. I can take it from here.'

'No. The deal is I see you safely inside your place. It's non-negotiable.'

Charlie shrugged her shoulders resignedly and climbed out of the vehicle. She moved up the stairs, fumbling in her purse for her keys, with Harley by her side. Her fingers closed around the ring of keys as she arrived at the landing outside her apartment door. She raised her head and staggered backward as if someone had hit her, bumping into her neighbor's door. Harley barked frantically. Charlie bent, clutched the dog, and ran down the stairs.

Halfway down, she collided with Simm. One of his hands grabbed her arm and the other the banister to steady the three of them.

'What is it?' he said.

Charlie was panting from exertion and fear. All she could do was point up the stairwell. Simm didn't need any further encouragement. He stepped around her and raced to the landing. When he reached the door, he staggered backward into the neighbor's door.

CHAPTER 15:

The same two police officers showed up at Charlie's apartment. Soon, the landing was crowded with uniforms and techs. Charlie had inched through her doorway to get into her home and sat huddled on the couch with Harley dozing in her arms. Simm paced back and forth between the woman and the scene at the door.

He was certain of one thing. The game had changed. The perpetrator knew where Charlie lived and wasn't shy about attacking her at home. She was no longer safe here.

After a closer look, Simm saw the technique the person had used was amateurish. It had the desired shock effect upon first glance, but everyone agreed he had used the most basic of materials.

Six posters of missing children had been plucked off bulletin boards and taped to Charlie's door. Each of them was slashed at least once with a sharp object. Then, a liberal amount of blood-like liquid had been applied. To top it off, a message, 'You can't bring back the children', was scrawled across the posters, again in a blood-red color. What that message was supposed to mean was anyone's guess.

'It's not real blood, Charlie,' Simm said, lowering himself onto the couch beside her.

'I know, but it's a shock all the same. And the worst part is, he knows where I live. He was here.'

Simm could just nod his head. How could he argue with her? It was precisely what he was thinking. Charlie scanned her living room, her lips curled in distaste.

'Why don't you go pack up some stuff? You can stay at my place tonight,' he said.

Charlie opened her mouth to say something, and Simm braced

himself for an argument, but she closed her mouth and stood up glumly. Harley moved over, setting his head on Simm's lap. He looked at the dog, and wondered how he would sneak him past the night watchman at his apartment building.

It was another hour before he had to worry about it. Pictures were taken, tests were made, and the neighbors were questioned. Charlie had two bags ready to be taken to the car, mostly filled with Harley's belongings.

Simm lived in a modern high-rise on Sainte-Catherine Street, one of Montreal's primary arteries, well-known for its shopping, restaurants and bars. There was a lot of traffic and activity in the vicinity, in sharp contrast to the relatively quiet neighborhood where Charlie lived. Despite the lateness of the hour, the street was still busy, and fortunately for Simm, the watchman was occupied elsewhere as they went through the lobby. But because of the security cameras, they took the precaution of carrying Harley in a tote bag.

His apartment was bright and spacious, but it only had one bedroom. Simm, being a gentleman, insisted Charlie take his room while he prepared the couch for himself. Once again, she didn't argue with him. He knew she had to be distressed if she couldn't make a decent argument against everything he suggested.

Her mood didn't improve during the night. A glum face sat across from him at the breakfast table, a coffee cooling in front of her.

'What time do you want to go to the pub today?'

'I don't know,' she answered with a shrug.

'Why don't you go have your shower while I take Harley out to do his business?'

'Okay.'

Concerned, Simm watched her shuffle to the bathroom. He glanced down at Harley.

'Okay, buddy, it's time to take care of you.'

Simm sifted through his closet and found the largest coat he owned. It happened to be a winter coat and would look strange on a warm day late in the month of May, but it was the only one big enough to hide a dog. He put a leash in one pocket, and gently picked up

Harley. He didn't want to squeeze him too hard for fear his bladder couldn't handle it. Meeting the watchman with a trickle of liquid running down his leg could raise questions Simm would rather not have to answer.

They made it outside without incident, but to be extra cautious, Simm waited until he was well out of sight of the apartment building before releasing Harley from his coat. Within a few minutes, his job was done, and they sneaked back inside in time to hear Charlie shutting off the shower.

When they arrived at Butler's, Simm witnessed Charlie's transformation. She immediately stepped into her role as the person who called the shots. Employees were scheduled, and alcohol was ordered to boost the inventory. A handyman was called to repair some chairs, and lists were made for supplies that needed restocking.

She may not be her usual cheerful self, but at least she seemed to have regained a purpose in life, Simm thought. He filled Frank in on the latest event and left Charlie under the bartender's watchful and concerned eye.

Simm's first stop was the police station to check with Detective Ranfort, only to find he had wasted his time. They had nothing new to tell him about the incident from the previous night and no leads to work on. Simm felt at loose ends, not sure in which direction he should be looking.

The memory of Charlie's expression disturbed his thoughts. He knew it wasn't part of his job description to keep his client cheerful and upbeat, but he couldn't help feeling bad for her. An idea popped into his head, and he mentally crossed his fingers, hoping he could make it work. Grabbing his cell phone, he sifted through his list of contacts.

Chapter 16:

Charlie was spooked. There were two films playing in the cinema of her brain. One starred the bag filled with bloody organs, and the other featured the pictures on her apartment door, dripping with red liquid.

Trying to take her mind off them, she threw herself into her work with even more enthusiasm than usual, but the images were impossible to escape. The fact that Frank and Simm argued over who would stay stuck to her side did nothing to put her mind at ease or improve her mood; it made things worse.

There was no denying she was disturbed by the events. To think someone had removed an animal's organs to send a weird and incomprehensible message to her was difficult to accept. And to think the same sick person had defaced her apartment door upped the ante from difficult to frightening.

She made it through the day, but not without a string of comments and questions from her regular customers as to why she was so quiet and pale. It drove her to go sit in the office and pretend she was doing paperwork or social networking, just to get away from everyone for a while.

Even Harley sensed something was wrong. Charlie felt him staring at her, and the more she tried to ignore him the more he whined, until she finally gave in and showed him some attention. He then insisted on sitting on her lap instead of on the floor at her feet, as if he could defend her from the evil that stalked her.

Charlie detested the idea of returning to her apartment, but she didn't have any choice, unless she stayed at a hotel. Simm had been nice enough to offer her a place to stay the previous night, but she knew it wasn't a long-term arrangement.

She didn't have any family left, and she didn't have a lot of friends, at least no one she felt comfortable enough to call and ask to take her in. She knew her shortage of close friends was a direct result of having her own business and spending seven days a week, including evenings, nurturing that business. After this was over, she would make it a point to get a life, like a regular person. The problem was she loved her life the way it was. She liked owning and working in a bar. She liked her customers with their familiar faces. She liked Frank and her other employees, and she liked the fact that she could walk around the neighborhood with Harley and be greeted by all the shop owners. She had always felt safe, up until now.

But all of those positive points meant she didn't have anyone she could call to help her out in a pinch. Sure, she could ask Frank to let her stay at his place –he had already offered- but she knew he and Paul had a small apartment, and she didn't want to be in the way.

No, she would have to suck it up and stay alone. After all, the guy probably knew she had called the cops. It might have the desired effect of making him back off.

Charlie's thoughts strayed to her tormentor. Simm's suggestion that it was Jim's past coming back to haunt her still burned. She had a hard time accepting that theory, but the cops would leap on it with both feet if they found out about Jim, and that led her to wonder why Simm hadn't told them. Most likely, he wanted to keep the case for himself and didn't feel like sharing it with the authorities. Truth be told, Charlie had more confidence in Simm than she had in the cops, although it would be a very cold day in July before she would tell him so.

The door opened and the subject of her thoughts stepped into the room. Her cheeks grew warm, and she hoped he wouldn't notice.

'You ready to go?' he said.

'Go where?'

'Home. Where else?'

Charlie glanced at her watch.

'It's eleven o'clock. The pub isn't closed yet.'

'And you're not out there either. I don't think you're getting much done in here, so you should go home and get some rest.'

Charlie didn't intend to go back to her apartment until it was absolutely necessary. She shuffled papers around her desk and tapped a few computer keys.

'I have tons of work to do here, so I'll stay a bit longer. There's no need for you to hang around. You can get going.'

'I don't think you understand, Charlie. I'm not taking you to your place to stay. We can pass by and pick up some things if you want, but you're going to stay at my place. I won't leave you alone. Not until we find this guy.'

Charlie fought to keep the look of relief off her face, but felt she had to make a minimal objection for the sake of form.

'There's no need for you to sleep on the sofa,' she offered.

'All right. But, just to let you know, I like to sleep on the left side of the bed.'

'What? That's not what I meant!'

Simm grinned.

'I'm just yanking your chain.'

Charlie grumbled a few words of protest and tried to look unhappy. She tidied up her papers and filed them away. Harley, probably noticing the change in atmosphere, stood up, stretched, and yawned before padding over to Simm to receive a comforting scratch behind his ears.

When she was ready to leave, Charlie went out to the bar and approached Frank.

'I'm going to take off now.'

The bartender looked at her in surprise before glancing at Simm. Silent communication seemed to pass between the two men.

'You don't have to worry about anything here. It's under control,' Frank said, no longer questioning her decision to leave.

'Thanks. I'll be in early tomorrow.'

'No need. I'll be here.'

Charlie gave him a quick hug of thanks before tugging on Harley's leash.

'Thank God for Frank,' Charlie said, as she slid into Simm's car and lifted Harley onto her knee. The little dog took his position as point man, his paws on the dash. 'I can really depend on him.'

'Uh huh.'

She scrutinized Simm as he maneuvered the car out of the parking lot and onto the street.

'You don't trust him, do you?'

'I don't trust anyone until I'm sure.'

'You can be sure about Frank.'

'Uh huh.'

Charlie snorted and shook her head. There was no winning with this guy.

A few minutes later, when she faced the door of her apartment, a shiver tickled her spine. The posters had been removed, supposedly taken to the police station for further testing, but whatever liquid had been used to simulate blood had stained the wood of the door.

Simm must have noticed the direction of her gaze.

'I'll scrub it clean,' he said.

Charlie shrugged and stepped over the threshold.

Once inside the apartment she stood in the entranceway and considered the space she had called home for six years. The apartment had lost its appeal. It had been invaded by a stranger, and she no longer wanted to live there. She doubted she would ever get over the feeling of intrusion.

Charlie glanced over to see Simm staring at her. She smiled weakly and headed to her room, hoping to avoid conversation. She packed a bag with a larger collection of clothing, so she wouldn't have to come back anytime soon. She made a mental note to talk to her landlord about breaking the lease.

As soon as possible, they were in Simm's car and on their way to his apartment. As he helped carry her bag into the building while she took care of Harley, Charlie had the sense he was preoccupied with something other than the fact that he would have a roommate for an indefinite period.

'What's wrong?' she said, as she started to make up the couch. Simm yanked off his cap and ran his fingers through his hair, a habit she had learned meant he would bring up an uncomfortable subject.

'How much do you know about the West End Gang?'

Charlie stiffened.

'Are you implying I'm connected to them somehow?'

'Of course not,' Simm said, spreading his hands. 'I'm investigating. It's my job. Investigating involves asking questions and, whether you like it or not, a lot of my questions will be directed to you. It's the nature of the beast.'

Charlie sighed. She knew she would have to stop being so suspicious of Simm's motivations. He had done everything he could to help her today, and she had to think of him as being on her side. She sat heavily on the couch, gathering in her lap the sheet she had been unfolding.

'I know the bare essentials. It's a criminal organization led predominantly by people of Irish descent, thus the a.k.a. of 'The Irish Mafia'. And they're principally involved in the distribution of illegal drugs. Apart from that, I don't know an awful lot.'

'Did Jim O'Reilly ever discuss them?'

'No, never. He tried to distance himself fully from them. The only way I knew of his connection was through my father. He told me about Jim's history.'

'Which was?'

'Jim's father had a bar in Pointe-Claire. Jim was brought up in the business, and when his dad retired, he continued in his footsteps. At some point, for a reason I don't understand, Jim became involved with the Gang, laundering money for them. Unfortunately, he was arrested and spent three years in jail. Meanwhile, his wife and baby son were on their own. The bar was taken over by the gang, and when Jim got out he had nothing. He gave up all connection with the Irish mafia, bought another pub, which is now mine, and started over. He learned his lesson and never wanted to be separated from his family again.'

'You believe all that to be true.'

'Absolutely. I know it, and my father knew it.'

'Okay, fair enough. But you must admit it's a hell of a coincidence for you to have a connection to a man who had a connection to a mob, and now you're being harassed and threatened by someone.'

'Yes, I admit it's a coincidence, but I honestly can't understand why, almost thirty years later, someone would want to get back at Jim by hurting me. He's dead. He can't be hurt.'

'I know that, and you know that, but stranger things have happened.'

Charlie agreed. She had been thinking a lot about Simm's theory, and no matter how much she denied it, it had her worried. She didn't want to be a target of a criminal organization. It had always been a fear of hers and part of the reason she never wanted to discuss Jim's connection to the mob. She had loved him dearly, but his past had scared her.

'How did he and your father become friends?'

She blinked at him.

'I don't know. I never asked. Jim was consistently a part of my life. I don't remember him never being there.'

'How did your mother feel about him? Was she friendly with Jim's wife?'

Her expression was thoughtful as she remembered all the times her family had been together with the O'Reilly family.

She could picture her mother, an otherwise talkative woman, becoming quiet as the conversation flowed around her whenever the other couple was present. Charlie had no recollection of the two women spending time with each other when the men weren't there. It surprised her that she had never thought about her mother's uncommon reaction before.

'No, they weren't best friends. I guess they put up with each other because their husbands were friends. They were polite to each other, but no more than that. And when Jim died, Mom never had anything further to do with her.'

'Why do you think that was?'

She shrugged.

'I don't know. I guess they didn't have much in common. I remember Sylvie as being a nice enough lady, but she acted a bit high-class, while my mother was more down-to-earth. Sylvie seemed to love

Jim and supported him. I guess the two women just didn't click.'

'Do you think the fact that Jim was a convicted criminal had something to do with your mother's animosity?'

'Perhaps. I know she wasn't thrilled about me working for him. Maybe she thought I would be badly influenced by him, but I didn't care. I wanted to work at the bar and nothing would stop me.'

'It's too bad she's not around now. There may have been something she could've shared with us. What about Mrs. O'Reilly? Is she still alive?'

'She's in a senior's home on the West Island.'

'Was she ever involved in the business?'

'No, never. She was the opposite of Jim. She was quiet and reserved. She didn't drink, and she didn't like to party. I don't know how the two of them got along, but they were devoted to each other.'

'You keep talking about her in the past tense.'

'I shouldn't do that,' she said, shaking her head. 'She's alive, but she had a severe stroke many years back, shortly after Jim died, and she's almost in a vegetative state.'

'Were you close to her?'

'Not nearly as close as I was to Jim, but she was his wife, and I saw a lot of her as I grew up. I would've liked to stay in touch with her, but it wasn't meant to be. Terry said she can't have visitors.'

She felt a wave of sadness, not just for what she was going through now, but for all that was lost from her past. She had no family left, and the other family that had been so much a part of her life was essentially gone.

CHAPTER 17:

'So, you used to be a cop,' Charlie said.

'How'd you know?'

'Lucky guess. Isn't that how most private investigators start?'

'Probably.'

'Why'd you give it up?'

Simm didn't roll his eyes, but he was tempted. He knew he was in for a game of forty questions. He had just taken his spot at the kitchen table with his morning coffee and his tablet, hoping to catch up on the scores of the hockey games from the previous night, when he saw Charlie set her cup on the opposite end of the table. As she pulled out the chair and settled in, he sensed his peaceful period of sports reviews wouldn't happen.

'It wasn't for me anymore,' he responded.

'Why not?'

His hope that his generic answer would satisfy her died a painful death.

'I'd seen enough. Enough death and gore. I needed a change.'

'You mean constantly having to deal with dead bodies and grief-stricken families became too difficult for you both psychologically and emotionally?'

'Something like that.'

'You see that a lot in the movies.'

Simm looked at her out of the corner of his eye, feeling her sarcasm and wondering where this was leading.

'I didn't think it actually happened that much in real life,' Charlie persisted. 'After all, this is Montreal, not downtown Detroit or New York City. It can't be that bad.'

'Have you ever been a cop?'

'Of course not.'

'Then don't give generalized opinions about something you know nothing about,' he said brusquely.

'So, during an average week, how many dead bodies would you see?'

Simm set his mug down with an exasperated clunk.

'Are you serious? You want details?'

She looked pensive for a moment, and said with a shrug, 'Yes.'

'Don't you give up? I could be suffering from severe post-traumatic stress disorder. You could set me off.'

She had the nerve to laugh.

'No, you don't look like you're suffering from anything more serious than a severe case of avoidance.'

'And you're some sort of expert on PTSD, I suppose, besides being an expert on cops?'

'No, but I know people. I see all kinds of people in my profession, and, let's face it, bartenders have to be pseudo-psychologists on a regular basis. You don't have PTSD, and you're lying about why you left the police force.'

Simm was stymied. How could he respond to such a blanket statement?

'You're really something, you know that? You'll have to send me your bill, Dr. Butler.'

Charlie chuckled.

'I'm glad I could provide some amusement for you,' Simm added. 'I have something else that may make you happy.'

Charlie straightened expectantly.

'What is it?'

'I should reconsider. I could find any number of people to go with me, people who won't pick apart my character and laugh at me.'

'Tell me what it is. I love surprises,' Charlie said, sitting on the edge of her seat.

He reached into his jacket pocket and pulled out two tickets. He flashed them in front of her face, yanking them out of her reach when she tried to grab them.

'Are those what I think they are?' she said, almost bouncing with excitement.

'Yes, they are.'

'When?'

'Tonight.'

'You've got to be kidding me. The first game! How did you get those?'

'I have connections.'

'Connections? What did you have to do to get them?'

'I had to call in a favor or two.'

'And?'

'Sign over my firstborn child.'

'And?'

'My left kidney.'

'God, I'm not surprised. But you're offering me the other ticket? What about one of your guy friends.'

'I don't have any,' he said, shrugging.

'Yeah, that doesn't surprise me either. Great! I'll be your friend for a night.'

Chapter 18:

'Frank, I need you to cover for me tonight.'

His expression was almost comical. Charlie knew her friend had never heard those words coming from her mouth, and he looked like he couldn't believe his ears.

'Do you mind?' she thought to ask.

'No, of course not. I know it's none of my business, but in light of recent events, I'd like to know if whatever plans you have are safe.'

'I'm going to the game,' Charlie said, smiling widely. She was rewarded with a shocked look.

'Not...'

'Yes, the first game of the Stanley Cup Finals!'

'How did you get tickets? How could you afford it?'

'Simm got them.'

'How could he afford it?'

'I don't know. Something about a firstborn child. I don't care. I'm going!'

'Wow, lucky you. In that case, I don't mind covering for you.'

From then on, the day dragged by sluggishly. At five o'clock, with the after-work crowd shuffling in, preparing to watch the game on the TV screens, Charlie and Harley hopped in a taxi –she was no longer allowed to walk home alone – and went back to her apartment. She hardly noticed the stains on her door as she rushed to her bedroom and excitedly searched through her closet. After finding what she needed, she got to work in front of the bathroom mirror. It was a long time since she had gone to a game and she wanted to do it right.

At six fifteen, the doorbell buzzed and Charlie smiled in satisfaction. She had timed it flawlessly. She flung open the door, expecting an approving look, but she was thrown off by his appearance, hardly noticing his shocked expression.

'You're kidding me, right?' he said.

'You're the one who's got to be kidding,' Charlie said. 'You're going like that?'

She looked him up and down, taking in his jeans, plain black boots, black leather jacket, and a Montreal Canadiens cap, the sole concession he had made.

Charlie glanced at the mirror by the door. The red Montreal Canadiens jersey hung mid-thigh, with the sleeves rolled up past her wrists. On each cheek, she had painted the logo of the team in bright red and navy blue, and her hair was pulled back and tied with a red and blue official hair tie. What could he possibly find wrong with her outfit? On the contrary, he looked dead boring compared to her.

'Okay, never mind,' he said. 'We have to get going.'

They weren't far from the Bell Center, but the streets were congested with cars and pedestrians, and it turned a typically ten-minute walk into one that took almost half an hour. When they were eventually seated, Charlie was speechless, but just for a moment.

'Really? Behind the player's box? I don't believe this! I expected to be in the nosebleed section.'

'Yep. They're good tickets.'

'Good? They're fantastic! I hope your firstborn is worthy of these seats.'

The arena buzzed with excitement. The Habs had made it to the final round, and the fans were pumped and ready. Charlie knew her clientele back at the pub had their eyes glued to the screens right now, and business would be brisk. She felt a momentary flash of guilt, but told herself she was being silly. She hadn't taken a night off in years. She deserved it.

Simm waved over a vendor and bought two beers.

'We'll get something to eat after, is that okay?' he asked.

Any answer she could have given was drowned out by the cheers of the crowd as the MC announced the arrival of the teams on the ice. The Chicago Blackhawks were politely received, but the crowd went mad for the Habs.

The game started with a bang as the Canadiens scored two goals in the first period. During the first intermission, Charlie and Simm stood up to stretch, but didn't leave the vicinity of their seats. They knew the food concession stands would be mobbed with people.

When the Blackhawks caught up during the second period, the mood was a little less jubilant in the arena. But, after having two beers each, both Charlie and Simm had to use the facilities during the next intermission. While Charlie went to the ladies' room, Simm stood guard outside the entrance. When it was Simm's turn, he told Charlie to wait by the door and not move a muscle. She was instructed to not hesitate to go into the men's room to find him if she noticed anyone suspicious-looking. Charlie grimly nodded her acquiescence. She didn't appreciate being reminded of her status as a victim, not when the hockey game had temporarily shoved the black cloud from above her head.

A matter of seconds after Simm left her alone, Charlie was approached by a teenage boy, skinny and pimply-faced. He smiled shyly at her. When he spoke, it was with a heavy French accent.

'Here, this is for you,' he said, handing her an envelope.

Charlie was too stunned to react, staring at the object as if he offered her a tarantula.

When she didn't instantly take the envelope, the boy shoved it into her hand, bringing her to her senses.

'Where did you get this?' she said to him.

The teenager turned and hurried away from her.

'Hey! Wait a minute!' she shouted, not letting him out of her sight as she shoved the envelope into her pocket.

Charlie ran after the boy, but he watched her over his shoulder and took off at a sprint, weaving between the people crowding the food concessions. Charlie didn't intend to let him get away. She ran without consideration for the people with their trays of food, or their plastic cups of beer. A cacophony of shouts and jeers followed her down the hallway, but she ignored them. She thought she heard her name being called, but she ignored that too. Her entire focus was on the skinny, little runt ahead of her.

She watched with satisfaction when he ran into someone and they both fell, sprawling across the floor in opposite directions. The teenager scrambled to his feet, jumped over his hapless victim, and ran for all he was worth. But, he had lost a lot of time, and Charlie was gaining on him. When she was just a few feet behind him, she leaped, worried she had poorly gauged her distance, but felt a measure of satisfaction when her hand caught hold of the leg of his baggy pants.

He went down hard. So did she, her ribs crying in pain when they hit the floor, but the element of shock and surprise was on her side. She crawled over him and sat on his back, straddling him. The boy gasped for air.

'Who are you? Where did you get that letter?' she demanded, her breathless voice not sounding as severe as she had hoped.

The boy started to mumble a reply when two arms grasped Charlie around the middle and dragged her off him. She shrieked in protest and tried to swing around to strike her assailant. Her body was still twisting when she was released, and the momentum made her fall on her rear-end beside the teenager. In her peripheral vision, she saw arms descending, and she braced herself for a blow, thinking she was being attacked by an enraged bystander.

But it was the boy who was lifted off his feet and shoved up against a wall with a bit more force than was perhaps necessary.

'Who are you? What did you do to her?'

Simm's face was a matter of inches from the tip of the teenager's nose. Charlie was shocked by his sinister look, and she knew she'd be shaking in her boots if he ever turned that expression on her.

The boy's face crumpled and tears rolled down his cheeks. He hadn't bargained for this.

'Nothing. He asked me to give it to her.'

'Who?' Simm asked, with a rough shake.

'I don't know. A man.'

'Who? Where is he?'

'I don't know.'

Simm gave him another shake. Charlie couldn't take it anymore.

She grasped Simm's forearm.

'Leave him alone. He doesn't know anything.'

'He knows what he looks like,' he said, turning his fierce gaze on her, never letting go of the boy.

'What's going on?'

The overweight security guard panted heavily and had a sheen of sweat on his face as he appeared at their side. He seized Simm's arm with one hand while reaching for his baton with the other.

'The kid harassed this woman,' Simm said.

Charlie thought the term of 'harassment' was a bit strong, but she wouldn't correct him. She would let Simm do the explaining.

However, the term apparently struck a chord with the guard, because he switched his attention from Simm to the still-sniffling teenager. Immediately, the boy was defensive, speaking in French, explaining that a man had given him twenty dollars to give an envelope to Charlie. He didn't know him, didn't know where he was, and he never thought there'd be any harm in it.

Simm let go of the boy and let him wipe his face, ridding it of tears and mucus, using the tissue Charlie dug out of her pocket and handed to him.

'Did he hurt you?' the guard asked Charlie, looking her up and down, taking in her disheveled appearance.

'No, I'm fine, but I need to know who gave him the envelope.'

Again, the boy spewed the same litany of explanations about his innocence, trying to make himself look like an innocent victim. Charlie's sympathy for him diminished. After all, he could have refused the twenty bucks and minded his own business.

'What do you want to do, Mademoiselle?'

Charlie leaned against the wall behind her. Now that the adrenaline rush had faded, she was drained of energy.

'Let him go. He doesn't know anything,' she said.

Everyone took a step back to let the kid walk away.

Chapter 19:

Charlie and Simm returned to their seats and pretended to watch the third period of the game, but they didn't participate in the cheering or the shouts of encouragement. Charlie's mind was preoccupied by the incident. As they sat behind the player's bench, they both read the note that had been passed to her by the misled teenager, and it only served to upset her further.

Dear Charlene,

My name is John. I can see you're a big fan of hockey. I would have liked to have played the game. I'm sure I would have enjoyed it. Even attending a game would be fun. You're so lucky you can do that.
Maybe someday we can get together and talk about it.

Charlie didn't understand what was happening. What was the point of these letters? They made no sense to her. They weren't threatening, but they seemed to be the product of a sick mind. The sheep organs and the damage done to her apartment door backed up that theory. To top it off, she now had proof he was following her. He could be watching her right at this moment. She looked over her shoulders uneasily.

'Damn it.'

Simm's exclamation startled her.

'What?' she said.

'He's here somewhere. We're so close.' Apparently, his thoughts were treading the same line as hers.

'Yeah, but so are twenty thousand other people.'

'I know. It just pisses me off, that's all.'

Suddenly, he swung to face her.

'And do you know what else pisses me off?'

Charlie opened her mouth to respond, but he didn't give her a chance.

'The fact that you didn't listen to me. Did I not tell you to stay by the door? Did I not tell you if something happened you were supposed to come in and get me?'

Charlie knew these were rhetorical questions. She would shut up and let him get it out of his system.

'Do you know how I felt when I came out and saw you were gone?'

No, she didn't.

'Then, I hear shouting and screaming, for God's sake!'

Yes, that would have been caused by her.

'Do you know how I felt?'

Again, no, she didn't, but she could tell it could be summarized in, 'not good'.

'And I could see all kinds of commotion happening down the hallway.'

This was said with much waving of hands to indicate commotion.

'What the hell were you thinking?'

Finally, a question she could answer.

'I was thinking I wanted to get the guy. Tiptoeing into a men's washroom, keeping my gaze above waist-level, trying to find you, was just going to slow me down. He would have gotten away.'

'You put yourself in danger.'

'I got him.'

She could see he wanted to argue, but she knew she had won a point.

'How can I protect you if you take off like that?' he said, changing tack.

'I didn't hire you to protect me,' she reminded him.

'I refuse to lose a client because she's running around unprotected.'

'Simm, I won't argue with you. I'm too tired. Let's just agree to disagree.'

'You must be very tired if you aren't willing to argue with me.'

The Habs won the game, but Charlie and Simm hardly noticed. They forced smiles onto their faces so they didn't appear to be rooting for Chicago, but the fun had been wrenched from the evening by a teenage boy and a man with a note.

Chapter 20:

'You're kidding me.'

'Nope.'

'He was there?'

'Yep.'

Charlie filled Frank in on the eventful evening at the Bell Center. He was fittingly stunned by the news.

'So, you never really saw the guy.'

'If I saw him, I didn't know it was him. He could have been sitting next to me, for all I knew.'

She shivered at the thought. It was entirely possible. She looked up from her perusal of The Gazette when she heard a chuckle.

'What's so funny?'

'I'm trying to picture you doing the Wonder Woman routine.'

'I was less Wonder Woman and more Sandra Bullock from 'Miss Congeniality'. I don't think I was all that graceful or powerful-looking.'

'Next time.'

'I hope there's no next time.'

'Did you sleep at Simm's place again?'

'Yes,' she said. 'On the couch,' she added when she saw the arched eyebrow of her friend.

'You should get in the bed. He's cute. I think it'd be worth the effort.'

'Get your mind out of the gutter, Frank. I have bigger problems to worry about right now.'

Apart from the obvious, those problems included a delay in the shipment of her most popular brand of scotch, a television screen that had decided to give out during the game last night and needed to be replaced before the next game, and a part-time employee who quit after being mauled by a drunken customer.

Unfortunately, these were all common problems to have in this particular type of business. Being stalked by a madman wasn't common, and it left her distracted and less able to deal with her day-to-day challenges.

'What's he up to today?'

"Who?'

Frank gave her a look.

'Simm? I have no idea. He dropped me off and left. Since he's a private investigator, I guess he's investigating something privately. I'm sure he'll let me know if it has anything to do with me.'

She still stung from the talking-down he had given her the night before. She believed she had reacted appropriately when the boy approached her, and if she had to do it over again, she wouldn't do anything differently.

During the evening, Simm dropped by Butler's, a scowl on his face. Charlie noticed him as soon as he walked in, but she didn't approach him. She watched as his gaze skimmed the bar, hesitated when he saw Frank, and then continued until he spotted her standing by a table of clients. His frown deepened. He came over to her and motioned with his head to her office door.

Charlie bristled, but decided not to cause a scene in front of everyone.

As the door shut behind her, she swung toward him.

'What's with the attitude? I happen to be working, you know.'

'Drop it. I'm not in the mood.'

'What the...'

'Why didn't you tell me about Frank?'

'What are you going on about now? You've decided to pick on Frank again?'

'With reason. Why didn't you tell me he had a record?'

'What? Frank doesn't have a record.'

'Yes, he does.'

He said it with such conviction Charlie knew it had to be true. That didn't make it easier to accept. She sat dejectedly in her chair.

'I didn't know. For what?'

'I don't have the details. He was a juvenile, so they don't release any information, but I know it involved an assault against a girl.'

'I don't believe it. Frank wouldn't hurt anyone. Besides, if they don't release information, how did you find out about it?'

'I have connections, and I could get the basics.'

'Your information is wrong. He wouldn't do it. I don't believe it,' she said, crossing her arms.

Simm sighed.

'Believe what you want, Charlie, but I'm going to have to question him.'

'No!'

'I have to. He's a suspect.'

'That's crazy! Besides, do you not think the kid last night would have noticed the person was a black man built like a tank? He would have mentioned it. And Frank was here last night. He was in charge of the bar.'

'He could have hired someone to follow you. He couldn't go himself. You would've seen him.'

Charlie shook her head vehemently.

'I can't let you question him. If you must know, Frank didn't have an easy life. When he came out at fourteen, his father wouldn't accept it. It was only because of his mother that he stayed in the house until he was eighteen. He would've been better off living on the street. His father made his existence a living hell. When he was of age, he was out of there, and he worked his way through university. When I hired him, he was a shy, quiet, young man, not quite what I was looking for in a bartender. But I took a chance, and he really blossomed here. Look at him now. Everyone loves him, and all it took was a little acceptance.'

'Okay, I get it,' Simm said, his expression grim. 'But, I still have to ask him about it. I have no choice.'

'No, you won't question him. I'll talk to him.'

'I want to be there with you.'

Before she could protest, he held up his hand.

'Look, whether you want to acknowledge it or not, I'm a trained investigator. I know how to do this. If you insist, I'll let you take the lead, but I need to be there.'

'There's no need to do this. He's innocent. I'm sure of it.'

'If he's innocent, he won't mind talking to us.'

'You'll hurt his feelings.'

'He's a grown man. He'll have to suck it up.'

Charlie ran her hands through her hair. She couldn't believe this was happening. He was making her doubt Frank, something she never could have imagined. Harley came over and sat at her feet, looking at her balefully. Even he seemed upset by the news.

'It's Tuesday night. What time do you close tonight?' Simm said.

She glanced at her watch.

'At midnight. In an hour.'

'We'll talk to him then.'

The next hour was one of the worst Charlie had ever lived through. She couldn't even look at Frank without feeling guilty, and he noticed.

'What's going on? You look upset. What did Simm have to say?'

'I'll talk to you later. After we close up.'

She kept herself busy, moving from the bar to the tables, continually checking on customers. Simm sat at a corner table, nursing a beer, trying to kill time. Charlie noticed Frank glancing at him suspiciously, wondering what he had done to upset his boss.

Finally, the last customer was ushered out the door and the 'closed' sign was put in place. Charlie, resigned to her fate, asked Frank to sit at a table with her and Simm.

'What's happening? Charlie looks like she lost her best friend.'

She grimaced. She hoped his statement wasn't prophetic.

'It's nothing serious, Frank. We just have a couple of questions, that's all,' she said.

'For me? This has to do with me?'

'Yeah, but it's nothing to worry about.' She tried to smile before continuing.

'Simm was doing his checking, like we hired him to do, right? And he came across some information. I'm sure there's a perfectly good explanation, and I know it has nothing to do with what's going on these days, but is it possible you have a juvenile record?'

She knew she had handled it clumsily when Frank's face contorted in anger, and he stood up so fast his chair fell over with a loud bang.

'You've been trying to pin this on me all along, haven't you?' he said, pointing his finger at Simm.

Simm unhurriedly got to his feet. He was almost as tall as Frank, but he wasn't as bulky, and Charlie didn't think he would fare well if it came to a physical fight. She also didn't want to have to choose sides. She stepped between the men, facing Frank.

'No one is pinning anything on you. We just want to clarify some things, that's all.'

Frank lowered his gaze to look at Charlie. The look in his eyes sent a pain through her chest.

'Clarify things? Have I not made anything clear to you over all these years? I thought we were friends.'

'We are! Please don't take this the wrong way, Frank,' she appealed to him, placing her hands on his forearms. She could feel him trembling with rage, and she knew she had made a terrible mistake. His face blurred in front of her, her eyes brimming with tears.

'How can I not take it the wrong way? You're accusing me of harassing you, sending you crazy letters and animal organs! What have I ever done to give you the idea I would do something like that?'

'Nothing, nothing at all. I know you wouldn't do it.'

'It's him,' he said, pointing at Simm. 'He's convinced you I'm some sort of psycho.'

Charlie had no idea how Simm reacted to that accusation, and she didn't care. She was much more concerned about Frank at the moment.

'Do you want to know what happened?'

'No, I don't...'

'I'll tell you. I was fifteen years old, and I was confronted by a bunch of bullies.' he said, glaring at Simm. 'There were three of them, two boys and a girl. The two boys held me down while she had fun kicking me, in the face and the groin. I was big then too. I managed to shake them off, and one of them fell on top of her, and she broke her arm. Of course, I was blamed for it. And who would they believe? Let's blame the black guy, right?'

Charlie was crying now, both for the fifteen-year-old boy and the kind-hearted man who had been by her side for the last five years, and who she was now afraid she would lose.

'I'm outta here.'

He turned to storm out of the pub, but not before picking up the chair and putting it back where it belonged.

When the door slammed behind him, Charlie's heart plunged lower than she thought it could ever go.

'Charlie…'

She held up her hand. Her back was still turned to Simm, and she knew she couldn't look at him. It hurt too much, and she was too angry.

'Leave me alone. I'm going to his place to talk to him. I have to make this right.'

'I'll drive you.'

'It's not far. I'll walk.'

'You can't…'

'I can, and I will. I can't deal with you right now.'

Charlie gathered up her things and attached Harley's leash to his collar. Without looking at Simm, she waited for him to step out of the pub before she locked up. As she trudged dispiritedly up the street, she saw him walking to his car. A few minutes later, she heard a vehicle following close behind her. Her heart beat faster. Had she taken a risk she would pay for?

She cautiously glanced over her shoulder and breathed in relief. It was Simm, following at a crawl.

Chapter 21:

The look on Frank's face broke her heart all over again. She had argued with Paul for a few minutes before he agreed to let her into the apartment. That was the easy part. The hard part was facing Frank.

She had expected him to be simmering, but instead he resembled a little boy who had lost his favorite toy. During the walk over, she tried to decide how she would approach him, but seeing him now, all her carefully-planned strategy flew out the window. The best way was to speak from the heart. She sat beside him on the couch.

'Frank, please forgive me. I'm an idiot. There's no excuse for what I did. I'm so sorry.'

She paused to see if there was any break in his expression. Seeing none, she went for broke.

'You're my best friend. God, you're my only friend. I spend more time with you than I've ever spent with anyone else. I depend on you. You're always there for me, through thick and thin. I made a mistake, a horrible mistake. I should never have listened to him. But, if it makes you feel any better, I never believed you had anything to do with the letters. I told him so.'

'He was going to talk to you about the juvenile record,' she continued. 'But I didn't want him to do it. I thought, if anything, it would be better if I was the one to ask you about it. But I messed it up. I messed up everything. Frank, you know I love you. I hate myself for hurting you. It was a terrible thing to do. I don't deserve to be forgiven, but please forgive me anyway.'

The silence was long and excruciating.

'I would never hurt a woman.'

'I know that. You wouldn't hurt anyone,' she hurried to say.

'You're wrong. I would hurt someone. I would hurt someone really bad. Anybody that messed with you would have to deal with me. And I wouldn't be gentle with them.'

Charlie blinked her eyes several times, trying to hold back the tears, until she gave up and let them flow. She leaned over and wrapped her arms around the big man's neck, laying her head on his shoulder. His body was stiff and tense. Despite his words, she worried that she'd be rejected, and she began to pull away, until she felt two strong arms circling around her and pulling her close.

'You're my best bud, Frank. Please don't leave me.'

'I won't. Unfortunately, I'm stuck on you too.'

'I never doubted you. I just...'

'Shh. Let's forget about it, okay? I don't want to talk about it anymore.'

'You're right. We won't discuss it.'

'And if that asshole Simm dares to imply anything, I'll...'

'Don't say it. It won't happen. I think he learned his lesson.'

'The only reason why I don't send him packing is because he does a good job of watching out for you.'

'I know.'

'And if he'll ever get his head out of his ass and start looking for the real culprit, maybe we can get past all this.'

'I agree. I'll pass on the message.'

An hour later, when Charlie and Harley came out of Frank's apartment, Simm's car was still parked at the curb. She hadn't expected him to wait. When she walked over to the car and peered in the window, she couldn't help but laugh, despite her lingering anger with him. He was sound asleep. Some bodyguard he was, she thought.

She rapped sharply on the window and was satisfied to see him jump in reaction.

'Keeping an eye out for me, were you?' she asked, when he lowered the window.

'I knew you were there.'

'You're such a bad liar, Simm.'

'Everything okay with Frank?'

'Yes. Thank God, and no thanks to you.'

'I had to check every angle.'

'Well, that's one angle we'll put to rest. And, just so you know, he thinks it's time you pulled your head out of your ass.'

Simm snorted.

'Let's get home. I'm tired,' he said.

Charlie was silent on the way home, but she wouldn't let it go entirely. As the door of the apartment closed behind them, she turned to face Simm.

'Just so you know, I don't appreciate what you put me through today, not to mention what it did to poor Frank.'

Simm ran his fingers through his hair.

'I know. I got it. But you have to realize I wouldn't be doing my job if I didn't look at all the possibilities.'

'Could you stick with possibilities that are at least plausible?'

'All of them are plausible. Even Frank was plausible. Incorrect, but plausible.'

'All of them? How many do you have?'

'A few.'

'Who?'

'I'll tell you when you need to know.'

'I can eliminate some for you if you tell me who they are.'

'That's exactly why I'm not telling you.'

Charlie narrowed her eyes. God, he could be frustrating.

'I think I should be involved in the investigation.'

Simm barked out a laugh as he threw himself into an armchair.

'No way. I work alone. The worst thing to do is partner with someone on a job, especially the victim.'

'And why would that be?'

'Because they're often too emotional, not to mention inexperienced.'

'I could be a good asset. I've worked in a bar all my life. I know people. I know how to read them.'

'Thanks all the same, but the answer's still no.'

'You can at least keep me informed. You could tell me about the next suspect on your list.'

'Need to know.'

'You're a pain in the ass.'

'You didn't hire me to be a nice guy. You hired me to find out who this freak is.'

'I didn't hire you at all. Frank did.'

'You didn't un-hire me.

'There's still time for that.'

Chapter 22:

Simm was at the pub, having a beer along with the after-work crowd without mingling with anyone, preferring to sit back and watch.

Most of his attention was drawn by Charlie, who buzzed around taking care of customers with her usual zest. Simm had finally gotten used to Charlie's looks. After all, there were differences. Helen's skin had been perpetually tanned, having spent most of her life outdoors. Charlie was fair-skinned, with a very faint dusting of freckles if you saw her in the right light. Her hair also had a bit of a reddish glow in certain lighting, while Helen's had been a true brown.

Their builds were similar, both of them slim, but Charlie was taller. Simm remembered how high the top of Helen's head reached in comparison to him. Charlie had an inch or two more on her.

He told himself he had to stop comparing the two women. It was something he never did with women he dated, and he knew it was because Charlie reminded him so much of Helen that he did it now, but it was unhealthy. Too many memories had resurfaced, and most of them were not good.

Thank goodness Charlie's character was the opposite of Helen's, or he'd lose his mind altogether. He remembered the gentle, unassuming woman he had known most of his life, with her easygoing personality, always ready to forgive and forget. How many times had she told Simm life was too short to worry about other people and their actions? She believed you had to enjoy the moments you had, and everything would work out for everyone.

Helen had been wise beyond her years, almost prophetic. Except, it hadn't worked out for either of them. On that point, she had been wrong.

Simm stiffened when a hand landed on his shoulder. The familiar voice did little to make him relax.

'Here you are. I finally tracked you down.'

'And I thought I was the investigator. How did you find me?'

Surprisingly, Walt had the grace to color a bit.

'To tell you the truth, I followed you.'

'I didn't think skulking around was your style. Hiring someone to follow me would have been more believable.'

Simm turned away to sip his beer, and caught Charlie looking at them with curiosity. He knew he had to move this discussion to another location if he wanted to keep her nose out of it. But it was too late. Charlie converged on them before Simm could barely move a muscle.

'Hey Simm, who's your friend?' she said, without taking her eyes off Walt. 'You guys must be related. You look so much alike.'

'You have a good eye,' Walt answered, clearly enchanted by the megawatt smile Charlie had pulled out for the occasion. 'I'm Walt, Simm's brother.'

'Isn't that great? At long last, I get to meet Simm's brother,' Charlie said, giving every impression Simm had told her about his sibling's existence. 'Sit down. What would you like to drink? It's on the house. Any brother of Simm's is a brother of mine.'

She sounded genuine, but the undercurrent of sarcasm was glaringly obvious to Simm. From the look on Walt's face, all he saw was a beautiful woman pouring on the charm.

When Charlie sauntered off to get Walt's whisky on the rocks, the bedazzled man turned to Simm.

'Who is that? Is she yours?'

'Her name is Charlie Butler, and she owns this pub. And to answer your question, no, she's not mine. She's a client.'

'She hired you?'

'Don't sound so surprised. There are people who hire me, you know.'

'Of course. It's just…what did she hire you to do?'

'Investigate. I can't discuss the details.'

'Is she single?'

Simm ground his teeth together. Walt was three years younger than him, and Simm had always been patient with him, as he believed a big brother should be, but sometimes Walt was irritating to the extreme.

'I don't know. I think so. But she's just a lowly bartender,' he said, with a meaningful look at his brother.

'Not at all. She's a businessperson.' Walt said, Simm's message going over his head.

'Why are you here?'

Simm knew the answer, but hoped to get past this episode as soon as possible.

'Susan told you he's dying,' Walt said, his attention moving from Charlie to Simm.

'Yeah. There's no need for you to look for me just to tell me again. It won't change anything.'

'He's your father.'

'I gave up considering him my father years ago.'

'He wants to see you.'

'That's too bad. It won't happen.'

'Simm.'

'Drop it, Walter.'

The younger man got the message this time. Simm's tone of voice and use of his brother's full name left no doubt that he was serious. Walt took a sip of the drink that had been set on the counter by a woman who had known when to leave the two men alone. He downed it in two gulps.

'You know where to find us,' he said before he turned and walked out of the building.

CHAPTER 23:

Simm knew Charlie wouldn't be happy with him, but what else was new? He had to decide who to investigate and how. He couldn't and wouldn't let her run the show.

His next suspect wasn't very difficult to find. A few minutes on his smartphone, and Simm was on his way. He didn't know what he had expected, but it certainly wasn't what he found. Charlie's comments had led him to picture something thoroughly different.

He had to drive very carefully to avoid damaging his car in the potholes, and he raised the windows to keep the dust from invading his vehicle. As he went along the road, the homes seemed to become more desolate-looking. Eventually, he spotted the number '25' on the side of a mobile home, and he pulled over to the side of the road. There was a driveway, but it was small and otherwise occupied by a beat-up pickup truck.

Simm studied the home for a few minutes, looking for a sign of life. Getting out of his car and being careful to lock it, he noticed a woman's face peeking out of a window of the neighboring mobile home. He smiled at her and nodded. She briskly stepped back and drew the curtains shut.

He returned his attention to number 25. Since a truck was in the yard, he assumed the occupant was home. He hesitated again when he reached the door and saw the condition of the front steps. Would they hold his weight? He guardedly went up one step, and then another, until he was close enough to knock on the door.

There was no sound from within, so after another half-minute, he knocked again, louder. This time, he heard a man's growl, followed by a bang that shook the structure, followed by more growling.

The door opened with such force Simm took a step backward, almost toppling down the steps. Just in time, his hand latched onto the rusty, black railing. It wasn't only the surprise that kept him tottering, the man's breath required a certain distance be maintained. Even from three feet away, he reeked. The blue of his irises was overpowered by red veins, and his skin was sallow, reminding Simm of a vampire.

'What do you want?' the man said, slurring slightly.

'Are you Terry O'Reilly?'

'Who are you?'

'My name is Simmons. I'm a private investigator. Are you Terry O'Reilly?'

'What? A private investigator? I didn't do nothin'. Go away.'

The man started to close the door. Having no choice, Simm took a step forward and placed his palm on the inside of the cobweb-covered door.

'I'd like to ask you a few questions. It won't take long. It's about Charlie Butler.'

The man released his hold on the door.

'What about her? Is she dead?'

Simm had difficulty interpreting that remark. With the slurring of the man's words and the dullness of his expression, Simm couldn't say whether he was concerned or hopeful.

'She isn't dead.'

'Oh.' Again, the reaction was too vague to interpret.

'Can I come in?'

The man stepped back, leaving enough room for Simm to squeeze by. Simm almost gagged as he walked into the home. Directly ahead of him was the kitchen table, which was littered with beer cans and liquor bottles, all apparently empty. Amongst the mess were two ashtrays overflowing with cigarette butts and ashes. The smell was bad enough to fell a buffalo.

To his right, were a couch, an armchair, and an old television. There were additional cans, bottles, and butts on the floor and on a three-legged coffee table. The fourth leg consisted of two cement blocks. To Simm's left, was a hallway, which in all likelihood led to a bathroom and at least one bedroom.

When Charlie told Simm that Terry was doing all right for himself, he hadn't imagined this level of squalor. Obviously, they had different definitions of 'doing all right for himself'. Either that, or Charlie wasn't up-to-date on Terry O'Reilly's current status. Simm favored the latter explanation.

'I'm glad to catch you at home. I thought you might be at work.'

The sound of the flick of a lighter drew Simm's attention back to Terry O'Reilly, and he watched as the other man popped open a beer can as smoke curled around his face. He knew from his research Jim's son was thirty-five years old, but he looked twenty years older. His bad habits were not good for his health.

'I'm temporarily unemployed.'

Simm also knew from his research Terry had been 'temporarily unemployed' for at least four years.

'So, what's up with the lovely Charlene?' O'Reilly said.

'She's been getting strange mail.'

This information elicited a reaction. Terry's teeth seemed to be his only feature that hadn't been ravaged. They were yellowed, but they were straight and even, and Simm saw he had a full mouth of them when the man threw back his head and laughed.

'Mail? She hired a private investigator because she didn't like her mail? She's got way too much money, that girl.'

He threw himself onto the couch and flicked ashes in the general direction of an ashtray, still shaking his head and chuckling.

'Do you see her often?' Simm said.

'Charlene? Nope. Not often since the old man died.'

'How often? Once a month? Once a year?'

'Coupla times a year, I guess.'

'Does she come here?'

This earned another loud guffaw, followed by a vicious bout of coughing. He washed it down with a long swig of beer.

'She wouldn't set her fancy little foot in here,' he continued when he could speak again. 'I usually meet her somewhere.'

'You just get together to chat? Have a little visit?'

'Somethin' like that.'

Terry was concentrating on putting out his cigarette. It seemed to be a process that required a lot of attention.

'Why did your father leave the pub to Charlie?'

'Charlene was his little sweetheart, the little girl he never had. I guess he really wanted a daughter and not a son.'

Terry didn't bother masking his bitterness.

'What about your mother?'

'What about her?' Terry's normally dead eyes sparked with something resembling anger.

'Did she have any say in the matter? She must have wanted the business to go to her son.'

Simm knew he was pushing dangerous buttons, but experience had taught him button-pushing frequently delivered information that otherwise would be held on to securely.

The lighter flicked again. Simm didn't know how long he could stay inside this place if Terry continued to fill it with smoke.

'She didn't have any say. She couldn't say anything.'

'Why not? Your old man wouldn't let her give her opinion?'

'No! She can't talk, for Christ sake! She can't do anything.'

Simm could see tears forming in the other man's eyes.

'Anyway, piss on it,' Terry continued. 'I never wanted that shithole place. More work than it's worth. She can have it.'

'So, you get along okay with Charlie? No hard feelings?'

Terry showed off his teeth again with a smile that didn't reach his eyes.

'How could I not get along with little Charlene? Everybody loves Charlene.'

'You know, you're the first person I've met who calls her Charlene. Most people call her Charlie. Why's that?'

Another big smile.

'Because she hates it.'

Chapter 24:

Despite the cool misty weather, Simm drove with the windows fully open. As soon as the door of his apartment closed, he removed his clothing. By the time he reached the washing machine, he was naked. He threw his clothing into the machine, added detergent, and turned it on.

Next stop was the shower. He ran the water as hot as he could stand it and scrubbed away the smoke and heebie-jeebies he had picked up at Terry O'Reilly's place. As he massaged the shampoo into his hair, he tried to reconcile Charlie's description of her mentor's son to the man Simm had visited. It didn't match, and he had a strong feeling Charlie's eyes were covered with wool.

He also knew he couldn't eliminate Terry as a suspect. Despite the fact that he was physically and mentally limited by his addictions, he was smart enough and sneaky enough to harass a woman via the postal service. Would he, or could he, go so far as to attack her physically? Had he been personally responsible for the organs and the assault on her apartment door? Maybe not, but that didn't mean he wasn't the guy behind it.

One thing was definite; Terry O'Reilly was not okay with the fact that Charlie had inherited the bar. He resented her and seemingly hated her. His body language and his sarcasm sent Simm the message loud and clear. Simm hesitated from accusing him outright simply because of his reaction to the news that Charlie had hired an investigator as a result of 'strange mail'. The surprise and the laughter had seemed genuine.

Drying himself off, he made the decision to keep the news of his meeting with Terry to himself for a while. He didn't want Charlie to get bent out of shape because of what he had done and possibly throw off any progress Simm made in his investigation of the man. He would continue to work on a need-to-know basis.

Meanwhile, he had another direction in which to look – the West End Gang. Simm didn't have much experience with organized crime, but the Irish Mafia was well-known in Montreal. Perhaps not as well-known as the Italian Mafia, but it had an established presence. It had been a part of the criminal landscape in the city since the early 1900s, running the usual gamut of organized crime activities. They were strong in the drug trade in the 1970s and developed ties with the Montreal Mafia and a few other organizations to ultimately make up a consortium with which they could fix drug prices and map out their respective territories. It was a dangerous and powerful organization in its own right, and a smart person shouldn't assume the Irish heritage of its members meant they were a jovial, party-loving bunch.

In his past life as a police detective, Simm had occasion to investigate some of the many crimes perpetrated by the West End Gang, but didn't have many solid contacts within the gang, with the possible exception of one.

If John Flynn was still alive and well, he might be willing to give Simm a lead. The challenge would be in finding him.

He began by contacting an old friend of his in the department.

'Jamie, how's it going?'

'Simm, you old dog. I haven't heard from you in a while. What are you looking for now?'

'You know me too well.'

'You don't call me without a good reason.'

'You're right. I need to know if John Flynn is still in circulation.'

'He's alive, but not in circulation. He's in Donnacona.'

'I hadn't heard that. Since when?'

'It must be a few years now. He was picked up for eliminating a bad debt,' the cop said.

'Is there any way I can get a fast track to meet with him? I don't want to have to do the paper route.'

Without his badge, Simm no longer had the advantage of being able to visit a prisoner without having to go through the technicalities required by Canadian Correctional Services. He would have to fill out a form, attach two passport-sized photos of himself, and send it all via snail mail. It could take weeks to get permission to visit a prisoner.

'I could try making a couple of calls and see what I can do. I'll get back to you.'

'I appreciate it, Jamie. And the next time I call you, it'll be to invite you out for a beer.'

'Yeah, right, promises, promises.'

Simm mentally crossed his fingers when he disconnected the call. It would save him a lot of time to have a fast-track approval for a visit to Donnacona prison. Meanwhile, he had to do some research on the gang. He'd clearly been out of the loop for too long. He hadn't even known Flynn was imprisoned.

Two hours later, he was much better informed. His internet research had given him an update on the organization and a link to a book that had been written a few years back by a former West End Gang member. Simm purchased and downloaded the book and worked his way through the pages.

The gang's activities hadn't evolved very much over the past years, but the leader's names had changed, either by natural attrition or by means of assassination. The current head was Marty Sullivan. He was the nephew of the previous head who had been murdered in his own home a couple of years earlier.

Sullivan was known to be tough and unforgiving, but not ruthless. All he wanted was to make money. He didn't encourage bloodshed unless it was necessary, or at least as much as he judged it to be necessary.

Simm flinched when his cell phone chirped. He had been fully concentrated on the documents on his laptop. He recognized the number on his phone screen and answered at once.

'That was fast. I hope it's good news.'

'Very. You owe me one. You have an appointment tomorrow at ten o'clock.'

'Fantastic. I couldn't have hoped for better. I owe you more than one, buddy. Believe me.'

Simm smiled as he hung up. Jamie had pulled some impressive strings to get him in so quickly. He did a rough calculation in his head. Donnacona prison was close to Quebec City. Factoring in the morning traffic in Montreal, he would leave at seven, grab breakfast along the way, and he'd be in Donnacona with a bit of time to spare if everything went well.

His phone rang again. He answered without looking at the screen.

'What did you forget to tell me?'

Silence.

'Hello?' Simm said. 'Are you there?'

'I'm here, but I don't know what you're talking about,' a feminine voice said.

'Sorry, Charlie. I thought you were someone else.'

'I got that.'

'What's up?'

'Just wondering where you were today.'

'Do you miss me?'

'Yeah, about as much as I miss a skin rash. It's because you didn't tell me what you're up to these days.'

'I'm working on cases. I can't tell you about all of them,' he said, fibbing a little.

'Someone else's case?'

'Yep,' he said, fibbing a lot.

'I see. You didn't go see your brother today?'

'No. Why would I do that?'

'I didn't want to bug you about it last night, but it definitely looked like you two had some things to work out.'

'Families always have things to work out, Charlie.'

There was silence on the other end of the line, and Simm wanted to kick himself. That was a pretty callous thing to say to a woman with no family left.

'Sorry. That came out wrong.'

'You should consider yourself lucky, Simm.'

'I know. I am lucky,' he said before the line went dead. But he had told Charlie the biggest fib of all.

CHAPTER 25:

The drive to the prison in Donnacona was uneventful. There were a few traffic snags in Montreal, but when he was on the highway he made good time, arriving twenty-five minutes before his scheduled appointment. He was admitted into the facility without a hitch, having only a moment of worry when the burly officer at the desk was searching for his name on a list. It crossed his mind that his authorization may be lost in the bureaucratic paper trail, but the guard finally found it and let him through. Since the prison was maximum security, and there were problems in the past with the smuggling of illegal substances, he was subjected to a thorough scan. His jacket, his belt, and the contents of his pockets were left in a basket in the admittance area.

Simm was escorted by another heavily-armed officer to an interview room. Again, he was impressed by Jamie's magical powers. Somehow the cop had gotten Simm the special privilege of a private interview room. Regular visitors, including family, could see the prisoners in a common area, talking to them through a Plexiglas window while surrounded by guards. Lawyers and police officers were fortunate enough to have a private meeting with the incarcerated.

John Flynn was already in the room, shackled and handcuffed to a chair that was itself bolted to the floor. There was one other chair in the room, on the opposite side of a table separating Simm from the prisoner. There were cameras in the corners. Simm knew every movement was recorded, and if he so much as leaned over to touch Flynn, someone with a gun would be coming through the door behind him.

Flynn had aged since the last time Simm had seen him, looking much older than his forty-five years. His once thick, curly hair was now graying and thin. The same description could be given to the rest of his appearance. Flynn, although not particularly tall, had been a heavyset man, but any excess had disappeared, and his skin was drooping and sallow. He looked like a cancer patient, but Simm knew the change was the result of prison life. This was Flynn's first incarceration, and it wasn't looking good on him.

'What are you doing here?'

'Not happy to see me, Flynn? I thought you'd be thrilled to have a visitor.'

'You're not a cop anymore. You have no business being here.'

'I have some questions for you. About Jim O'Reilly,' Simm said, ignoring his remark about his former profession.

'O'Reilly? He's dead.'

'I know he's dead, but that doesn't mean I can't ask questions.'

'I didn't know him too good.'

'What did he do for the gang?'

'Why should I tell you anything? You can't do nothin' for me.'

Simm had expected this. Giving information to the authorities worked under the barter system, and Flynn was aware Simm didn't have much influence since he had left the police force.

'I can still put in a good word for you.'

'Who cares what you have to say now? You're a nobody.'

'Not true. I still have lots of connections. How do you think I got this room?'

The prisoner narrowed his eyes and scrutinized the room, as if just realizing where he was. When his gaze returned to Simm, his attitude had changed.

'I'm up for parole in six months.'

'I'll send them a letter. But I need something that will move my case along.'

'What do you want to know?'

'What did Jim do for the gang?' he repeated.

'Small stuff. He went down for money laundering.'

'What do you know about his bar on Drummond?'

'Not much. He didn't own that one when he was with the Gang.'

'Did he do any dealing?'

'No, just small stuff, like I said. He would've gotten off on the other stuff, but he wouldn't turn, so he had to do the time.'

'Loyal, was he?'

'Yeah. Or scared. He had a wife and kid.'

'Anybody have a beef against him?'

'Not that I know of. He got along with everybody.'

'Do you know Charlene Butler?'

His face scrunched up tightly until he resembled a raisin.

'Nope. Who's she?'

'Who was O'Reilly's boss?' Simm asked.

'Kelly, but he's dead.'

'Who could I talk to that would give me further information about O'Reilly? Someone close to him.'

'He was pretty tight with Sullivan at one time. I think that's why he could walk away without being touched.'

'Marty Sullivan?'

'The one and only.'

Chapter: 26:

The drive home went by quickly. Simm was so preoccupied with thoughts of his meeting with John Flynn he didn't notice the time. He couldn't leave the prisoner without promising once again to send a letter of recommendation to the parole board on behalf of Flynn. Simm would see through on his promise, but he didn't know if it would bear fruit for John. Simm knew Flynn had committed murder on multiple occasions, even though he had only been convicted for one. He was a dangerous felon who had a solid membership in a powerful criminal organization. Those facts alone would keep him in prison for at least twenty-five years, and a letter from a private investigator would do little to help him.

For Simm, the most disturbing element about the interview was the news that he would have to deal face-to-face with Sullivan to get more information about Jim O'Reilly. The idea of sitting down with the head of the Irish Mafia to discuss a former colleague of his was not very palatable. Just getting access to the man would be a major feat. The miracle Jamie had performed to get him into the Donnacona prison was small potatoes compared to what it would take to get a meeting with Marty Sullivan.

Flynn had given him the name of another person to contact, someone who could perhaps set it up for him, but Simm would do his research first. He wouldn't put his life into the hands of a total stranger, especially someone who also happened to be a mobster.

In the interim, he wanted to pay a visit to Mrs. O'Reilly. If Charlie's information was correct, and Terry said the same, the wife of the mobster probably couldn't communicate with him. But Simm had to see for himself. Charlie had mentioned which home Sylvie O'Reilly lived in, and he made the decision to go see her first thing in the morning.

He checked the clock on the dashboard of his car. It was three fifteen. He would stop at the pub and check on Charlie, even though he knew it wasn't necessary. Frank was more than capable of protecting her, but Simm thought he could use a beer right about now.

The pub was moderately quiet, but since it was manned entirely by Charlie and Frank, they were busy. Simm didn't mind not having their attention. He didn't need anyone to keep him company. He enjoyed sitting, sipping his beer, and watching Charlie at work. She definitely had a knack for this business. She could mix drinks, pour beer, and carry on a lively conversation with everyone, all simultaneously. Looking at the men lined up at the bar, Simm estimated more than half of them were more than half in love with her.

It occurred to him he may also fall into the same category.

He shook his head and looked at his beer glass in confusion. He had just had one so far. He shouldn't have such strange thoughts only partway through his first beer.

'What's up?'

Simm looked up guiltily at the sound of Charlie's voice. He hoped his thoughts weren't transparent.

'Nothing. Just having a beer.'

'Where were you today?'

'Quebec City.'

'What for?'

'I had to go see someone for a case.'

'My case?'

'I told you I have other cases.'

'I was under the impression I was the only one in your life.'

Her smile was teasing, but Simm was uncomfortable with the comment. His smile was more of a grimace.

'So, when will you let me in on what you're doing?' she continued.

'Need-to-know, remember?'

Her eyes flashed with irritation. She leaned across the counter and answered through gritted teeth.

'This is my case. I have to know.'

Simm heard someone calling her name from the opposite end of the bar. He caught a glimpse of the warm, customer-oriented smile before she turned her back to him and went to tend her client. He knew it was just a temporary reprieve. She would come back at him at the end of the day.

CHAPTER 27:

The huge glass windows on the facade of the building reflected the lush, green lawns and the flowering shrubs. Simm half expected to see a valet offer to park his car for him, but he eased his old Toyota smoothly into a spot with a Mercedes on his left and a Porsche on his right.

The reception area was just as impressive. The space, which was manned by one woman dressed in white, was the size of a basketball court. The ceilings were twenty feet high, topped with a frosted glass skylight. All the furnishings were made of a rich mahogany wood and included a huge reception desk, four chairs, and a few tables on which magazines were methodically stacked. The rest was open space. Simm felt like he was in a swanky lawyer's office, not a home for the aged and infirm. It made him wish he had worn dress trousers instead of jeans with a small rip in the back pocket.

The woman in white didn't seem to mind his attire. She welcomed him with a warm and gracious smile.

'I'd like to see Mrs. Sylvie O'Reilly please?'

'No problem,' the woman answered with an oh-so-patient smile. When asked, he explained he was an old friend of the family and was in the area. Apparently satisfied with his answer, she said, 'I'll call for someone to come and get you. It won't be long if you'd like to have a seat.'

Simm didn't sit. He gazed around him at the rich furnishings and the doubtlessly expensive artwork on the walls, and wondered how much money Jim O'Reilly had left behind if his estate could bankroll a setup like this. After having seen Terry's situation, he knew the younger O'Reilly wasn't footing this bill.

He heard the faint sound of padded footsteps behind him and turned to see a young man dressed in a pristine white uniform with creases sharp enough to slice cheese. He also had a smile that displayed several thousand dollars' worth of dental work.

'Madame O'Reilly? Venez avec moi, monsieur.'

Simm did as the man said and followed him along a wide corridor of high ceilings, cream-colored walls, and wood railings. After a short elevator ride to the second floor and a shorter walk along another hallway, he was shown into a suite of rooms that were larger than his entire apartment. Within those rooms, he was escorted to a sitting area complete with a pair of floor-to-ceiling windows overlooking a beautifully-maintained flower garden.

Sitting in a chair facing the windows was an elderly woman. From the back, Simm saw she had a full head of silver-white hair. Her shoulders were thin, draped with a royal blue shawl. Simm went around to face her as the man in the white uniform pulled a stuffed Victorian-style chair over to accommodate him. He thanked the man and settled into the chair. He heard the soft footsteps heading for the door as he stared at the woman before him.

Simm knew she must have been a beauty when she was young. She still had the look about her, despite the fact that her face was wrinkled and spotted. Her mouth was slack on one side, and she had a handkerchief clasped in her hand that she periodically used to wipe drool off her face.

Her eyes were pale blue, almost violet, and had doubtlessly been one of her best features in her youth. They were still filled with curiosity and intelligence. Simm was surprised she wasn't concerned about a strange man coming to visit her. Apparently, Sylvie O'Reilly didn't have many worries. Considering the circumstances under which she lived, it was hardly surprising.

'Hello, Mrs. O'Reilly,' he began.

She slowly nodded her head.

Simm introduced himself as a private investigator and said he had a few questions to ask her. He explained that he didn't want to tire her, and he would ask questions that would require exclusively a nod or a shake of her head. The look of curiosity increased as he spoke.

'I want to ask you a few questions about your family. I know your husband had connections to the Irish Mafia in his early days. He was convicted of money laundering and went to jail for a few years. When he was released, he gave up his work for the Gang and lived a normal existence with his family. Is that information correct?'

The older woman didn't move. She seemed to be frozen in place, and her expression could only be described as wary.

'Do you remember Charlene Butler?'

Sylvie O'Reilly's gaze dashed between Simm and the windows a few times before focusing on the wall ahead of her.

'I assume you do, since her family and yours had a long association. Her father was a good friend of your husband, wasn't he?'

Simm waited for a nod, or some kind of reaction, but nothing came. Instead, her gaze hardened, and he had the feeling she was almost in full shut-off mode.

'And you got along well with Mrs. Butler, didn't you?' Nothing. 'What about your son? Did he and Charlene always get along well?'

Her hand wiped unsteadily at the drool, which dripped from her mouth at a faster pace. There was definitely fear in her eyes now. Simm couldn't slow down. He didn't know how much more time he had before someone would come to check on her.

'Why did your husband leave Charlene the business, instead of your son?'

Her hands trembled violently.

'Do you know of anyone who would wish Charlene harm?'

Simm knew she couldn't answer these questions with a nod, but he wanted a reaction.

Her eyebrows drew together in surprise, and he knew he had thrown her off. The trembling in her hands slowed somewhat, but she continued to wipe at her mouth. He suspected she would like to ask him a few questions of her own. The first one would probably be whether Charlene was dead or alive. He decided not to enlighten her. Despite her regal good looks and the beautiful surroundings she lived in, Simm had difficulty warming to Mrs. O'Reilly.

Chapter 28:

Simm left the retirement home with more questions than answers, but nevertheless it was a worthwhile visit. It gave him a better impression of the O'Reilly family. It was evident both the drunken son and the holier-than-thou wife resented and perhaps hated Charlie Butler. This wasn't surprising, since the son had been pushed aside in the old man's will, and the mother likely sided with the son. But Simm sensed Sylvie O'Reilly was afraid of something. Was she afraid he would discover a deep, dark secret about the family? Did she fear for her own safety or her reputation? Was she afraid on behalf of her son? Did she suspect Terry was involved in the mysterious letters and perhaps had a more malicious plan for Charlie?

All of those questions gave Simm a lot to consider, but he also had to speak to Charlie about the wife of her mentor. He stopped for lunch on the way, choosing to arrive at the pub mid-afternoon when Charlie would have time to talk to him.

He found her in the back room, frowning at a pile of papers.

'What's wrong? Did you get another letter?'

'No, I'm paying bills. Again. They just don't stop.'

Simm let out his breath slowly.

'It has to be done,' he said.

'I know, but I'd love someone else to do it. It'd be less painful.'

'I have some questions for you.'

'Shoot,' she said, pushing aside the papers with relish.

'Talk to me about Sylvie O'Reilly.'

'What about her? I already told you everything. She had a stroke and she's living in a home now, unable to talk or take care of herself. It's very sad.'

'When was the last time you saw her?'

'At Jim's funeral.'

'What was she like when she was well?'

'She was beautiful, quite refined, and quiet. She was almost the polar opposite of Jim. He was loud and boisterous, someone who was more comfortable at a tailgate party than at a tea party, but as they say, opposites attract.

'You never went to see her at the retirement home?'

'No, Terry told me he was the only person allowed to go see her.'

Simm thought about how easy it had been for him to visit the woman.

'I was there today.'

Charlie's eyes opened wide.

'Did you see her?'

'I did. I said I was a friend of the family. I was told the woman could only nod her head to answer yes or no, and I said I was fine with that.'

'You talked to her? How did she seem?' Charlie said, sitting on the edge of her chair.

'Apart from the fact that she can't talk, and she isn't very mobile, she looked healthy. She has all her wits about her.'

'What did you ask her?'

Simm didn't hold anything back this time around. He told Charlie what he had asked Sylvie O'Reilly, and he described her reactions. Charlie leaned back in her chair as he talked, an expression of disbelief on her face.

'I don't understand. Why would she react like that?'

That was what Simm wondered. What was the old woman afraid of?

'Do you know anything about this place where she lives?'

'No, not at all. Is it nice?'

'Nice would be one word to describe it, but you could also say luxurious, lavish, ritzy, snazzy, fancy-shmancy, the list goes on.'

Charlie's eyes widened again.

'Really?'

'I googled it as I was having lunch. That place costs more per month than I earn in six. Jim's estate must have been worth a heap of money if it can pay for a home like that for an indeterminate amount of time.'

Charlie stared at him as if he had told her Sylvie O'Reilly was a prostitute in her free time. She shook her head.

'It's impossible. I know Jim did okay. This place was debt-free, but it was all he had besides the few investments he left to Terry. His house went to Sylvie, and I guess it was sold to pay for her care, but it wouldn't have been enough for her to live in that type of luxury.'

'Someone's paying for it. If it isn't the estate, who is it? And why?'

Chapter 29:

Charlie was more than a little perplexed. Things didn't match up. How could Simm get in to see Sylvie so effortlessly when she had been told it was only immediate family who could visit? Why was Sylvie living in such a posh place? Immediately after Simm left, she went online to check out the website belonging to Sunset Residences. It was an exercise she had never considered doing before today. What she found shocked her. It looked like a five-star resort hotel with all the bells and whistles. She could never imagine Jim and Sylvie being able to afford a place like that.

Charlie grabbed her cell phone, searched through her contacts, and hit dial. The voice on the line was slurred and feeble. Another surprise.

'Terry? Is that you?'

'No, it's Santa Claus. Who wants to know?'

'It's Charlie.'

'Charlene! You're cropping up everywhere these days.'

Charlie didn't quite know what to make of that remark, but decided to ignore it for the time being, since Terry wasn't sober and didn't have his wits about him.

'I'd like to see you. Could I come over to your place sometime soon?'

'I'll meet you at the coffee shop.'

Charlie hesitated. She was curious to see his home, a curiosity she had never felt before, but not wanting to alienate him, she agreed.

'When?' he asked.

'How about today? What time do you start work?'

'I'll meet you there in an hour.'

Charlie checked her watch. She could squeeze in a quick meeting with Terry before she had to be behind the bar mixing drinks.

'All right. I'll see you there.'

She hung up and went to find Frank. He agreed to take care of Harley while Charlie stepped out for a couple of hours. She had a few stops to make before going to the coffee shop, but she arrived fifteen minutes early and took a seat in the corner.

She always met Terry at the same place. He insisted on it and preferred to sit at the same table, if possible. Knowing his history, she tried to accommodate him as much as she could. The last thing she wanted to do was drive him to drink, but after her phone conversation with him, she suspected she was too late.

Charlie almost didn't recognize him when he came into the shop. It was several months since she had last seen Terry, but he had aged by years. He squinted and peered around the restaurant, looking for Charlie, apparently forgetting their usual spot. He didn't smile when he saw her. He dragged his feet, his shoulders were slumped, and he bumped against tables as he made his way to her. People stared at him, presumably noting his unkempt appearance and wondering if he was a homeless person looking for a handout. He certainly looked the part.

Terry slid into the booth across from her, but didn't offer a greeting. Instead, he looked around, searching for the waitress.

'Where is she? I need a coffee, real bad.'

'Hello, Terry. How're you doing?'

'Pretty good, Charlene,' he said, turning his bleary gaze on her. 'Why did you want to see me?'

'You know I like to check in with you every once in a while, just to see how things are going.'

'There's an awful lot of people checkin' in on me these days.'

'What's that supposed to mean? What's been going on?' Charlie remembered his reference to her name cropping up everywhere.

'Your friend came to see me. What's his name? Somethin' strange.'

Charlie had trouble pushing the word past her lips.

'Simm?'

'Yeah, that's it. What the hell's that about? You sent him to see me because you got some stupid mail? Are you losin' it, or what?'

'I didn't send him to see you. He went on his own.'

Charlie seethed. This is what Simm was hiding from her. She hated to be blindsided like this.

'Somebody musta told him about me, and it could only be you.'

He had her there. Drunk or not, Terry could still figure out the tic-tac-toe.

'I'll deal with Simm. He won't be bothering you anymore.' She took a sip of her coffee and used those few moments to calm down and concentrate on what she had set out to do.

'I wanted to ask you about your mom. I was wondering how she's doing.'

'Mom's good.'

'I'd like to go see her.'

'I already told you. Nobody can visit her except me. She's not well enough. She gets upset.'

'She knows me. She wouldn't be upset. Besides, I want to make sure she has everything she needs.'

That sparked a reaction.

'You think I'm not taking care of her? She's my mother. I make sure she has everything.'

'Are you supporting her? Financially, I mean.'

She was impressed with how swiftly Terry could leap ahead in his thinking. Charlie could almost hear the clicking of his brain. He looked at the table with a forlorn expression.

'I do the best I can.'

'I'm sure you do,' she said solemnly.

'I don't earn a lot at my job, but I get by and whatever extra I have, I give to Mom.'

'Very commendable.'

'It's not easy. Most times I do without.'

'Let me look into it. I'll try to do something to help you.'

'That would be great. You're doing so well with the bar. I can see why Dad left it to you.'

Charlie forced a smile to her face, although it was painful to do so.

She shoved her coffee aside and grabbed her purse.

'Speaking of which, I have to get back.'

'I'll wait to hear from you then, Charlene.'

Charlie mumbled something as she slid out of the booth and hurried out of the coffee shop. Never before had she felt the need to get as far away from Terry as possible. The fact that he insisted on calling her by her full name had forever grated on her nerves. She knew he did it to irritate her, but she had repeatedly forgiven him for that foible. But today, she had seen a different side to Terry. Or perhaps, she had belatedly seen the real Terry.

He had lied to her about his mother. She had needed some sort of confirmation after what Simm had told her and she had gotten it. She had also seen how he had tried to manipulate her into giving him money, which according to him, would have been used to support his mother. Charlie greatly doubted it. It would be spent on alcohol. Sylvie had another means of support, and Charlie wanted to find out who and what it was.

CHAPTER 30:

Charlie fumed during the walk of several blocks to the pub. She had promised Frank she would take a cab, but she had a lot of anger to walk off. She was angry with three people. Terry, of course, was one of those people. She realized now she had been a target for him. Often when she met with him, she would slip him an envelope filled with cash. She did it because she had never quashed the guilt she felt for having inherited the pub instead of him. He was Jim's son. He should have been the beneficiary. Even though she understood Jim's reasoning, and even though she was aware he had bequeathed his son a large sum of cash, she continually harbored a feeling of being undeserving. But today, the fog of guilt had cleared long enough for her to see his true character. And what she saw angered her.

The second person was, of course, Simm, who had lied to her. It may be a lie of omission, but it was still a lie. She resented the fact that he had gone to see Terry, and he hadn't told her. She deserved to know what was going on.

The third person she was angry with was herself. She felt naïve and gullible. Because of those two traits, she had been taken in by the first two people on her list, and it pissed her off. You would think with her experience running a bar frequented by all types of individuals, she would have seen it all and recognized it all. But, apparently, she was still innocent and easily fooled. Both Terry and Simm had taken advantage of her.

Frank looked up in surprise when the door banged against its hinges as she flung it open.

'What's wrong?' he said.

'Nothing,' she said. 'Everything.'

114

'Could you be more specific?'

'I don't like being taken for a fool.'

'Simm?'

'He's one. Terry's the other.'

'Oh, double whammy.'

'You got it. I'll be in my office for a while, making voodoo dolls.'

Harley greeted her affectionately when she opened the door, his little beige body shaking with excitement. She cooed a bit and scratched him behind his ears before she settled behind her desk. She hit the power button on her laptop and grabbed the stack of unopened mail. As her hand made contact with the top of the pile of envelopes, she was struck by a bad feeling. She hesitantly sifted through them to discover her bad feeling was justified. The now-familiar handwriting was scrawled across the front of the envelope. She warily opened it and spread the letter on the desk.

Dear Charlene,

My name is Tamara, although I'm sure my nickname would be Tammy. I think I would like that. Just like you prefer to be called Charlie instead of Charlene. Did you know we would be about the same age? I am also of Irish descent. Do you ever wonder about your roots, your heritage? Have you ever been to Ireland? It's beautiful there. I think you would enjoy it and find it very educational. Maybe we can get together and talk about it.

The phone was cold and hard in her hands as she dialed the number. She resisted the temptation to throw it across the room purely to vent her frustration.

'Please come over here,' she said, when she heard the voice on the other end of the line.

'What's up?'

'I got another letter.'

Simm hung up without another word. Charlie knew he would be with her within minutes.

Charlie's legs were not feeling very solid when she went out to see Frank, the paper in her hand. He read it without expression.

'I don't get it. What's it all about?' he said, his brows almost touching.

'I don't know, but I'll find out. I don't want to live with this anymore.'

Both heads turned when Simm walked into the room. His long legs brought him to their side within seconds, his gaze pinned on the paper lying on the bar. Nothing was said as he read the message.

'Charlie, could you get me the other letters please?'

'Why?'

For the first time since coming into the pub, he looked at her.

'Could you just get them without giving me a lot of hassle? I want to look at something.'

Charlie scowled, but slid off the stool and headed to the office. A couple of minutes later, Simm placed the letters in chronological order along the counter of the bar.

'What are you looking for?' she said.

'Shh.'

'Don't shush me! This is my place, my letters, and I'm paying you with my money. I want to know what you're looking for.'

Simm ignored her. Charlie resisted the temptation to hit him. Instead, she counted to ten in her head. Luckily, that was long enough for Simm to read the letters.

'Do you notice how the tenses are all mixed up?'

Charlie forgot about hitting Simm and concentrated on looking at the letters, trying to figure out what he was talking about.

'Tenses? What do you mean?'

'I mean the 'would haves' and the 'I ams'. 'I would have been your age.' That implies that she's dead. But then she says, 'I am of Irish descent', which is present tense.'

'Maybe it's just bad writing. Maybe this person isn't very educated,' Frank chimed in.

'And the third letter, from Ben. I will never have that chance. Why not? Is he dead?' Simm said.

'How can he be dead if he's writing letters? And they always want to meet with me to discuss things. They can't be dead.'

'It's the same handwriting. It's one person, guy or girl, writing these letters and using different names. I think we can all agree on that,' Simm said. 'He can do whatever he wants with the characters he's creating. They can be dead. They can have regrets, desires, opinions. But, I find this last one interesting. The mixed tenses intrigue me.'

'Let's say you have a point. I don't necessarily agree, but let's just say. What good does it do us? Does it lead us somewhere?' Charlie said.

'Maybe. Maybe not.'

'Wow. You're pretty good at this.'

Judging by the look Simm gave her, her sarcasm wasn't appreciated.

'Leave it in my hands,' he said.

'No, you won't get away with that anymore.'

'With what?'

"Leave it to me', 'It's on a need-to-know basis', 'I'll take care of it'. That won't cut it anymore, Simm. I want to be in on this from start to finish. I want to know what you're doing and when you're doing it.' Charlie stabbed him repeatedly in the chest with a finger.

'There's no need for that...' Simm tried to say, grabbing her finger and hanging on.

'Oh yes there is. I had a very interesting visit with Terry this morning.'

Simm let go of her finger and developed an intense interest in a spot on the counter, rubbing it long after it had disappeared.

'You went to see him,' Charlie continued. 'You told him I was getting strange mail. You pried into my personal life. And his.'

'That's my job,' he said, looking at her again. 'I have to pry into people's lives if I want to get information. It's called investigating.'

'You could've told me.'

'I knew you would say no.'

'No, I wouldn't have.' Her face was reflected in the mirror behind the bar, and it seemed to look at her accusingly. She had to confess. 'Okay, yes, I would have.'

Out of the corner of her eye, she noticed Frank nodding in agreement.

'You have to trust me. You have to let me do what I'm trained to do,' Simm said. 'You can't keep throwing spokes in my wheels.'

'Fine. Let's make an agreement.'

Simm threw his head back and rolled his eyes. Frank chuckled and rubbed his hands together.

'No, you'll like this one,' Charlie said to Simm. 'I'll give you complete leeway to investigate however you please. Well, pretty much complete leeway. And, you'll keep me informed about what you're doing and who you're talking to.'

'Wow. That sounds like a wonderful deal.'

Charlie heard a snort coming from Frank's direction.

'It is. I just gave you carte blanche.'

'I wasn't looking for carte blanche from you. I don't need it.'

'You do, if you want to get paid.'

'Ha! If you only knew how many times I've thought the frustration I put up with is not worth all the money in the world.'

'Frustration?' she said, looking at Frank. 'What's he talking about?'

Her friend grinned and held up his hands.

'No comment. I'm not getting involved in this one.'

Chapter 31:

Simm escaped to his apartment shortly after his visit with Charlie. He didn't know how it had happened, but he had given in to her agreement. The last thing he needed was to have someone breathing down his neck at every turn, but he seemingly had a weakness somewhere that she exploited. Before he knew it, he had told her about his visit to the prison in Donnacona and the information he had learned.

Charlie didn't seem surprised by anything he told her. She was, however, very interested at the prospect of a potential meeting with the head of the Irish Mafia.

'I want to go with you.'

'Are you out of your mind?'

'Why not?'

'Because he's the head of a large criminal organization, and it could be dangerous.'

'I doubt it.'

Simm threw up his hands.

'How can you say that? Crime. Criminal. Danger. Those words all go together.'

'Jim wasn't dangerous. He was a teddy bear.'

'Jim was a little cog in a big wheel. He was a guy who was looking for an easy buck. He may even have had a conscience. I doubt Marty Sullivan falls into the same category.'

'I'm not worried.'

Simm bit his tongue. He could already see their little agreement flying out the window. There was no way he would expose Charlie to that kind of danger. He wasn't even sure he wanted to expose himself to it.

'We'll see.'

Charlie narrowed her eyes, but withheld comment.

Simm researched the contact name John Flynn had given him. Billy Connor was the guy who was supposed to set him up for a meeting with Marty Sullivan. The guy had a prison record, but had never been arrested for murder or anything involving bodily harm. Simm took that as a positive sign. Connor seemed to be more of an enabler.

Simm's call was answered on the second ring with a barely audible grunt. Simm introduced himself as a friend of John Flynn.

'So?' Billy Connor said.

'He said you could help me out with something.'

'Johnnie says a lot of things that aren't true.'

'Well, let's see if he's right this time. I want to meet with Marty Sullivan.'

There was a brief silence.

'Why would you want to do that?'

'I want to talk to him about a mutual friend.'

'Who?'

'Jim O'Reilly.'

'The bar guy?'

'That would be him.'

'He's dead.'

'I know that. It doesn't mean I can't talk about him,' Simm said. He seemed to have to say it often. 'So, what about it? Can you set it up for me?'

'I can't guarantee anything. First, I gotta know who you are and what it's about.'

Simm knew he had to be honest. They would find out anyway, and if they caught him in a lie, it wouldn't go good for him.

'I'm an ex-cop. I work as a private investigator now. I've been hired for a case that may be connected to Jim O'Reilly, and I need information.'

'Who hired you?'

Simm didn't like to give her name, but he couldn't hide it.

'Charlene Butler.'

'Give me your number. I'll get back to you.'

The conversation ended the instant he finished reciting his cell phone number. Connor's voice didn't give anything away. Simm would have to wait and see how it unfolded.

Chapter 32:

Charlie hurried inside the bank, anxious to get her business finished. She hated hauling around cash. Normally, she sent Frank to do the errand for her, but she needed to get out of the bar. She spent her days like a prisoner, either at the pub, or escorted to and from it. It took a lot of coaxing and cajoling to get Frank to let her run a few errands in the middle of the day while she was surrounded by crowds of people, but she eventually got her way. She cursed the mysterious letter sender once again. It was because of him that she lived this way.

Charlie also felt her normally optimistic outlook slipping away. It was inconceivable to her that one person could change the shape of someone's personality, and she didn't want him to succeed. But she didn't know how to stop him. Not yet.

When the deposit was made, she ran one other errand, which took her longer than she expected, and it was almost four thirty before she made it to the pub. Frank was busy, trying to furnish the larger-than-usual crowd drawn by the nice weather and the scent of summer on its way. Melissa was running the tables and looked a little harried by all the action. Charlie pitched in without hesitation.

At six o'clock, Nathalie showed up, and they spread out the load. Charlie made a sign to Frank to tell him she was heading to the back to check on Harley.

As usual, the door squeaked noisily when she pushed it open. Most times, it roused the pug from his siesta. Charlie smiled when she was ignored.

'Harley. Wake up, you lazy lug.'

She circled her desk and peered underneath. His doggy bed was empty.

'Harley? Where are you?'

The room wasn't big enough for many hiding spaces.

'Harley,' she said gruffly.

She didn't appreciate this game. She circled the room, pushing aside boxes and chairs, looking for the dog, but he was nowhere in sight. Her heart rapped against her ribs. Where could he be? Had he slipped out the door? Was he hiding in the bar area? Wouldn't someone have noticed him?

She left the office and rushed along the corridor, only to backtrack when she thought to check the washrooms along the way. Two men, who stood facing the urinals, jumped in surprise and scrambled to cover themselves when she barged into the men's room. She didn't care.

'Did either of you see a pug in here?'

Their twin looks of incomprehension were answer enough.

She repeated the search in the women's washroom to no avail.

When she reached the bar, her fingers dug into Frank's arm and wrenched his attention from a customer.

'I can't find Harley!'

'What? He's not in the office?'

'When did you last see him?'

'Not since you took him for his walk. I was too busy to go to the office.'

'He's not there. We have to find him.' Her voice shook with desperation.

'He has to be around here somewhere.'

Frank took charge. He sent Melissa to the door to make sure no one left with a pug under their coat. Then, he put two fingers into his mouth and emitted an ear-piercing whistle that brought complete silence to the crowded room.

'I want everybody to check under their seats and tables to see if there's a little dog there,' he boomed.

No one argued or questioned his demand. Simultaneously, all heads ducked to scour the area around them. The silence continued for a few moments. No one shouted, 'Here he is!'. Charlie's heart sank into her stomach. She saw her look mirrored on Frank's face as conversation gradually resumed.

'Someone took him,' she said, clutching her elbows, trying to stop the trembling. 'Who would do that?'

'It has to be someone who walked right by me. The back door can only be opened from the inside.'

'My poor baby. He must be so scared.'

Tears filled her eyes. Frank hauled her into his arms and mumbled platitudes, but she knew he had no more of an idea what to do than she did. Nothing he said would console her.

'Do you think it's the same guy?'

Charlie leaned back to look at him, confused.

'Who?' she asked, but her eyes widened as his meaning became clear. 'Oh my God. Please, no.'

Frank grasped her shoulders.

'Don't panic, Charlie. I don't know. I just said that. I'm probably way off base.'

Charlie pulled free and raced back to the office. The door slammed loudly again as she grabbed the phone.

Chapter 33:

Once again, Simm raced to Butler's. Her message had been almost incomprehensible, something about 'the guy' and Harley. All he knew was she was very upset, and if any harm had come to her pug, it would explain her level of panic.

He swept through the bar and caught a look from Frank on his way to the office. It was enough to prepare him for Charlie's state of mind.

'Finally. It took you so long to get here. We have to find him.'

'First, you'll sit down and tell me what happened,' Simm said, prying her hands off his forearms.

'What happened is that someone came in here and took Harley. And it must be the same guy.'

'Let's not jump to conclusions.'

'What will happen to him?' she said between sobs. 'He'll hurt him, maybe even...' She bit her lip, obviously unable to think about the, 'maybe even'.

'There's nothing to say it's the same guy who took him. It could've been anyone. It could be someone who wants to love him and give him a good home.'

'And I'll never see him again,' she wailed.

'Look, the first step is to search for him. He could have slipped out the door as someone entered. He could be wandering around outside.'

'He'd never do that. He's a good dog. He wouldn't go outside without Frank or me.'

'Maybe he spotted another dog, or a cat. Let me call the SPCA to see if a stray dog was reported. And we'll get a few people together to go out and search around the neighborhood.'

Before she could argue with him, he turned on his heels and

headed to the main room. He had spent enough time here that he could spot the regulars and know who he trusted to think about Harley's well-being. He gathered together a group of five twenty-somethings and explained their mission to them. Cell phone contacts were exchanged so news, good or bad, could be transmitted as rapidly as possible. Without hesitation, they set out to search a two-block radius. Simm didn't think Harley would have strayed any farther than that on his own.

He returned to the office to find Charlie on the phone. By the tone of the conversation, she had taken it upon herself to contact the SPCA. When it came time to describe her pet, her face crumpled, and she couldn't go on. Simm took the phone and provided the rest of the information. When he hung up, he turned and pulled her into his arms. There was nothing he could say, but he hoped the physical contact would help calm her.

'I want to go look for him,' she mumbled.

'I'll go with you. You're not going out there alone.'

She looked up at him.

'You think it's him.'

He did, but he wouldn't tell her that.

'I'm not taking any chances,' he said.

'Should we call the police?'

'Let's see if our search party turns up anything first. We'll give it an hour.'

An hour later, Simm talked to Detective Ranfort on the phone. All the members of Simm's search party had returned to home base empty-handed, and it looked like Harley's disappearance was not due to an innocent wandering-off. Normally, a lost or stolen dog would not be given a high priority by law enforcement, but with Charlie's recently-received attention, the detective took the phone call seriously. A team was on its way.

Charlie was inconsolable. Simm and Frank tried to change her mind by drawing her attention to small incidents in the busy pub, but their efforts were fruitless. She was convinced Harley was being tortured, and any argument to the contrary was rejected.

'He didn't hesitate to hurt those poor sheep, did he? Why would he take pity on a dog?'

'In all likelihood, he stole those organs from somewhere,' Frank said calmly. 'The police told us the people at MacDonald College thought they were missing some. He didn't massacre the sheep.'

'He's got a sick mind. Look at the letters. He's not sane.'

'Yes, he's got a loose screw, but that doesn't mean he'll hurt Harley,' Simm said.

'Why would he take him?'

'Maybe, he wants to send you a message.'

'Like what?'

Simm hesitated. He didn't know if he should voice his thoughts, but as it turned out, he didn't have to say anything.

'He wants to let me know he can get close to me and the things I love. That's it, isn't it?'

'Maybe.'

'There's no maybe about it. He's threatening me through Harley.'

Charlie was pacing the small office floor, at times bumping up against her desk or chair, without seeming to notice. Her brows were lowered, and her lips were pressed tightly together. Gone was the desolate and heartbroken expression. She had turned into Mama Bear.

'I'll kill him.' Definitely Mama Bear.

She turned and shook a fierce finger at Simm.

'I'll put *his* organs in a plastic bag. I'll take great pleasure in yanking them, bit by bit, out of his body. Let's see how he likes that.'

They were interrupted by a knock on the door. The police had arrived. And so began another round of questioning for Charlie.

Chapter 34:

It was a long night. Charlie couldn't sleep. Simm snuck off to his bedroom and tried to catch a couple of hours of rest, but he heard her pacing, mumbling, and banging around in the kitchen, making coffee to fuel her restlessness.

There was little they could do to find Harley. The police and the SPCA would be in contact with them if he crossed their paths. A team of friends had put up posters around the neighborhood asking for information. If it was the letter-writer who had taken him, Simm hoped he would get in touch with them somehow. His only wish was that the dog be returned unharmed, but he was worried it wouldn't be the case. His plan was to intercept whatever packages were sent to Charlie, and he spoke to Frank to make sure he also kept an eye out for anything suspicious.

At seven in the morning, Simm and Charlie were on their way to the pub. It was a ridiculously early hour to open a bar, but Charlie was too restless to hang around Simm's place any longer.

'Let's scoot by the apartment for a minute,' Charlie stated as soon as she settled into the passenger seat.

'You need to pick something up?'

'Yep.'

Simm knew it was an excuse to check the premises for any sign of Harley, but since he thought it was a valid reason, he didn't hesitate to play along. Unfortunately, the apartment was exactly as it had been the last time they had seen it. Harley wasn't there.

Her face grim, she wordlessly slid into the car, and repeated the exercise at Butler's Pub.

'I don't know whether to be relieved or disappointed,' she said, blinking back tears. 'I wanted him to be here, but I was deathly afraid of what condition he would be in when I found him.'

'Why don't you let me do the searching from now on?'

'I hate doing nothing! It's so frustrating.'

'I know, but you have a business to manage, and that's what you should be doing. At the very least, it'll provide a distraction.'

She conceded, setting to work with a vengeance. The already-spotless bar was cleaned again. Frank would be impressed. Next, she tackled the storage boxes in her office. Items she had hung on to preciously were now considered of no use and were tossed in the garbage bin. Whenever Simm offered to help, he was told he would just get in the way. After her third trip to the outside bin lugging boxes half her weight, he stepped forward. His conscience wouldn't allow him to stand back and watch.

'Let me take that.'

'I'm okay.'

'Charlie, you're sweating like a dock worker. You're so red in the face, I'm afraid you'll have a stroke.'

'I'm fine.'

'Stop it. Killing yourself won't bring Harley back.'

It felt good to yell at her, but seconds later he regretted his lack of constraint. When she bent over to set the box on the floor, she remained hunched over it, her head lowered. Her shoulders shook, and the sound of her sobs broke his heart.

'Come here.'

He grabbed her forearms and pulled her into his arms. All the toughness and all the fight left her body. She felt as limp as a wet noodle. He sat on the box and lowered her onto his lap, pressing her head against his chest. He let her cry until the sobs turned into sniffles.

'He's not coming back, is he?'

'Honestly, I don't know. I hope so, but the more time goes by, the less chance there is of him coming back.'

'I won't replace him. No other dog could take his place.'

'You may change your mind.'

'No. I can't go through this again. It hurts too much.'

They sat in silence for several minutes.

'I'm exhausted. Every muscle in my body hurts,' she said.

'I'm not surprised. You're a machine.'

'It felt good for a while, but now I feel like hell.'

'The bad news is, it's time to actually start your workday. The good news is, it'll keep you busy.'

Chapter 35:

It was a warm, sunny Saturday, and the customers were thirsty and happy to socialize on the outdoor patio. Some of them were under the green canvas awning they had unfurled for the occasion, others preferred to soak up the sun. Usually days like this made Charlie happy, but today was just another day. A busy one, but nothing more than that.

Saturday bled into Sunday, and it was more of the same. At least, she had slept the night before. She was so tired by the time she got to Simm's apartment she was almost comatose. Putting one foot in front of the other had required an enormous effort.

On Sundays, the pub closed at eleven in the evening. By eleven fifteen, they were in the car and headed to Simm's place.

'I want to go home,' Charlie said

'That's where we're going.'

'No, I mean my home, my apartment.'

Simm sighed audibly.

'Charlie, we were there yesterday morning, remember? There was nothing. We're both tired. We'll stop by tomorrow morning on our way to work.'

'No. I want to go now.'

Charlie caught the eye-roll, but she ignored it. The fact that she hadn't checked the apartment yet today bothered her. She should have gone whether she was there the day before or not.

They found a parking spot in front of the building, and Charlie hurriedly climbed the stairs. She heard Simm's heavy steps following her at a slower pace. She tried the door, hoping to find it unlocked, but it was as they had left it the previous morning. The air inside was stuffy and warm. She heard Simm opening a window in the living room as she made her way to the kitchen.

'What?' she asked, spinning around to face Simm.

He gave her a confused look.

'I didn't say anything.'

'Are you sure?' she said.

'Of course, I'm sure. I'd know, wouldn't I?'

Charlie was certain she had heard a noise. She raced along the hallway, throwing open doors.

'Harley? Are you here, baby?'

Each room was undisturbed. There wasn't a dog, or any sign of anything unusual. When she stepped back into the corridor, Simm stood at the end, staring at her.

'Don't look at me like that. I was sure I heard something,' she said.

'It was probably a noise from outside, a horn or something.'

Her shoulders slumped. He was right. She was going crazy, imagining things that didn't exist.

'Okay. Let's go,' she said.

As they walked by the closet near the door, she thought she heard a snort. Doubting herself, she looked up at Simm. His eyes were wide, and she knew he had heard it also. She flung open the closet door and saw her coats hanging as they should. Her shoes and boots were neatly arranged on the floor. Nothing had changed. She heard a soft snuffle. She thrust her hands among the coats, frantically pushing them aside. A large canvas bag that didn't belong to her hung from a hook on the bar behind her long, winter coats. Charlie gingerly placed her hand on the bag. It contained something solid. She lifted the bag off the hook and peered into it, holding her breath. Inside, was a fawn-colored dog curled in a ball, his breathing weak and uneven, his eyes closed.

'Harley?' she whispered.

She rushed to the couch and gently set down the bag. With Simm's help, she lifted out the dog. He whimpered faintly.

'Oh, Harley, my poor baby.'

She could barely see him as her eyes brimmed with tears, of joy or sorrow, she couldn't be sure.

She lowered herself to the couch and set her pet tenderly on her knee. He whimpered softly, but his eyes remained closed and his body was limp.

'Oh God, Simm, what did he do to him?'

Simm knelt beside her and ran his hands over the dog.

'He doesn't seem to have any wounds or broken bones. We'll get him to a vet.'

'There's a twenty-four-hour place over on Metcalfe.'

Charlie sat in the back seat of Simm's car with Harley lying on her lap. She bent over him, whispering words of encouragement during the short drive to the clinic.

Simm opened doors for her as she carried the dog into the brightly-lit building. Without delay, she was met by a young, white-coated man, who took charge of Harley while he asked Charlie all the pertinent questions. She filled him in as much as she could.

Charlie paced the floor as Harley was taken to the other section of the clinic to be seen by the vet. After a tense half hour another white-coated person, a woman this time, came to see her.

'Ms. Butler, my name is Dr. Boisclair. I've examined Harley, and he hasn't been beaten or abused. Someone seems to have given him a strong sedative, which is gradually starting to wear off, but since I'm not sure what he was given, I'd like to keep him here overnight for observation.'

'Do you think he'll be okay?'

'Yes, I'm reasonably sure. I just don't want to take a chance.'

Charlie looked at Simm uncertainly.

'I hate to leave him here.'

'There isn't much you can do before the drug wears off,' Simm said. 'They'll take good care of him, and we'll come back in the morning to get him.'

Charlie reluctantly and quietly agreed, but when they were in the car, she vented indignantly.

'That bastard! How dare he drug my dog.'

'At least Harley's still alive and relatively unharmed,' Simm said.

'I know. But he shouldn't have done anything to him. He should never have taken him in the first place.'

'We have to call the cops and go back to your apartment. He may have left something behind, either intentionally or not.'

'I hadn't thought of that. I was so concerned about Harley I didn't pay much attention to anything else.'

Simm grunted his agreement as he placed a call to Detective Ranfort.

'Don't touch anything until the cops get here,' Simm said, as they stepped into the building and climbed the stairs. 'It's not likely he left fingerprints, but we can't take a chance.'

Charlie let Simm explain the sequence of events to Detective Ranfort. A few minutes later, her heart picked up a beat when the bag was examined, and an envelope was found taped to the bottom. All eyes turned her way. She gestured to the police detective.

'Why don't you open it this time?'

With his gloved hands, he slid open the envelope and removed the letter. He read it to himself, then read it aloud.

Dear Charlene,

How did it feel to lose something you love? Did it hurt a lot? I hope it did. You're very lucky I have a kind heart and I love all living beings. I didn't hurt him. Not this time. I'm giving him back to you. Not everyone is lucky enough to deal with someone like me. Not everyone is lucky enough to get back the people they love. Did you know that? Some people have no respect for others.

This time you're lucky.

'He's crazy. I don't know what he's talking about. And why me? What have I ever done?'

'For some reason, he's targeted you,' the detective said. 'It's important to find out what the reason is. And I'd say sooner rather than later. These letters are starting to sound a lot more threatening.'

The cop gave Simm a significant look as he spoke to Charlie. Simm nodded his agreement.

Chapter 36:

Charlie stepped into Simm's bedroom. He lay on his back, the covers pulled halfway up his bare chest. One arm was flung over his head and the other stretched out by his side. He took up a good chunk of the king-size bed. He was also fast asleep. Her intention had been to wake him so they could go to the vet's, but she felt a flash of pity for him. She had been keeping him up late every night, and last night was no exception. He didn't get more than five hours of sleep.

She tiptoed out of the room without waking him, deciding to take a taxi to the clinic.

The receptionist at the vet's office beamed at her when she gave her name and said she was coming to get Harley.

'Of course. He'll be happy to see you. What a cutie he is!'

'Is he better?'

'Much. I heard the story when I came in this morning. What a horrible thing to happen to a little dog. Come this way.'

Charlie was led to an examination room and asked to wait. Within a few minutes, the girl returned carrying Harley. When the pug recognized his mistress, he started to whimper and wiggle.

Charlie gathered him in her arms and was immediately slathered with kisses. He whimpered for several more minutes as Charlie cooed and comforted him. She looked up when the vet arrived with an update.

'He seems to have recovered from the sedative, but expect him to be a bit groggier than usual, and his appetite may be off for a couple of days. Make sure he has lots of water, and bring him back if he doesn't bounce back soon.'

Charlie thanked her, paid the bill, and hailed a taxi to take them back to Simm's apartment. On the way, she called Frank to let him know Harley had been found and was doing all right. The dog sat on her lap and rested his head against her body. When she got out of the cab and tried to set him on the ground, he cried and pressed himself to her legs. She had to sneak him into the building in a large tote bag and hoped he would stay quiet during the journey. She didn't have to worry. He dozed off in the elevator on the way up.

There was no sign of Simm in the living area when they entered, so she went to his bedroom door and peeked in the room. He was still sleeping, this time curled up on his side. She went to the bed and gently set Harley next to him. The dog stretched out against Simm's back.

'Helen?' Simm mumbled.

Charlie's eyebrows lifted. She leaned over and shook his shoulder.

'Who's Helen?'

'What? What's happening?' Simm was instantly on alert, jumping out of bed and grabbing his jeans.

'Who's Helen?' Charlie asked again.

Simm focused on Charlie, and glared at an equally confused Harley, until it dawned on him what she was asking him. He held his jeans in front of him.

'What's Harley doing here?'

'I went to get him. Who's Helen?'

'You went to get him by yourself? You're not supposed to do that.'

'Stop changing the subject. Who the hell is Helen?'

'God, I'm tired.'

He dropped his jeans and crawled back into bed.

'Simm, don't go to sleep,' Charlie said, shaking his shoulder.

'She's an old friend, that's all. Look, I just woke up. I'm tired, and it's not a time for conversation.'

'An old girlfriend?'

Simm rolled onto his back and stared at the ceiling.

'Yes, an old girlfriend,' he grumbled.

'Do you still love her?'

'No, it was a long time ago. Can we drop it please?'

'Why were you calling her name in your sleep?'

'I don't know, and I don't care,' Simm said, scowling.

'Is she the reason your brother came to see you? Does she want to get back together with you?'

'No, on both counts.'

'Did you discuss her with your brother?'

'Not at all. Not one word was said about her.'

'But his visit triggered something.'

'I guess. Don't worry about it, Charlie. I'm sure some other night I'll call out another girl's name for no reason. It's just a thing I do.'

'Impressive.'

'Yep, that's me,' he said, as he dragged the covers over his head.

Charlie, exceptionally, let him off the hook. She was so happy to have her pet back she was willing to be generous, but she filed the subject of Helen away, to be dealt with another day.

Charlie paced the floor, waiting for Simm to shower and get ready to drive her and Harley to the pub. When she arrived, she spent time in the office with Harley at her feet, but when she went to go out to the main room to tend customers, he tried to slip out the door with her. She urged him back into the room, but his whimpers broke her heart. Unable to help herself, she acquiesced and moved his bed to the area behind the bar. It was a Monday, she reasoned, so it would be quiet, and she could stay within his sight. In a few days, he would get over his separation anxiety. She couldn't help but repeatedly curse the person who had brought on all this misery for him.

CHAPTER 37:

The call came at a very unfortunate time. Simm and Charlie sat outside Butler's Pub at a bistro table, Simm having a beer and Charlie a glass of wine. It was rare for either of them to drink at two o'clock on a weekday afternoon, but it was summer and the weather was nice. They both had a rough weekend behind them, and the timing seemed to call for a drink. They discussed nothing in particular, but were interrupted when Simm felt his phone vibrating in his pants pocket.

It may have been the beer, the warmth, or the sun reflecting off Charlie's hair, but Simm didn't check his call display before answering.

'Hello.'

'Simm?'

He recognized the voice, avoided Charlie's eyes, and tried to sound casual. He could have stood up and walked away from her, but he knew such a move would merely peak her curiosity and make her follow him. He decided to go for vague.

'Yeah.'

'I set it up. Tomorrow, ten o'clock, Terrasse Beauchemin, The Old Port. Go to the main bar and ask for Marty. Someone will tell you where to find him.'

'Okay.'

A hundred questions ran through Simm's mind, but he knew he would sound ridiculous asking any of them. Most of all, he wanted to know if he would survive the visit or not. Or would he be found at the bottom of the Saint Lawrence River wearing cement shoes? He didn't dare look at Charlie, certain his face would give him away.

'You gonna be there?' the man said.

'Of course.'

'No funny stuff.'

'Of course not.'

The line went dead. Simm had no intention of doing any funny stuff, which he took to mean no cops, no wires, no weapons. He would play this clean and hope for the best.

'Who was that?'

'A friend.'

'You're not very chatty with your friends.'

'What can I say? I'm not a chatty kind of guy.'

'Simm.'

'What?'

'Have you forgotten our agreement already?'

'That call had nothing to do with our agreement.'

'You're a terrible liar. Tell me.'

'Charlie, you don't have to know everything.'

'You promised.'

He had, damn it.

'I have a meeting tomorrow with Marty Sullivan.'

'Great. What time do we go?'

'You don't go. I go.'

'I want to be there.'

'It's too dangerous.'

'Not at all. What time?'

'Charlie…'

'What time, Simm?'

'I'm going to be there at ten o'clock. Alone.'

'I'll be ready at nine thirty.'

'Charlie…'

The following morning, at nine forty-five, Simm waited in his car outside his apartment. Charlie had shouted from the bedroom that she was almost ready and she'd be out in a minute. He thought he must be crazy, brain-dead, or a little of both. Why the hell could he never say no to her?

His eyes widened as he saw her saunter out of the apartment building wearing a sleeveless summer dress in a floral pattern. The dress ended well above her knees, and her feet were clad in a pair of strappy, pink sandals. Simm had never seen Charlie in anything but jeans, and the sight was breathtaking. He couldn't speak. Suddenly, he realized the effect this same sight may have on Marty Sullivan and his cohorts.

Simm was out of the car and blocking her passage long before she made it to the sidewalk.

'You ready?' she asked.

'No. You have to go change.'

'Why?'

What could he say? You're too beautiful to be seen by a pack of criminals? I won't be able to concentrate on what we're supposed to be doing?

'You shouldn't dress up. You should be wearing jeans or something very plain.'

'I disagree. I think this is the perfect outfit.'

'Oh, yeah? That's what you think? How many times have you met a mafia boss? Is there some etiquette we're supposed to follow?'

'I just know, okay. It's women's intuition.'

'Cop's intuition tells me it's a mistake.'

'Women's intuition overrules cop's intuition any day.'

Simm's lips were pressed together for the ten-minute duration of the drive to the Old Port. Surely the day would come when he would win an argument with her.

They had no trouble finding a parking spot at the Old Port. It was, after all, a Wednesday in early June. The crowds would start in earnest in a couple of weeks, and continue until October.

The day was warm enough that Simm was glad he was dressed in light clothing. He purposely didn't wear a jacket so it would be obvious he wasn't carrying a weapon.

Under normal circumstances, Simm would like to spend time with Charlie strolling along the section of the city near the waterfront. It was an area filled with boutiques, food trucks, restaurants, and bars. And of course, most restaurants and bars had a patio area, so customers could enjoy the view and the weather. Yachts of all shapes and sizes were docked at the marina, and the Clock Tower, a Montreal institution since 1921, watched over it all.

The restaurant was inside a building named Terrasse Beauchemin, which housed a few businesses aimed for the tourist crowd. Once inside, it took a couple of minutes for their eyes to adjust to the sudden darkness after the brilliance of the sunshine. As soon as they could focus, they made their way to the bar.

'Do you know where we can find Marty Sullivan?' Simm asked the bartender.

The man looked them both over, but didn't ask if they had an appointment. Simm was sure Billy Connor had informed everyone about their imminent arrival.

'Go to the upper level, to the last room on the right. Somebody'll be waiting for you there.'

'Sullivan seems to have his own private room here,' Simm said, as they climbed the stairs.

'I guess he's an important man,' Charlie responded.

As they approached the door, two men dressed entirely in black stepped out of the shadows. Simm laid a restraining hand on Charlie's arm, letting her know they couldn't go any farther without approval.

'Hold up your arms,' the man on the right said.

Neither of them argued. One of the men ran a wand over them. It looked like those used by airport security. The other man stared at Charlie the entire time. She didn't seem to notice, or if she did, she didn't appear to mind. But Simm minded. He didn't like the look, and it didn't make him feel any better about agreeing to bring Charlie along.

Apparently satisfied they were unarmed and unwired, the staring man moved to the door and opened it wide. As they walked across the threshold, Simm noticed the thug stared again, and he resisted the urge to tell him to stop. He didn't think it would be a good idea to rock the boat at this point.

The room was large. It contained about twenty-five round tables, all covered with white tablecloths and nothing else. Only one of the tables was occupied, at the rear of the room. A man of about fifty years of age and medium build sat alone, a glass of what looked like straight whiskey on the table in front of him. He had a head of thick, black hair with several strands of gray working their way through it.

His expression was very serious, and his eyes were narrowed as he watched them approach. As they drew closer, and he focused on Charlie, his attitude changed altogether. Simm found himself ignored. The man smiled brilliantly, stood, and extended his hand to the woman by his side.

'You must be Charlene Butler.'

'Yes, I am. Pleased to meet you, Mr. Sullivan, and please call me Charlie.'

'Then feel free to call me Marty. All my friends do.'

Simm had the sensation he was at a social event, not a meeting to question a criminal mind. It also occurred to him the meeting would not be so sociable if he had come alone. Charlie was smart enough to understand, and canny enough to dress the part. She also acted the part, gushing and simpering like a southern belle.

'This is such a beautiful spot. I can see why you like to spend time here. It's almost like a vacation resort,' she said, motioning with her hand toward the panoramic view offered by the expanse of windows.

'It's convenient for me. I hear you have a great place too. I haven't been there for years, not since Jim had it, but I remember you. You were just a young thing then, helping out around the place.'

'Did you know Jim well?'

'Oh yes, we were close. But where are my manners? Sit.'

He pulled out a chair for her, and for the first time, seemed to notice Simm, the person who had asked for the meeting in the first place.

As Charlie settled in her chair, the two men shook hands. The smiles weren't quite as brilliant or simpering.

Out of nowhere, a waitress appeared and asked them if they would like something to drink. Both Charlie and Simm asked for a coffee. For them, it was too early to drink whiskey.

Chapter 38:

Charlie was nervous about the meeting, but she did her best to hide it from Simm. Her choice of outfit served the purpose of boosting her confidence a little, knowing she looked good in it. She wanted to impress Marty Sullivan enough to get him to cooperate. Whether she would succeed or not was yet to be seen. After all, he was an experienced criminal. He had seen it all and wasn't apt to fall for false pretence.

He was a handsome and charming man. It made the act of pretending that much easier. She was certain she could chat with him for hours without any difficulty. She was more worried about Simm. His jaw was clenched, and his spine was stiff. His usual affability was gone, and she didn't understand why. He should be playing along with her.

Marty drew her attention again.

'I didn't know your father so well. I had my own dentist.'

As if to prove his point, he displayed his perfect, brilliant smile again.

'So, what is your problem, Charlene?' he continued. 'Why did you hire a private investigator?'

He gestured in Simm's direction.

'I've been receiving some disturbing mail. Simm thought it may have to do with Jim and his past.'

'Mail? What kind of mail?'

He frowned at Simm, as if he was the person responsible.

'Strange letters sent by the same person, but invariably claiming to be someone else,' Simm explained. 'They aren't overtly threatening, but one of them was a package, delivered to her home. It contained organs.'

'Organs? Human organs?'

'They turned out to be from sheep, but they gave us quite a scare,' Charlie explained.

Marty Sullivan was no longer smiling. He laid his hand on the table, palm up, reminding Charlie of Frank.

'Let's see them.'

Charlie reached to pick up her handbag from its spot on the floor. She withdrew a large brown envelope from which she extracted the small pile of letters and handed them to Marty.

He took another sip of his whiskey before pulling his eyeglasses out of his pocket and starting to read. His brows remained furrowed and his lips tight. Charlie let him finish going through the letters before she continued.

'That's not all. He knows where I live. He put torn posters of missing children, and fake blood on the outside of my apartment door. Then he took my dog.'

'He took your dog?'

He seemed so upset by the idea Charlie hastened to finish the story.

'I got him back a couple of days later. He wasn't hurt, but he was heavily drugged, and it took a while for him to get over it. In the meantime, I was frantic.'

'What kind of guy would use an innocent dog to send a message?'

Charlie and Simm exchanged a quick glance. She knew Simm was having the same thought as she was. A head of a criminal organization, responsible for multiple acts of violence, was concerned about the welfare of a small dog?

Marty Sullivan returned his attention to the letters, looking them over once again. He removed his glasses and set them on the table, his gaze still lowered. He rose and stood facing the plate-glass window, his hands on his hips, and stared at the magnificent view of the Saint Lawrence River with the Clock Tower in the foreground. Charlie sensed he wasn't actually taking in the sight.

Sullivan seemed upset by the letters and Charlie didn't understand why.

'I don't like this,' the older man said, still facing the window.

'I can tell you honestly, I don't like it either,' she said. 'Do you think Simm is right? Do you think it has something to do with Jim's past?'

The mafia boss turned and returned to his seat. He finished off his glass in one swallow, and, like magic, the waitress appeared with a refill. He didn't acknowledge or thank her. He seemed to be deep in thought. Neither Charlie nor Simm said a word. After several long, uncomfortable minutes, he spoke.

'Maybe.'

Suddenly, he sat forward and reached for Charlie's hand, meeting her gaze again. His hand was cool and dry. She sensed Simm stiffening beside her, and she hoped he remained calm long enough for them to get the information they wanted.

'Charlie, you have to understand that Jim was a good man.'

'I know that. I always knew it,' she reassured him.

'He did some work for us, nothing dangerous. He didn't like danger. But we made use of his establishment for certain things, and he helped us out. After he got out of jail, he wanted all the way out. We understood. We're very understanding people, so we let Jim off the hook. He was a good guy. And he remained a good friend. He was like a brother to me. I was broken-hearted when he died.'

Charlie didn't remember seeing this man at Jim's funeral, but he may not have attended. It wouldn't do to have someone of his stature in a criminal organization showing up at a funeral. It would definitely get rumors going once again.

Marty didn't seem to be finished with his story, so Charlie waited patiently for him to speak.

'We continued to do favors for each other over the years,' he said. 'Sometimes, Jim would have some small hassle with a client or a supplier, and I would arrange for someone to have a conversation with this person.'

He dropped Charlie's hand and went over to stand by the window again, his back to them.

'We helped each other out, but we never did anything malicious or harmful.'

He turned to face them again.

'I don't like that you're getting these letters. It makes me angry. I know Jim thought of you like a daughter, and I know he'd be angry too. I want to find out who's doing this.'

He looked at Simm and pinned him with a glare.

'I know who you are and who you used to be. I got no beef with you. My sources say you're a good private eye, and you do things straight. I'll help you find who's doing this. But, there's two things you gotta know. If you don't succeed, I'm going to take over. The second thing is, you better be careful with the information you may find. I appreciate discretion. Remember that.'

Charlie knew a threat when she heard one, and she hoped Simm wasn't planning to do anything Marty Sullivan didn't like.

'Do you know who's doing it, sending these letters to me?' she asked, pulling his attention back to her.

'No, I don't, but I want to. I want to know who it is, and where I can find him.'

His tone was enough to scare Charlie on the perpetrator's behalf.

'I can't point this guy out for you,' Marty continued. 'But, I think I know where you can find more information.'

'Good. That'll be a big help,' Simm said.

'I hope you have a passport.'

'I do, but why?'

'Because you're going to Ireland.'

Chapter 39:

'I've always wanted to go to Dublin.'

'You're not going to Dublin.'

'You need me,' she insisted.

'I'm capable of handling this on my own.'

'When will you admit I was a big help today?' Charlie said.

'I already did. I told you that you did a great job. That doesn't mean you're coming to Ireland.'

'Do you remember the letter I received? I think it was from Tamara. It talked about Ireland and how I should go there to find my roots. That's where we'll find the answers. I can feel it. The key is in Ireland.'

'I'll find it for you. You can stay here where it's safe.'

'If you don't want me to go with you, that's fine. I can go on my own. My passport's ready.'

Simm banged his hand on the steering wheel.

'Why do you have to be so stubborn? Why can't you just let me do my job? I promised you I would keep you up-to-date on whatever I find.'

'I've always wanted to go to Dublin,' she repeated.

'Then go there. On vacation, when this is all over. It'll be much more enjoyable, believe me.'

Simm had a sudden thought.

'Besides, what about the pub?' he added. 'And Harley? You can't just pick up and leave.'

'I have Madame Lafrance for Harley and Frank for the bar. He's entirely capable, and I'll get Marie to come in and work full-time while I'm gone.'

Simm gritted his teeth. This was not going as planned. Ever since Marty Sullivan mentioned Ireland, the wheels were turning in his head. All they had was a name and a last-known address. Aidan Connelly and Thomas MacDonagh Flats. Simm had research to do and a flight to plan, and he didn't need a complication named Charlie.

He dropped her off on the sidewalk in front of Butler's. When she suggested he come in so they could discuss their plans, he declined. He gave an excuse about having to work on another case for a while. His smile felt stiff, and he hoped his sunglasses helped to hide his true feelings.

Back at his office, he turned on his laptop and opened the internet search engine. After an hour, he sat back and ran his hands through his hair. He had discovered quite a bit, but it wouldn't give him much.

First of all, the number of people with the name of Aidan Connelly in Ireland was staggering. Second of all, the address that Marty had given him, Thomas MacDonagh Flats, no longer existed. The apartment building had been in Ballymun, a northern suburb of Dublin, but it was demolished in 2005. If the Aidan Connelly they were looking for had indeed lived there, Simm had no idea where he could be found now. He had his work cut out for him. He was tempted to call Marty Sullivan and ask him for further details, or better yet, what it was all about, but he didn't think the man would be forthcoming.

Simm had the impression Sullivan knew a lot more than he was telling. For some reason, he was holding back information, and his threat about what Simm did with the information he found confirmed there was something he didn't want revealed, possibly something that affected the mafia boss personally.

Simm thought his best bet would be to get to Dublin as soon as possible, before Charlie had time to get her act together. From there, he would contact the local authorities and see if he could track down Aidan Connelly.

CHAPTER 40:

'I'll tell you a secret, if you like.'

The only reply was a grunt.

'I've never done this before.'

Simm opened one eye and peered at her.

'Never?'

'Nope,' she said, smiling. 'It's a bit scary, but exciting at the same time.'

'There's nothing to be afraid of.'

'I bet you've done it a few times.'

'Much more than a few.'

'There's no need to brag.'

'Just stating the facts, that's all.'

She crossed her legs and leaned back. Simm closed his eyes again. They were at Pierre-Elliot Trudeau Airport waiting for a late-night flight to Dublin. It was the best he could get on short notice. Again, he didn't know how she had done it, but Charlie had wormed her way into his plans. As he checked the flights online, she showed up by his shoulder, passport in hand. The next thing he knew he booked two seats.

'If you've never travelled before, why do you have a passport?' Simm said.

'I wanted to be prepared, just in case. Aren't you happy I was?'

Simm thought it would be better not to respond to that question. Instead, he closed his eyes again and thought ahead several hours.

They would arrive in Dublin at 11:00 in the morning local time. He would have a few hours to try and make some contacts before the close of the business day. They would get to sleep at a normal hour and, hopefully, would get their biological clocks in sync by the next day. But, that was likely wishful thinking.

He jolted upright when Charlie seized his knee.

'Our flight is boarding now,' she said.

'Okay, there's no need to panic. We're right here. They can't leave without us.'

He watched her fidgeting impatiently as people lined up. He sighed, sat up, and grabbed his carry-on bag.

'Let's go,' he said, knowing she wouldn't relax until she was on the plane.

It didn't take any further encouragement. She was in the line-up before Simm had a chance to stand.

Once they were on board, Charlie looked around her with fascination. She insisted they put on their seatbelts right away. She removed a book and a notepad from her carry-on bag and put it in the pouch in front of her. She fiddled with the fold-down table and the window shade. When she reached up to check on the light switches, he captured her arm.

'That's too much activity, Charlie. Why don't you relax for a while?'

'The flight is six hours long. We can't relax during that time?'

'Let me put it this way. You're driving me crazy with all your fidgeting. Give it a rest.'

She scowled and leaned back in her seat. Everything went smoothly until the plane fired up the engines for takeoff and raced down the runway.

'Oh God. Oh God. It won't make it.'

Charlie's hand gripped Simm's knee with surprising strength. The more the engines roared, the harder she gripped. He thought her fingers would puncture the skin of his leg.

'We're going to crash!'

'We're not going to crash. Everything's fine.'

'Listen to that. The engines are forcing too much. They can't lift us.'

As she said this, the plane was already halfway to full altitude.

'It'll be over in a few minutes, Charlie.'

Simm winced when he witnessed the look of shock on her face.

'I mean we'll be at cruising speed, and they'll slow the engines. Don't worry.'

She didn't speak again or relax her grip until the engines quieted to some degree. When she removed her hand, and looked out the window, Simm surreptitiously rubbed his leg, trying to regain circulation. Charlie finally relaxed, but refused to remove her seatbelt or close her eyes.

However, Simm closed his eyes to try to catch up on some much-needed sleep.

'How will we find him?' Charlie asked.

'I'll figure that out when I get there,' he answered, not opening his eyes.

'What if he's dead?'

'I'll figure that out when I get there.'

'Don't you ever do any preplanning?'

'All the time, but have you ever heard about the best-laid plans?'

'Well, of course, things can go wrong, but you have to have somewhere to start.'

'I have somewhere to start. Aidan Connelly in Ballymun.'

'Is it nice?'

'What?'

'Dublin. Ballymun.'

'I don't know. I've never been there, but apparently Ballymun was not a very nice place a few years back. A lot of crime and drugs.'

'Do you think this all has to do with drugs?'

'Maybe, but I doubt it. And don't ask me why I think that. I just do.'

'Fair enough. We'll soon find out.'

Charlie managed to remain silent for a few more minutes.

'Apparently, it's not that warm, even in the summer.'

Simm sighed. There was nothing to be done. He straightened up in his seat and prepared for conversation.

'You've been doing your research, I see.'

'Of course, you can't travel without doing research first.'

'I didn't think you knew much about travelling. This is your first time on a plane.'

'You're right. I know nothing about travelling, but I can still figure things out.'

'Did you never go on family vacations as a kid?'

'No, not at all. My father worked very hard, and when he took a vacation, he just wanted to rest and get things done around the house. He was a homebody more than anything.'

'What about your mom?'

'I don't think she liked to go anywhere either. At least, she never complained or talked about travelling. She seemed to like to stay close to home. My dad went to Ireland once, but he went with Jim.'

'He went to Ireland? When did he go? Why would he go with Jim?' Charlie had Simm's full attention now.

'I don't know when he went. Maybe before I was born. I just remember him mentioning he went to Ireland with Jim. I didn't ask why.'

'Your mother didn't go with them?'

'No. Now that you mention it, I remember her not being happy about the conversation. She seemed very annoyed with my father for bringing it up. I guess she wasn't happy about not going with them.'

'What about Jim's wife? Did she go?'

'I don't know. Again, I didn't ask.'

Simm had a feeling this information was significant for some reason. It was odd Pat Butler and Jim would go off to Ireland together. As if reading his thoughts, Charlie piped up.

'I never thought it was a big deal. I mean, Dad and Jim were good friends. Jim went to Ireland many times before. I guess he just wanted to share the experience with my dad. It wasn't that unusual.'

She sounded as if she wanted to convince herself.

'Why did Jim go to Ireland so often? What was he doing there?'

'I don't know exactly. Jim was very proud of his Irish heritage. He was born in Canada, but his father was born in Ireland, and he had a large extended family over there. Whenever he met an Irishman, he treated him like a member of the family. I imagine he travelled to Ireland to visit his relatives and to stay close to his roots.'

Simm thought she may have a point, but there were too many coincidences to make him comfortable with the explanation.

'You never thought it strange that an outgoing, back-slapping mobster was friends with a quiet, introverted dentist?'

'Don't call him a mobster. He wasn't like that.'

'He was arrested as a person who had a connection to the mob. That makes him a mobster.'

'If you want to be technical about it, you're right. But he wasn't like that. He was such a nice, friendly, kind man. He would give the shirt off his back to whomever needed it. I think his problem was that he couldn't say no. That's probably what happened. The West End Gang asked him for something, and he said yes. You heard Marty Sullivan say Jim was a great guy. They were friends. Sullivan is another Irishman. Jim would do anything for another Irishman.'

'I understand, but you didn't answer my question. Didn't you find it strange that Jim and your dad made such an odd pair?'

Charlie stared out the window for several moments. Then, she turned and looked at Simm with a sad expression.

'Yes, I did.'

CHAPTER 41:

'We could die today.'

'We're not going to die. We're perfectly safe.'

'If this plane crashes, there's no way we'd survive.'

Simm had succeeded in distracting Charlie for a short while, but when their conversation ended, she reverted to worrying about the flight.

'It won't crash. There are less deaths by air travel than there are by car. It's proven.'

'At least in a car you have a chance of survival.'

'Stop being paranoid. It'll be okay.'

'I've always had a fear of dying alone, with just a stranger by my side.'

'That's not the case. I'm here.'

'I hardly know you.'

'What are you talking about? We've known each other for weeks.'

'Superficially. I know nothing about you or your background.'

Simm banged his head against the headrest.

'That's what this is all about? You're trying to manipulate me into telling you about my family?'

'You know about mine.'

'That's not true and you know it. I've been trying to find out about your family since day one, and it's like pulling teeth.'

Charlie stared out the window for a minute, and then twisted in her seat to face him.

'All right, I'll make a deal with you. I'll tell you about my family if you tell me about yours.'

Simm considered the offer thoughtfully. He felt he needed to know more to move the case along, but he detested the idea of revealing his life to Charlie. On the other hand, if he was crafty enough, there was sure to be a way to sugar-coat it.

'Deal. You first,' he said.

Charlie looked at him with narrowed eyes, obviously trying to read him. He worked on giving her his most innocent face. It apparently worked, because she turned face-forward again, put her head back, and began to talk.

'I had a great childhood, or at least, it was great from my standpoint, and I guess that's what counts. My parents doted on me, probably since I was the only child. I was a bit of a tomboy and spent a lot of time with my father, playing ball, going hiking and fishing. I really looked up to him.'

'What about your mother?'

'I loved her, but she was more of a background player for me. She took care of me physically, and kept me organized, clean, and healthy, but she wasn't the type to get overly involved in my activities. It was my dad who did that.'

Simm saw the sadness creep into her expression.

'And then he didn't anymore,' she said.

'He left,' Simm said.

'You knew?'

'I knew they were divorced, but I don't know the reasons behind it.'

'You and me both. One day he was there, and we were all happy, and the next he was gone, like we never existed.'

'You didn't see him again?'

'Yes, but it was awkward, and it was obvious he didn't want to be there.'

'Was there another woman?'

'No, apparently not. He changed. It's as simple as that, but at the same time, it wasn't all that simple.'

'What was your mother's reaction?'

'Strange. It was very strange. It was more of a non-reaction, as if she expected it. When I asked her, she said they had grown apart, but that was bullshit. You don't grow apart from one day to the next. And, she also changed after he left, or maybe it all happened simultaneously. I can't say. She became…I don't know…bitter, I guess. She would say things about my dad, like how weak he was. I never thought of him as weak.'

'How old were you?'

'Fifteen.'

'You were pretty young. Maybe everything had seemed great between them, but they'd succeeded in hiding it from you.'

'Maybe you're right.'

'What happened after that?'

'Jim stepped up to the plate. He took me under his wing. As a friend of my father, he had continually been a background presence in my life, but he moved into the foreground. He gave me a job in the pub and became my mentor.'

'Why do you think he did that?'

Charlie shrugged. 'I always assumed it was because he loved me.'

'That's believable.'

'So, that's my story. Your turn,' she said, turning to face him. He sighed.

'I had a pretty normal childhood. I have a brother and a sister. Walt, you've met. Susan is my sister, the youngest of the kids.'

'Are your parents still together?'

'They might have been, I guess. My mom died of cancer when I was thirteen, Susan was eight.'

'That's awful.'

'It was. My father remarried a few years later. They're still together.'

'Do you like your stepmother?'

'Yeah, she's okay. She was good to us.'

'And?'

'And what?'

'What's the issue you have with your brother?'

'I don't have an issue with him. We get along fine.'

'Do you see him often?'

'Not really. We're both busy. Charlie, you're looking for something that isn't there. You won't find anything interesting in my life story,' he lied.

'We'll see. I still need more details about Helen.'

Simm laid his head back and closed his eyes. He had dodged the bullet for now, but he knew it would turn around like a boomerang and come back at him someday soon.

'There aren't any more details to give. Besides, we agreed to discussing only our families today.'

'I know. That's okay. I'll be patient.'

Simm gave a short laugh. 'That'll be something new.'

CHAPTER 42:

The remainder of the flight, for the most part, was uneventful. There were two other instances when Simm's knee was attacked. The first time was when they had some turbulence, but luckily for him there was only one incident of rough skies. The second, of course, was on landing. Simm knew that would be another tricky part. If she reacted badly to takeoff, the landing was likely to be worse, but he came out of the experience relatively unharmed.

They landed in Dublin to rare, clear skies and 15-degrees Celsius temperature. After they picked up their luggage, they grabbed a taxi for the ten-minute ride to the hotel. Simm had booked adjoining rooms for three nights, hoping that would be long enough to track down Aidan Connelly and get the answers they needed.

The rooms were clean and comfortable, as expected. Charlie wanted a refreshing shower before setting out to Dublin center. It occurred briefly to Simm he should take off without her while she was in the shower, but he knew the recriminations would be painful. He also knew she would find him, and it would be nothing short of embarrassing.

Within half an hour, they were on their way, again by taxi. Their destination was An Garda Siochana Headquarters. Simm was sure he had botched the pronunciation of the name, but the good-spirited taxi driver didn't blink an eye.

When they arrived, it was to a locked-down and gated establishment. Both Simm and Charlie had to produce identification, be searched for weapons, and give a reason for being there.

Simm's statement that he was a private investigator from Canada, searching for the key to a crime in said country, was enough to allow them entrance.

The taxi driver, however, wasn't allowed to drive through, so Charlie and Simm walked through the gate and over to the main building. It was a large stone building, undoubtedly built several decades earlier. The inside was modernized, giving it a bright, efficient look.

The desk sergeant spoke in a particularly heavy Irish brogue, and they had to ask him to repeat himself twice before they knew what he asked them. Finally, they were shown to a waiting area that was decorated with enlarged photographs taken from various periods in the police station's history. Charlie remained standing and browsed through them as they waited. She had changed from her jeans into a pair of beige dress pants and a light sweater. Her hair was shiny and thick, standing out against her sweater. Simm noticed she had added a touch of lipstick. The only other occasion he had seen her wearing lipstick was when they visited Marty Sullivan.

The same desk sergeant showed up and said something in his unintelligible accent, but from his hand movements they understood they were being shown to another room. The man they met there was not tall, but very round. He had wisps of red hair circling his head with a shiny pate on top.

'Hello to you both. My name's Inspector James O'Reilly.'

They took turns shaking the man's extended hand. Charlie gave Simm a quizzical look, as if to say, 'Could it be a relation?'. Simm shook his head slightly to ask her not to pursue it. The amount of O'Reilly's in Ireland would be astounding.

'Would you know Jim O'Reilly?' she asked. 'His family's here in Ireland, and he used to come visit them frequently.'

Simm wondered why he went to the trouble of sending her a mental message when she chose to ignore it.

'Well now, there are a lot of us O'Reillys in Ireland, and a good many would be named Jim, as I am meself. Is this the nature of your business here? Are ya looking for this Jim lad?'

Simm stepped in, hoping to gain control of the situation.

'Not really. Jim passed away a few years ago. We're looking for a man who may have been an acquaintance or associate of his, Mr. Aiden Connelly. Would you have any information about him?'

'Another common name. Would this man happen to be a criminal? I ask because ya chose to go through us to find him. That leads me to believe he may not have always walked the straight and narrow.'

Simm and Charlie exchanged a glance.

'Possibly,' Simm offered. 'All I know is that he was from Ballymun.'

'Oh, Ballymun. Well that may narrow it down a bit. Let's see if I can help ya out with that. Sit yerselves down now.'

Charlie and Simm waited while the policeman entered information into his computer. Simm noticed his expression became grimmer as the minutes went by. The man sighed.

'Well, I have a few Aidan Connellys from Ballymun in the system. We would have to try and narrow it down by a bit more. Would ya know how old the fella might be?'

'Jim would have been in his late sixties by now. I'm not sure if they were contemporaries or not, but let's see if anyone fits into that age group,' Charlie suggested.

'Yes, there would be one about sixty-five years of age.'

'Is he still alive?' she asked.

'Well now, that's a bit hard to say. He was alive about ten years ago when he was released from prison.'

'What did he do time for?' Simm wanted to know.

'He was involved in a variety of crimes. Worked for the mafia, he did.'

'I think he's probably the one we're looking for. Do you have any information that would tell us how to find him?' Simm said.

'Not a lot. I can give ya his last known address.'

The policeman hesitated and glanced at Charlie before addressing Simm again.

'I could give ya some names of his past associates, but I don't think they'd be the friendly sort, if ya know what I mean. It could be dangerous.'

'We'll take the information, and we'll decide how we'll handle it from there. But, don't worry, we won't take any unnecessary risks.'

'I'd appreciate that, lad. I don't want to get called out just to find the two of you in deep trouble, or worse.'

Chapter 43:

'So, will we go to the address now?'

'Not yet, we're going back to the hotel and we'll sleep for a bit.'

'I'm not tired,' she said.

'You will be. To keep ahead of the jet lag, a little nap is called for. Then we'll check out the address.'

Charlie frowned, but didn't put up an argument. Simm took that as a good sign. He deposited her outside the door of her room, and continued to his. Once inside, he didn't lie down. He stood at the window for a few minutes, paced the floor, and occasionally listened at the adjoining door. He heard the toilet flush and a small noise as if someone had sat on the bed. He guessed he was safe.

He opened the door to the corridor and closed it softly behind him. The elevator was around a corner and far enough away from the room. He knew she wouldn't hear the noise.

In the lobby, he stopped by the desk to ask for a map of the Ballymun region. Map in hand, he turned to leave and bumped into Charlie. An angry-looking Charlie.

'I knew it. This was your plan. Dump me in a room and then leave.'

'I couldn't sleep. I decided to go for a walk, get to know the area.'

'You are such a liar, Mr. Simm Simmons.'

'Okay, I'll admit it. I was going to check out the address, but just to see what the area's like, nothing else.'

'Liar. C'mon let's go.'

'Charlie, I don't want you to come with me. We don't know what this place is like. It could be dangerous. Let me check it out first, and I'll come back for you.'

'No way. I'm going with you now.'

Simm didn't think he had ever met anyone so hard-headed before. There was no reasoning with her. And there was no way around it. Either they turned back and returned to Montreal, or they did what they had set out to do. Since Simm didn't want to waste his time or this trip, he gave her his fiercest scowl and turned to the door.

The car rental agency wasn't far. Simm took care of the paperwork as Charlie chatted with, and charmed, one of the clerks. They got directions to where they wanted to go and went to the parking lot to get their car, a small European model. There was a moment of confusion when Charlie went to climb in the right-side door only to see a steering wheel.

'Oh, I forgot,' she said. 'We have to drive on the opposite of the road. Can you do that?'

'Why wouldn't I? How difficult can it be?' Simm replied, still feeling frustrated.

He intended to give every impression he knew what he was doing, but the car had a manual transmission, the stick-shift was on the left, and within seconds he was disoriented. They moved at a snail's pace, and he heard little exclamations of concern coming from the passenger seat.

'Stop it,' he snapped.

'I can't help it. Don't you notice all the people honking at you?'

'Of course, I do. I'm not deaf, but I don't feel like having an accident either. And you're not helping to keep me focused.'

'Sorry. What can I do to help?"

'Keep quiet.'

That lasted a few seconds.

'Oh my God! You're going the wrong way.'

'No, I'm going the right way, which is the opposite way. Be quiet!'

He was in a roundabout, driving in the opposite direction from what he was accustomed, and not quite sure how to get out without running into someone. He felt a trickle of sweat creep down his spine.

Finally, he saw his chance, made it out, and onto a street. He had no idea if it was the right street, but at least he was no longer turning in circles. He pulled over and checked the GPS signal on his phone.

Letting out a breath of relief, he glanced over at Charlie. She stared straight ahead, her hand holding on to the handle above the door as if the roof of the car was threatening to leave them.

'We're okay. We're going in the right direction,' he assured her.

She looked at him out of the corner of her eye, without saying a word.

'Why don't you help me out with this?' he said, handing her his phone. 'Just listen to whatever it says, and you can navigate.'

Charlie took the phone from his hand, looking at it dubiously.

'It's okay. It won't blow up or anything. Haven't you ever used a GPS before?'

'No. I've never gone anywhere unfamiliar before.'

'Don't worry. You'll love it.'

Simm put the little car in gear, and moved along the road at a faster speed, feeling more at ease.

Within a few minutes, he didn't see anything to be at ease about. The farther they drove the less appealing were their surroundings. The buildings took on a shabby look, weeds growing on the few patches of ground visible underneath the garbage. Paint and plaster peeled from walls, and graffiti covered most surfaces.

Once again pulling over, Simm locked the car doors and took the phone from Charlie to see the name of the street they were on. They weren't that far from their destination, with only another block and a half to go.

They stopped in front of 157 Gosford Street, and Simm's heart sank even further. It was one of the more rundown buildings on the street, and that was hard to beat. Windowpanes were broken, and the door was missing a hinge. There was a cord with one end tied to the doorknob and the other end tied to a nail hammered in the exterior wall to keep the door from falling on the sidewalk.

He glanced at Charlie. Her jaw had dropped and her eyes were wide.

'Stay behind me,' he warned.

He heard Charlie's footsteps crunching on the stones behind him as he approached the house. He knocked lightly on the dilapidated door. There was no sound from inside. He put his left hand on the door to hold it in place, and he knocked noisily with his right. This time, he heard a crash, followed by a loud voice. The words were indistinguishable, but the tone was clearly unhappy.

The dirty curtain on the other side of the door was pushed aside, and a man with long, greasy hair and bloodshot eyes peered through the cracks in the glass.

'What do ya want? Do ya have ta make enough racket to raise the divil?'

'Are you Aidan Connelly?' Simm asked.

'Aidan Connelly? What the hell would ya want with Aidan Connelly now?'

'Are you him?'

'Of course not. Do I look like an old man to ya?'

Simm held his tongue. The man may not be old, but it was very hard to tell from the unhealthy lines on his face and the stoop of his shoulders.

'So, you know him then? Could you tell me how I could find him?'

'I don't know him well. He used to live here. I haven't got the foggiest where he is now.'

He plucked a cigarette out of his pocket, and for a moment, Simm had difficulty seeing his face through the cloud of smoke as he lit it. He squinted first at Simm, then leaned over to get a better look at Charlie, who was half-hidden behind Simm. The man's face broke into a grin, revealing yellow and black teeth.

'Who's lookin' for him? The little lass here?'

'We happen to know a friend of his, and we thought we'd look him up.'

'Ya don't say now. Who would this friend be?'

'I'd prefer to speak to Mr. Connelly about it myself. Could you tell me how to find him?'

'Let me know where I can find ya, and if I happen to see him, I can tell him where to go.'

'I tell you what, we'll come back here tomorrow around the same time. Just tell Mr. Connelly we're friends of Jim O'Reilly.'

The man's eyes narrowed. The curtain fell back into place without another word being spoken.

CHAPTER 44:

It took them a little longer than it should have to get back to the hotel.

'I don't remember going on this street on the way over. Are you sure you're not lost?'

'I know exactly where I am,' Simm answered.

'But, I thought the hotel was in the other direction.'

'It is.'

'Simm, what's wrong with you? Do you want me to drive?'

'I think someone's following us. I'm trying to lose them. No, don't turn around. Just look in the side mirror. It's a black Volkswagen.'

'What? Have you seen the number of Volkswagens here? And black? Most of them are black.'

'Yeah, well this one has a dent on the right-hand side and the guy's wearing a hat. He obviously doesn't know what he's doing if he's trying not to be noticed.'

'Do you think he's the guy from Connelly's house?'

'No, this guy doesn't have long hair. It's someone else.'

'I don't see him.'

'That's because he's not there. I think I lost him.'

Charlie looked closely at Simm. She wondered if jet lag or stress was getting to him. He could be imagining someone was following them. But she noticed they were again in familiar territory and approaching the hotel.

'Maybe we should have a rest when we get there. A real one this time, no running off.'

Her suggestion was accepted without argument, and she wondered if he was legitimately tired, or if he was up to something. She, on the other hand, was almost too tired to care. The lack of sleep on the way across the ocean had caught up to her. The excitement of the arrival and the search for Aidan Connelly had worn off, and all she wanted was a bed.

Once in her room, she quietly slipped off her shoes before she tugged back the covers and slid between the sheets. She fell asleep the instant her head hit the pillow. For all she cared at this point, Simm could spend his day running all over Ireland without her.

Two hours later, a heavy knocking on the door woke her. Groggily, she staggered out of bed and pulled open the door. Strangely, there was no one on the other side, but she still heard knocking. Slapping her forehead, she shut the door and went to the adjoining doors. There she found Simm, leaning against the door jamb.

'You were sleeping soundly. I was about to knock down the door.'

'I was tired. Did you sleep?' she asked, narrowing her eyes skeptically at him. After a bit of rest, she was back to caring whether he tried to disappear without her or not.

'Like a log. Now I'm hungry. Let's go get something to eat.'

'Where are we going?'

'I spoke to the guy out front. He gave me a suggestion.'

'What should I wear?'

'What you're wearing now.'

'Give me a sec.'

She went into the bathroom, ran a brush through her hair, and checked her makeup. It would have to do. She knew Simm wouldn't be patient enough to wait much longer. When she stepped out of the bathroom, he slid his gaze over her, but made no comment other than, 'Let's go'.

The car ride to their destination was short enough they could easily have walked it, but Charlie guessed Simm was extra cautious about them being out on the street, especially after his earlier suspicions about being followed.

Considering it was a Tuesday night, the pub was more crowded and noisier than Charlie would have thought, but she was instantly charmed. The atmosphere was warm and congenial. It had the same style of mahogany furnishings as she had back home, but with a touch of something else that she couldn't quite put her finger on. It was something that would make her want to return time and again, and she itched to discover what it was so she could copy it.

'Welcome to our humble pub. What might ya be looking for? Something to quench yer thirst? Or do ya have a hole in yer gizzard that needs to be filled?'

Charlie turned to the source of the welcome, and faced a middle-aged, red-haired man, a little on the short side, with a well-rounded belly. She returned his warm smile.

'We'd like a bit of both.'

'Ah now, I can tell by yer lovely wee accent yer not from around these parts. Where might ya be hailing from?'

'Montreal, Canada.'

'Isn't that grand? We love our Canadians, we do. Come and sit yerself down, and I'll get someone to help ya.'

They were swiftly seated at a table in the center of the room, with many nods and smiles from people along the way. A few seconds later, they were greeted by a pretty, young woman with long, auburn hair and a bright smile. It seemed to Charlie the smile was directed at Simm a little longer than it was at her.

Charlie ordered the traditional Irish stew while Simm asked for the fish and chips, which were highly recommended by the waitress. They soon had two glasses of Guinness set before them to drink while they waited and that seemed to be the signal for the locals to engage them in conversation. Charlie wondered if they were the only out-of-towners in the bar. She felt like a new arrival at the zoo, everyone curious about who they were and where they came from.

'Would you happen to know someone by the name of Aidan Connelly?' Simm asked to no one in particular, apparently deciding to take advantage of the local intelligence.

'Would that be Tim Connelly's lad?' asked an older man to Charlie's right.

Before Simm could answer, someone else said, 'No, Tim's lad was called Andy, not Aidan. It must be old Sonny's lad.'

'Is he a young fella?'

'He should be in his sixties, I think.'

'Oh now, that's another story. I don't remember an Aidan around here.'

There was a lot of head-shaking and mumbling. Most had to take another gulp of Guinness to help revive their memories.

'Are ya sure the name's Connelly? I know an Aidan Conway,' one ventured.

'No, it's definitely Connelly,' Simm responded.

'If the lass is looking for a man, I could give her a hand,' offered a rough-looking man in his fifties, with uncombed hair and large gaps in his mouth that had once held teeth. His remark was greeted with raucous laughter.

'Take a jump and run, Dan. You with a face like a horse's arse, do ya think she'd be interested?' The waitress set the plates in front of them, her scowl promptly turning to a brilliant smile for Simm. 'Here ya go. Get that inta ya now.'

The group around them quieted and concentrated on their task at hand, which seemed to be polishing off as many pints of Guinness as they could before they had to go home. Simm and Charlie dug into their meal, and it was every bit as good as expected. They were finishing up when a chair was pulled up to their table and the pub owner sat with them, introducing himself as Harry O'Shea.

'How was that then?'

'Delicious,' Charlie answered. 'I'd like to serve something like this at home. You wouldn't be interested in coming to work in a pub in Canada, would you?'

'Oh, ya have a business now, do ya?'

Charlie explained about the pub and was summarily offered the recipe for the Irish stew, but no plans for immigrating.

'I hear you're lookin' for an Aidan Connelly.'

Simm leaned forward, resting his elbows on the table.

'Do you know him?' he asked.

'Not personally, no. But I heard of one who used to be not far from here. He's gone now.'

'Gone as in moved, or gone as in dead?' Simm said.

'The last I heard he was alive, but ya never know with that sort.'

'What sort would that be?' Simm asked.

The man leaned ahead, and both Charlie and Simm did the same, all of them meeting in the middle.

'He was involved in some sort of shady business, maybe even the Mafia.'

Charlie studied Simm to see his reaction, but he remained stone-faced.

'You don't have any idea where he is? Or who could help us find him?' Simm asked.

'Well, I'm thinkin' maybe Tom O'Brien could be of some help. Ya could find him over on East 24th street. He's an old retired Guard, and he likes to keep up on what's happening with his past cases. Could be this Aidan fella was one of them.'

'That's a great help. If you could give me his exact address, we could look him up.'

'No problem there. And ya can tell him I sent ya. That'll help. He's a regular here.'

Chapter 45:

Charlie felt a little tipsy when they eventually left the pub. She wasn't much of a beer drinker, but she figured you couldn't come to Ireland and not drink a Guinness in an authentic Irish pub. She'd be laughed out of her own pub at home if she neglected the task. And it had tasted good, seemingly better than the same brand at home.

Simm, however, was his usual controlled self. His body weight, being larger, allowed him to indulge a bit more without having any of the effects. When Charlie weaved a little on the way to the elevator, he caught her elbow to steady her.

'I'm okay. The floor was a little uneven there,' she reassured him.

'Uh huh.'

'Do you have your key?' he asked, as they stopped outside her door.

'It's somewhere in here,' she said, rifling through her bag.

Simm took her arm and gently tugged her to his door, pulling out his key card.

'You can go through the adjoining door.'

He pushed open the door, hesitated a split-second, and shoved her behind him.

'Stay here.'

'What's wrong?'

Simm swung around, lowered his face to hers, and hissed, 'Stay here!'

Charlie, suddenly stone sober, knew he was very serious, and, for once, she didn't plan to disobey him. He noiselessly slid past the door and peered around the room before moving into the bathroom. Charlie heard the shower curtain being moved aside before Simm came back out, snagged her wrist, and tugged her into the room,

170

shutting the door behind her.

She had her first glimpse of what had alerted Simm. The room was ransacked. The covers were lying on the floor alongside the bed. The drawers were pulled out of the dresser and turned upside down. His bag was overturned on the floor. Glancing into the bathroom, she saw little was disturbed, probably because a can of shaving cream, a toothbrush, and toothpaste were hard to search.

That's when it occurred to her that her room had likely been searched also. She opened her mouth to mention it to Simm when she noticed him staring at the adjoining door. It was slightly ajar.

'Stay over there,' he said quietly, pointing to the corner near the closed door of his room.

She complied without a word. She was quite happy to let him go first.

The door opened soundlessly, and Simm slipped through. A minute later, he reappeared, looking grim.

'They went through your room too.'

Charlie grimaced, not surprised, but she had been holding on to a kernel of hope.

'Who do you think 'they' are?' she asked, as she stepped over the threshold.

'I don't know, but it's obviously connected to Mr. Connelly.'

Charlie's room had been searched in the same manner as Simm's. The bathroom was worse. Her makeup and toiletry bags were emptied into the sink, and a few things were broken. Unlike Simm's room, a message was left in hers. On the bathroom mirror, using her red lipstick, someone had written 'GO HOME'.

'Don't touch anything. I'm calling the police.'

He had his cell phone in hand, and he asked to speak to Inspector O'Reilly. He filled the policeman in on what had happened and hung up.

'He'll be over soon with a crew.'

The man was true to his word, appearing at the door in less than ten minutes. He stood with his hands on his hips and looked around the room.

'This must've put the heart crossways in ya, I suppose. Someone would rather ya head on back to where ya come from.' He turned to face Simm. 'I told ya I didn't want to see ya getting inta trouble. Ya didn't listen now, did ya?'

'We came here looking for someone, and we intend to find him.'

'By the looks of things, I don't think he wants to be found. Anyway, I'll have me men take a look at this. The doors aren't banjaxed, so they had a key. We'll have to talk to the manager and the rest of the staff.'

'I suspect you'll find a master key has been stolen.'

'Most likely, but I'll let ya know. Meanwhile, ya might want to find another place to lay yer heads, and either follow the advice written on the mirror, or be extra cautious with yerselves.'

'Ms. Butler will be travelling back to Canada, but I'll be staying.'

'What? I'm not going anywhere,' Charlie protested.

'Can't you see that it's become dangerous now? You have to go home,' Simm insisted.

'No way, I'm in for the long haul.'

She heard a short laugh coming from Inspector O'Reilly, and glanced over to see him looking at Simm with a glint in his eye.

'Sounds like ya got a powder keg here. Ya might be in for a clip around the ear if yer not careful.'

Chapter 46:

'Are we changing hotels?'

The cops had left at last. The rooms were dusted for fingerprints, the staff was questioned, and they were alone in the room. Simm threw his belongings into his bag.

'There isn't much point tonight. They've left their message. They won't be back this soon. Tomorrow, we'll move on, hopefully without them finding us. I spoke to the manager about giving us another room for tonight.'

He zipped his bag closed and hitched it onto his shoulder.

'C'mon, we'll get your stuff together,' he added.

Charlie went through the same process in her room, and they took the elevator to another room on another floor.

'It's only one room.'

'That's right,' Simm agreed. 'And that's the way it'll be. We can't be separated. It's too dangerous.'

'There's just one bed.'

'You have a talent for pointing out the obvious. This was all they had available. We'll make do. Besides, it's almost two in the morning. We don't have that many hours to worry about.'

Simm saw Charlie was uncertain.

'You don't have to worry. It's been months since I've attacked a woman. I think I'm over it.'

'Very funny.'

'Seriously, it's a big bed. I swear I'll be extra careful to stay on my side.'

'Okay. Just for tonight.'

Charlie looked in the closet and pulled out two extra pillows,

173

which she then placed under the blankets in the middle of the bed, effectively creating a mini-wall. Simm stood with his hands on his hips, wondering if she would set up traps to catch him if he dared cross over.

When the bed was protected and Charlie was in her pyjamas, they both settled under the covers.

'Good night,' Simm said, as he shut off the light and rolled onto his side, his back to Charlie.

She responded in kind to his good night wish, but a few minutes later, the light on her side of the bed came on, and Simm felt her adjusting her position.

'You've got to tell me. I think I've been very patient with you, but it can't go on any longer.'

Simm rolled over and studied her with a terrible feeling in his gut. She was on her side, facing him, her hand propping up her head.

'God, what is it now?'

'Simm.'

'What?'

'Simm,' Charlie repeated. 'I have to know what your real first name is. It's impossible for someone to name their child Simm Simmons.'

'Simm is a short form of my last name. I thought that was obvious.'

'It is, but the reason for not using your real name isn't. What is it?'

'I'm not telling you.'

'Come on. It can't be that bad. If I need to, I'll hire another private investigator to find out for me.'

Simm knew she would. There was no way to get past it.

'Winston.'

'Your name is Winston? Winston Simmons?'

Her head went back and a full belly laugh came out of her mouth. She eventually doubled over in laughter. Simm saw she wanted to say something, but it wouldn't come out lucidly. She controlled herself long enough to spurt out, 'It's a good thing you don't have a lisp. Winthun Thimmonths. Oh God, that's funny. Why would your parents call you Winston?'

'It's a family name,' he said defensively.

'You mean you're Winston Simmons, the second?'

'Third.'

This produced more gales of laughter.

'Winston Simmons, the Third. That's pretty hoity-toity for a private investigator.'

Simm didn't comment, but he saw her expression change when realization struck.

'Oh, I get it. You're the rebel, the black sheep of the family.'

'You're a smart one. You've got it all figured out.'

'Let me guess. Your father wanted you to run the family business, which is...lumber...or a distillery...and you didn't want to have any part of it, so you ran off and became a cop.'

'Printing and real estate.'

'Printing and real estate, that was my next guess. But, I'm right on all the rest, aren't I?'

'Yes, you're right. And I don't get along with my father, and that's why my siblings have been after me to reconcile with him.'

'He didn't want you to be a cop.'

'No, he didn't.'

'Did you give up the police force and become a private investigator to try and please him?'

Simm laughed abruptly and bitterly.

'Not at all. There was no pleasing him. Not unless I went into the family business and was at his beck and call twenty-four hours a day.'

'Then why did you make the change?'

Simm sighed. 'I guess I inherited a bit of his entrepreneurship. I wanted to be my own boss. It's a simple as that.'

'And now he's sick?'

Simm thought she was way too good at this game.

'Apparently, but it doesn't make any difference to me.'

'But what if he dies, and you never get to see him again?'

Simm shook his head and shrugged. He didn't care.

'Simm, my parents are both dead. I was angry as hell with my father for leaving me and my mother. I swore I never wanted to see him again, but when he became sick, I went to see him and we mended our bridges the best we could. And, I don't regret it. I would've regretted it forever if he'd died before I could see him again.'

'Those are different circumstances. I have no intention of seeing my father again.'

'You're making a mistake.'

'It's my mistake to make,' he said gruffly.

Chapter 47:

Charlie's eyes were at half-mast when she stumbled into the shower the following morning. She wasn't much of a morning person, which was a good thing, considering the business she ran. Add to that the jet lag and she wasn't disposed to being good-humored. Simm didn't seem to care about her humor and insisted they continue their investigation. Of course, his arguments made perfect sense. She was more than ready to put this whole experience behind her. But, why did it have to start so damn early?

'Where did you say we were going?' she asked Simm, when she came out of the bathroom, dressed and ready to go.

'Drink this. Maybe it'll help your memory a little.'

Charlie thankfully took the cup of coffee from him. It was almost enough to make her forgive him for waking her up.

'I'm not at my best this early in the morning. Oh, this is nice and strong. Where'd you get it?'

'Room service, of course. I asked them to add a little extra caffeine for you. There's some pastry things too. I think they called them scones.'

Charlie didn't care what they were called. She was hungry, and they disappeared in seconds.

'You didn't answer my question,' she said.

'We're going to see Mr. O'Brien, the retired cop. It may be a dead end, but at this point, it's the only end we have.'

The man wasn't hard to find. He lived in a small apartment near the center of Dublin, and he didn't seem surprised to have two unannounced visitors knocking on his door. He stood at the threshold for a moment, looking them over, scratching his abundant stomach through his threadbare t-shirt. His sparse grey hair looked like it hadn't been combed in a while.

'Mr. O'Brien, we were given your name by Harry O'Shea. He thought you could help us,' Simm said.

'Is that right? Well then, you'd better come in and sit yourselves down. Don't mind the mess. My housekeeper has been out for a while. Actually, she's been out for about three years.'

The old man laughed at his own joke. He shoved a pile of newspapers off the couch onto the floor to make room for them to sit, but made no effort to pick up or excuse the dirty plates and mugs on the coffee table.

'My name is Simm and this is Charlie Butler. If you haven't already guessed, we're from Canada, Montreal specifically.'

'I could tell you were foreigners, I could. I spent many of me years as a peeler. I can sniff out a foreigner a mile away,' he said, tweaking his nose and chuckling.

'I'm sure you can. We're looking for someone, and Harry thought you may have had contact with him during the course of your career.'

'And who might that be?'

'Aidan Connelly.'

His eyebrows rose and the corners of his mouth turned downward.

'Now why would you be looking for that scum bastard?'

Charlie sat back and let Simm tell the story. He didn't leave much out. He described the letters Charlie had received, the details of the initial investigation that had led them to Ireland, and everything that had happened so far during their visit to the Emerald Isle. The only snippet he withheld was the fact that they were helped by an Irish Mafia boss.

The retired cop didn't interrupt. His facial expression never wavered, his years of service having perfected his poker face. When Simm finished telling the tale, the man sighed deeply.

'I can't say I'm surprised. The chickens were sure to come home to roost at some point.'

He turned his attention from Simm and looked sharply at Charlie.

'So, Jim O'Reilly, was it?'

178

'You knew Jim?' she asked.

'Oh yes, I knew Jim. He was a real gentleman, despite his shady business. I always wondered how he tolerated such a desperate arse wipe as Connelly. I still do.'

'What kind of business did they do together?' Simm asked.

'Now that's a good question, it is. Connelly had his dirty little fingers in a few pies. Some of them were pies of his own making, and some of them were cooked up by our friends in organized crime. Ah yes, we have the Mafia over here too. It's not Montreal that invented it, you know.'

Evidently, Mr. O'Brien could figure out most of the details on his own.

'Can you tell us more about these pies? Did you ever arrest Connelly for anything specific?' Simm said.

'Oh, Connelly was in and out of the clink more times than I can remember, and always for something new. It coulda been thievin', or traffickin', or any number of things. By Jaysus, he'd even steal the blessing from the holy water, if he had half a chance. But he had a specialty, hooverin' it was.'

'Hoovering?' Charlie had heard of the British term for vacuuming, but couldn't understand how anyone could be arrested for it.

'Abortion. It's illegal here in Ireland, unless the mother's life is in danger. That's the only circumstance that's allowed.'

Charlie was too surprised to speak.

'Is he a doctor?' Simm asked.

'He liked to call himself a doctor. He was at one point, but he lost his license to practice medicine early on. That didn't stop him from using the title. Many young women banked on him having the smarts to do a good job, and many of them didn't survive to tell the tale.'

Charlie was horrified. In her mind's eye, she pictured a dirty back room in an apartment, and a man wearing a blood-stained lab coat as a woman lay dead on the table in front of him. She felt her stomach turn, and she prayed she would keep down the morning's scone.

'Why wasn't he put in prison for life?' she managed to choke out.

'We couldn't make anything stick. He had powerful connections, on both sides of the law. He could always pull in a favor.'

'A favor? What kind of favors?' she asked.

'We don't know. That was the big secret, and we could never get a handle on it, but it certainly served him well.'

'How was Jim involved with him? I can't imagine Jim condoning illegal abortions,' Charlie insisted.

'I got to know Jim a little. We had him in a few times for questioning, trying to discover a way to get at Aidan. They were acquaintances for some reason. I don't think I'd go so far as to say they were friends, but they had business dealings.'

He made quotation signs with his fingers when he said the word 'business'.

'But you never found out what kind of business they had?' Simm said.

'No, O'Reilly claimed they were just friends, distant relatives even. They were as different as a horse and a crow. I couldn't see it.'

'Neither can I,' Charlie agreed.

'But, I'm not a plonker. I checked out your man Mr. O'Reilly. I know he was connected back beyond. There was somethin' between him and Connelly. I never found out what it was, and it's bothered me ever since.'

'Do you know where Connelly is now?' Simm asked.

'Don't you worry. I've been keeping me eye on the gippo. He's livin' with a stick up his arse, all laudy daw, beyont in Arkwik, no doubt supported by some of those connections of his.'

'Arkwik? Where's that?' Simm took his mobile phone out of his shirt pocket.

'Just round the corner, it is. You'll be there like shite off a shovel if you take the highway.'

Chapter 48:

'I'm not sure I want to be anywhere like shit off a shovel,' Charlie commented when they were in the car.

'I think he meant quickly.'

'I hope so. Interesting old lad, though, isn't he?'

Simm chuckled.

'Yeah, he certainly is,' he agreed.

'What do you think about all this abortion business with Connelly?'

She had her own ideas about the information given to them by Mr. O'Brien, but she wanted to hear Simm's take on it.

'I think it's connected,' he said.

'Why?'

'Think about the letters. They were written from the perspective of someone who would have liked to live in Montreal, or worked in a bar, or whatever. Like they never would have the chance to do something like that. Why? Because they never had an opportunity to live. They were aborted.'

'That's what I was thinking.'

'And the organs you got? Body parts? Embryos? It could all have significance.'

'That's a good point. I hadn't thought of that one. But, I have one big question.'

'Let me guess. What does it all have to do with you?'

'Exactly. I never was involved with abortion. I don't even know anyone who's had an abortion. My parents were ordinary people. As far as I know, they didn't believe in abortions. I don't get it.'

'I think the key is Jim O'Reilly.'

'I know for a fact Jim was against abortion. We had the discussion once, and he said he would never condone it unless the mother's life was in danger, the same as the law in Ireland handles it.'

'I understand. But I still think he's the key. He's the connection between you and Aidan Connelly, the common thread.'

'But why should there be a thread between us? Why am I connected in any way with Connelly?'

'I don't know, but Sullivan knew. That's why he threw us in this direction.'

'Why didn't he just tell us what it was about, instead of sending us on this wild goose chase?'

'Again, I don't know, but I suspect we'll find out soon enough, when we get to Arkwik.'

As promised by Tom O'Brien, they arrived in Arkwik soon enough, but it turned out the last known address for Aidan Connelly was no longer the right one. The retired cop hadn't been keeping such good tabs on the man as he claimed. However, a few questions at the local pub led them to another house, this one farther out of the town limits, in a more isolated spot.

Charlie wasn't sure just how luxurious it was to live 'all laudy daw', but Mr. Connelly's present living quarters seemed very comfortable compared to those of Mr. O'Brien. He lived on a large property, in what was a nicely renovated farmhouse, although there wasn't any evidence of farm activity. The grounds were well cared for, and the flowers surrounding the house were lush and colorful.

They parked their rental vehicle beside a late-model car in the driveway.

'I don't know if I'm ready for this.' Charlie's voice held a slight quiver.

Simm looked at her with a puzzled look.

'This was our goal, to find this mystery man,' he said.

'I know, but I'm almost afraid of what we'll find.'

'Let's not be afraid of something we know nothing about yet. We'll have a chance to be afraid after, if need be. What you have to remember is we have to play this cool. We can't let him know we know what he's done. Let me handle the questions. Please.'

His eyes were very serious as they looked straight into hers. He expected a promise from her.

'I'll behave.' It was the best she could give him.

Simm looked around as he climbed the front steps with Charlie by his side. His obvious uneasiness with the surroundings did little to calm her already fully-stretched nerves. Their knock was answered immediately by a woman of around fifty years of age. Charlie was surprised. It had never occurred to her Aidan Connelly would have a wife, and she wondered fleetingly why she had assumed he was single.

As it turned out, she was right. The woman was his housekeeper, and after checking with her boss, she showed them into a small sitting room and told them Mr. Connelly would be along shortly. Charlie took in the Victorian-style furnishings, the chairs straight-backed, and the tables useful merely for holding a glass of sherry or two. Heavy drapes in a matching floral pattern covered the windows from ceiling to floor.

Charlie was studying the imposingly large portrait of a young woman when a man appeared in the doorway. He was tall and thin, and held himself very upright. His hair was more salt than pepper, but, for his age, which Charlie assumed to be at least sixty-five, he was quite young-looking. The smile he offered them didn't reach his eyes, which were more cautious than curious. She suspected he wasn't surprised to see them, despite his first words.

'My my, it's rare that I have visitors all the way out here. And Mrs. Wright tells me you have a foreign accent. Isn't this a pleasant surprise?'

He spoke with a British upper-crust accent. Charlie knew he had been born and raised on the streets of Dublin. Was the affectation exclusively for their benefit?

They both stood and shook the man's hand, and Charlie held back a shiver of revulsion when her skin came into contact with his. She couldn't push aside the thought that those hands were responsible for lost lives, both babies and mothers.

CHAPTER 49:

Simm saw Charlie had a difficult time hiding her emotions. Since Connelly focused his attention on her, ignoring Simm almost totally, he needed to take control of the meeting.

'May we have a few minutes of your time?' Simm asked.

The man released Charlie's hand, and turned to Simm.

'Certainly. Why don't we sit?'

He gestured at the arrangement of chairs beside them. Simm took Charlie's elbow and guided her to the couch, sitting beside her before the other man could.

'I'm trying to place the accent. American?'

'No, Canadian.'

'Ah, I've never been, but I've heard it's lovely.'

'It is. As is Ireland,' Simm answered.

Simm didn't want to have a polite conversation about their respective countries or the weather. He wanted to move on.

'We have a mutual acquaintance, Jim O'Reilly,' Simm said.

'Jim? Yes, I met him years ago. He also lives in Canada. How is he doing?'

'He passed away a few years ago,' Simm said.

The other man assumed a sad look and began to speak, but Simm interrupted him, not wanting to hear his lies, or a fake expression of sympathy.

'How did you know him?' Simm continued.

Connelly waved his hand in a dismissive gesture.

'Oh, he was just someone I had come across. I think I met him in a pub one night, and we hit it off. Whenever he came to Ireland he would look me up, and we'd share a pint. Nothing more than that.'

'We heard you had business dealings with him.'

'Is that so? Well, that's strange. He ran a pub back in Canada. I've only ever been on one side of the bar. No, I'm afraid you heard wrong. We were just acquaintances. But why are you asking?'

'Jim's son isn't well, and he asked us to come to Ireland to do research on his roots. We had found your name mentioned in some papers of Jim's, and we thought maybe there was a family connection.'

'Oh heaven's, no. Are you related somehow to Jim?'

He directed his question to Charlie, his eyes sharp.

'No, but we were close. He was a friend of my father.'

'What was your father's name? Maybe Jim mentioned him to me at some point.'

'Butler. Pat Butler.'

Simm detected a flash of recognition in the man's eyes, but Connelly controlled it instantly. His words belied his reaction.

'Butler? No, I never heard of him.'

His gaze remained on Charlie, and there was a gleam of pleasure and perhaps something else in it.

'Is this your first visit to Ireland, my dear? Surely, with a name like Butler, your roots are here also,' he said with a smile.

Simm felt Charlie fidgeting and inching closer to him.

'It's a first visit for both of us,' Simm interrupted, trying to draw attention away from Charlie. 'Are you retired now? This is a nice place you have.'

The chilling gaze moved to him.

'Yes, I've retired. I worked as a doctor for many years, and I feel I've earned my time here.'

'Where did you practice? In Dublin?'

'Yes, always in the city, but I much prefer my peaceful existence in the country. How did you find me, by the way?'

'Another mutual acquaintance, Mr. O'Brien.'

The man threw back his head and laughed genuinely.

'Poor old Tom. How is the old delusional bastard? He had such a wild imagination, he did. For some reason, he was terribly jealous of my success and went out of his way to invent stories about me. Of course, nothing was ever true.'

'Do you have other friends in Canada, Mr. Connelly?'

'No, as I said, I've never been.'

They witnessed his dead smile, his teeth revealed, but his eyes cold.

Chapter 50:

'He was lying.'

'Like a rug,' Simm agreed.

'About everything.'

'Yes.'

They had taken their leave. Charlie was never so glad to get out of a house than she was that one, no matter how gracious it looked. Simm headed the car toward Dublin.

'Now, what do we do? What did we gain from that, other than a serious case of the willies?' she asked.

'We got to look him in the eye. We let him know we're looking in to his past. We shook him up, even though he put on a good show of trying not to look shook up. Now the ball is in his court. We'll have to see how he reacts.'

'Are you sure he will?'

'Yes, he will. This man is not one to sit back and do nothing. He kept his ass out of jail this long, he has no intention of letting anyone put it back in there now.'

'What do you think he'll do?'

'He'll send us a message, a warning.'

'We already got a warning, in the hotel room.'

'And that was probably his doing. Someone let him know we were asking questions about him. He'll send us another one. He'll try to scare us off.'

Charlie didn't like the sound of that. The assault on their hotel room was enough.

'You should go home to Montreal,' Simm said.

'No. I'm going to stick it out.'

'Charlie…'

'Don't even think of it. What about you? This is dangerous for you too. And don't tell me you're a man, and you can handle it better than me.'

'It has nothing to do with me being a man. I was a cop. I have a certain amount of training that you don't have.'

'I know, but I'm not leaving.'

'If you stay, you'll have to listen to me at all times.'

'I will.'

'You never have in the past.'

'I will now.'

They drove in silence for several minutes.

'What kind of warning do you think it'll be?' she asked in a soft voice.

'I don't know, but we'll have to be very careful.'

'Do you think someone will try to kill us?'

'No, they don't want to ruffle any international feathers. I think it'll be subtler than that.'

Charlie held her breath as they unlocked their hotel room door, but the room was intact. It was their oasis for the time being.

'So, what do we do now? Sit around and wait?' Charlie asked.

'I'm going to do some online research, see if I can find any other leads on 'Doctor' Connelly's past.'

As Simm booted up his laptop, Charlie took the opportunity to call home for an update.

'It's the world traveller!' Frank said.

Charlie smiled. She hadn't realized how much she missed Frank until she heard his voice.

'How's it going? Busy?' she asked.

'It's busy like it normally is this time of year, but there's nothing to worry about. Everything's under control.'

'I wasn't worried. I knew I could count on you. How's Harley? Do you know?'

'He's great. I checked with Madame Lafrance. He misses you, but he's trying hard to hide it.'

She laughed, then grew serious.

'Any more letters or anything?'

'Nothing.'

'You wouldn't tell me if there were,' she said accusingly.

'That's true, but in this case, I'm not lying. It's been very quiet. I passed by your place to make sure everything's okay, and there's nothing out of place.'

'Great. Thanks, Frank. I owe you.'

'There's nothing to owe. Are you getting anywhere over there?'

'I think so. Nothing conclusive, but I'd say we've made progress.'

'You're being careful?'

She glanced over at Simm, hunched over his laptop.

'Yes. Don't worry. I'll be in touch in a few days and let you know when you can expect us home.'

They said their goodbyes and hung up, and Charlie was struck with a wave of homesickness. She wanted her life to revert to normal. She wanted to be back at work, with her friends and her dog. She didn't want to have the threat of a crazy person hanging over her head.

'What's wrong?'

She came out of her daydreaming with a jolt.

'Nothing.'

'You look upset. Judging by your conversation, it sounded like everything was okay at home.'

'It is. I just want to be back there.'

'You're not enjoying your first trip overseas?' he said with a wry smile.

'I would if it were a real vacation. I'd prefer to be touring and learning about Ireland. This isn't the same thing.'

'No, it isn't, but if we can get it over with, maybe we can turn it into a mini vacation.'

Charlie smiled feebly. She believed they had a long way to go before it would be 'over with'.

CHAPTER 51:

Simm's search for further information about Aidan Connelly turned up very little. He discovered a few archived newspaper articles about his run-ins with the authorities, and his subsequent releases, but it wasn't anything they hadn't already heard from Mr. O'Brien.

After a brief discussion, they decided to return to the same pub for dinner. The weather had changed and returned to what was considered normal for Ireland this time of year, cool and misty. Charlie added a cardigan to her outfit to provide a bit of warmth.

They weren't surprised to find most of the same customers as the previous night. Charlie had the impression it was a place for regulars, and they were two of the few outsiders in the pub. However, they were greeted with open arms, as if they had lived in the area for years. Charlie was charmed once again, as they were shown to the same table as the night before. This was the type of atmosphere she yearned to achieve with her place. Of course, she had her regulars, but not to this extent, and even her regulars moved on sooner or later and were replaced by others. She had the impression that didn't happen here.

'And, have you found yer man? Old Tom told me ya were over to see him.'

It was Harry O'Shea, setting a Guinness in front of each of them, even though they hadn't ordered them.

'Yes, we did,' Simm answered. 'Mr. O'Brien was a big help.'

'That's good news, now it is. So, will ya be takin' this Aidan fellow back to Canada with ya? Are ya arrestin' him?'

'No, I'm not a cop, and we have no reason to take him back to Canada. We just wanted to talk to him.'

Charlie was amused, but also worried about how the rumor mill worked around here. If word got out they wanted to extradite Aidan Connelly, God knows what kind of attention they'd attract.

Simm promptly changed the subject by asking to see the menu, but the locals were not ready to let it go. A man to her right leaned over to Charlie.

'So, is he a smarmy fella then?'

'Uh, no, I wouldn't say he was smarmy,' Charlie ventured.

'What is it he did that ya would want to take him back to Canada for?' asked another.

'We don't want to take him back to Canada,' she clarified again.

'I bet ya he's a spy,' offered a younger man sitting alone at another table.

'Aye, a spy, an international one. That's it.'

'Maybe he's a terrorist.'

The debate continued as Charlie and Simm looked helplessly at each other. It didn't seem to be worth the effort to argue. They placed their order, sat back, and drank their beer while listening to the debate and opinions flow around them.

Once they were full of delicious food and beer, they stood to take their leave. It took at least fifteen minutes longer before they made it out the door, since they had to chat with everyone at each table they passed on their way out. They had to reassure Harry they would return for another meal, or at least a drink, before they returned home to Canada.

Laughing, they stepped on to the sidewalk only to have a jute bag thrown over each of their heads, and their hands tied behind their backs.

CHAPTER 52:

Charlie woke feeling disoriented. It was pitch dark in the room, and when she turned her head to look at the alarm clock on the night table, she saw nothing. The bed was also unusually hard, and her arms ached horribly.

Suddenly, she remembered what had happened, or at least some of what had happened. Her earliest memory was of the bag being yanked over her head and tied around her throat, all but cutting off her air. By the muffled sounds coming from Simm's direction, she knew he suffered the same fate. Although she struggled as her arms were pulled behind her back and tied, it had little effect. The grunts of pain coming from beside her made her think Simm was putting up a better fight, and perhaps losing.

She tried to call out to Simm, hoping to make him stop fighting for fear he would be hurt, or worse, but as she breathed, the bag went in her mouth, and the best she managed was a muffled scream. They were shoved ahead, stumbling and tripping, until two strong arms picked her up and tossed her in the air. She landed on top of something firm, but not rock hard, more like bags of sand. A few seconds later, accompanied by other loud grunting sounds, something landed beside her, and she heard the sound of a tailgate being slammed shut. This was followed by more banging as doors were opened and closed again.

'Simm?' she said shakily.

'Are you alright?'

'Yes. Are you?'

'I'm okay.'

'What's going on? What will they do to us?' Her voice rose in panic, the implications of what had just happened beginning to dawn on her. 'Will they kill us?'

'Don't worry, we'll get out of this somehow. I don't think they'll take a chance on harming us. Since we're from Montreal, they may suspect Marty Sullivan is involved somehow. They won't want to provoke him.'

'I hope you're right.'

Charlie thought she heard him say, 'So do I', but his words were drowned out by the roar of the engine starting up, and they jolted forward roughly.

'Charlie, you have to remember to cooperate with them,' Simm said when the truck stopped temporarily, possibly at a traffic light. 'Do whatever it takes for them to set you free. We're not in this to sacrifice our lives.'

'What about you? You have to do the same.'

'Don't worry about me.'

'Don't worry? Of course, I'm going to worry. What if we're separated?' The thought of something happening to Simm sent her into a fresh spasm of panic. What would she do?

'It's possible we will be. If you get free, head straight back to the hotel, get your passport, and fly home. I'll meet you there.'

'Are you crazy? I can't just leave you here. I have to get help.' She fought to control the trembling in her voice. She knew she had to keep her mind clear if they wanted to have a hope of getting out of this.

'Tell the cops what happened, and then go home. You have to promise me, Charlie.'

She heard the desperation in his voice and knew it was important to him.

'I promise,' she said, knowing she was lying to him merely to put his mind at ease.

After several more minutes, the truck rolled to a final stop. Doors creaked open and banged shut, and heavy footsteps shuffled around them as the tailgate opened. Charlie felt a hand close around her leg. She was tugged backward by the ankle, but her hands hooked in something behind her. Her arms were dragged backward and upward, and she knew they would only go so far before they would break. She tried to scream, but it came out as a hoarse groan.

'Be careful, ya eejit. She's hooked.'

Loud cursing followed, and the bed of the truck dipped as someone climbed in to pick her up. Again, she was tossed, not knowing where she would land, but arms closed around her and eased her feet to the ground. She didn't think Simm was being handled so considerately, judging by the groans and noises coming from his direction. She wished he would follow his own advice and cooperate.

They were shoved and jostled blindly, until she felt a difference in temperature and assumed they were inside a building of some kind.

'There's stairs in front of ya. Pick up yer feet now,' a gruff voice commanded them.

Charlie tripped a few times, unable to balance herself with her arms, until someone became frustrated and threw her over his shoulder. She landed roughly on her feet once again when they reached the top of the stairs. She heard heavy clumping and thumping behind her, and was thankful to know Simm was being led in the same direction as her.

Her thankfulness was short-lived. She was shoved into an unlit room, pushed onto a cot, and her hood was removed in the dark.

'Where's Simm?' she said, knowing she was alone in the room with this stranger. He remained silent. She saw a sliver of light when he opened the door to leave, revealing nothing but a drab hallway and the large shape of the man leaving the room. When he slammed it shut, the sound echoed through the room, and she was in darkness.

Chapter 53:

Charlie had no conception of time. Her world consisted of blackness. She understood how prisoners in solitary confinement lost their minds. She tried to focus on her predicament, hoping to find a way to escape, but her thoughts kept straying elsewhere. She spent a lot of time worrying about Simm. They hadn't hurt her as yet, and there may be a reason for that, but she had a feeling Simm wouldn't be treated with kid gloves. If he put up a fight, which he undoubtedly would, they would reciprocate. Add to that the fact that there were more of them, and the likelihood they were armed, and things could get very messy.

She listened for even the tiniest of noises, but heard nothing. She was either in an isolated part of the building, or the walls were soundproofed. She shivered. Her sweater and lightweight pants were not enough to shelter her from the cold and damp.

She tried to figure out who was behind their abduction. It clearly was connected to Aidan Connelly, but would he have hired a bunch of thugs to take them captive? And for what purpose? Was it just to scare them? Or did he have a plan to get rid of them permanently?

Charlie thought about the possibility she would never see Simm, Frank, or Harley ever again. As more hours passed, the more pessimistic she was about her chances of surviving the ordeal.

She fidgeted on the hard mattress beneath her. Her shoulders were aching and her hands were numb. If they wanted to keep her tied, it had to be because there was something in the room she could access and use against them. She stood and shuffled around in the dark, hoping she would bump into something useful.

She found a wall and walked around the room while leaning against it, but she never touched another piece of furniture, a picture frame, or any other object apart from the bed. She tried to venture into the middle of the room, but became disoriented, and it took several minutes to find her way back to the bed. She sagged onto the mattress, discouraged. There was nothing she could do to help herself.

She remembered Simm's words, telling her to cooperate with them. She couldn't cooperate with them if she didn't know what they wanted, and she was impatient to find out what was expected of her. That was likely their strategy – make her desperate to do anything to escape this dark prison.

She must have drifted off to sleep, because she was jolted awake by the scraping of a lock, followed a moment later by the background light from the hallway as the door opened. She squinted and turned her head from the light, wishing she could look and learn something about her surroundings.

The door was shut again, dousing the room in darkness once more, but she heard someone walking toward her. A lantern was lit and set on the floor close to her. It barely illuminated her immediate area, revealing the bed, the dirty white linoleum floor, and the booted feet of the man before her.

'Are ye happy with your new home?'

She detected a hint of glee in his voice. Her heart pounded, and she fought to control her breathing. She didn't want him to sense her fear.

'The cat got yer tongue, did it?'

'Why are we here?'

'Ya know the answer to that one. It's Aidan. Ya were up his arse. We tried to warn ya, but ya wouldn't listen.'

'We're not doing you or anyone else any harm.'

'Askin' questions can be harmful, didn't ya know it. Yer diggin' up shite and ya don't even have a proper shovel.'

'Why are we here?' she repeated.

'We wanted to have a little chat with ya.'

'Where's Simm?'

'Don't worry yer little head about yer friend. He should be okay – in a week or two.'

His laugh sent chills up Charlie's spine. She hoped he was merely trying to scare her.

'Now, yer very curious about our man Aidan. I suggest ya leave him alone and hightail it beyont. Ya can forget ya ever saw him.'

'We won't hurt Mr. Connelly. We just wanted some answers.'

'Ya don't say. Now what might ya be wantin' answered?'

Charlie hesitated. Should she reveal her hand? In the spirit of cooperation, she decided to go ahead.

'Someone's been harassing me. We thought Mr. Connelly could tell us who and why.'

'Harassin' ya, ya say. And where would ya get the peculiar idea that Aidan could help ya? Why would ya be thinkin' he had anything to do with ya?'

'We had a lead that brought us here, to him.'

His laugh bordered on evil.

'Yea, I have a good idea where your lead came from. I tell ya what, I'll be gettin' back to ya on that one.'

He bent to pick up the lantern, but kept it too low for her to see anything but his lower body.

'I want to see Simm.'

'Yer not in a position to be makin' demands, are ya now? Ya can hold yer horses for a bit longer.'

'Could you at least untie my hands? They've gone numb.'

He set down the lantern again. His hand dug into his front pocket and removed an object. He pushed a button on the handle and a blade shot out. Charlie held her breath. Had she gone too far with her demands?

She leaned back as he stepped toward her.

'Do ya want me to cut ya loose, or not? Sit still.'

She almost choked on the putrid smell rolling off him as he leaned over her and sliced through the rope tying her hands. The pain in her shoulders eased as she pulled her hands in front of her and rubbed her wrists.

'Thank you. That's better.'

He chuckled.

'Ya owe me one now,' he said, as he brushed a finger along her cheek.

CHAPTER 54:

Hours passed, perhaps a day, she wasn't sure. The monotony was broken up twice by a silent person who brought in a plate of almost inedible food and a lantern. He returned several minutes later to pick up the plate and the lantern, but she was ridiculously thankful to have the brief reprieve from the interminable darkness. She used the lantern to look around her room, but it was as she had suspected, empty and windowless, except for the bed she was sitting on. Charlie asked the man questions about where they were, how Simm was, and when they would be released, but he ignored her completely, without any indication he had even heard her.

At some point, the door opened and the other man came in. She recognized the boots and the pants. He was also of a stockier build than the food delivery man, as she had come to think of him. Like before, he set the lantern on the floor beside her.

'Well, ye've been providin' some conversation for us. We're all very curious about this harassment ye've been talkin' about. What happened to ya?'

'I received anonymous letters talking about strange things. Once I received a package with animal organs in it. Another time, someone put posters of lost children on my door with something that looked like blood.'

'Ya don't say now.'

The words were casual enough, but there was something in his tone that sounded like concern. She doubted it was concern for her well-being.

'And what did the letters talk about?'

'To me it sounded like nonsense. It was written by the same person, but repeatedly using a different name. He'd talk about how he'd have liked to live in Montreal, or how he would have liked to play sports, or things like that. It didn't make any sense to me.'

'I see. So, ye and yer friend decided to take it upon yerselves to find this person. And, somehow ya decided Aidan was yer man.'

'No, we don't think Aidan sent the letters, but we think there's a connection, that's all. We just have a few questions for him.'

'And how would ya make such a grand leap from letters ye're getting' in Montreal to a man livin' in peace here in Ireland?'

'I told you. We got a lead.'

'Don't take me for a blitherin' eejit. Someone gave ya a name. Who was it?' he said, almost shouting.

Charlie swallowed. She sensed he was nearing the end of his patience, but handing over Marty Sullivan's name was not something she was willing to do. They had been warned by the Gang boss, and she took the warning very seriously. A little white lie would do the trick.

'We got another letter, an anonymous one, telling us to go see Aidan Connelly in Ireland.'

She hoped the lie was plausible enough for him to believe. But, he didn't answer or react in any way. He picked up the lantern and left.

Charlie prayed she had handled it the best possible way. She lay in the darkness and second-guessed herself for hours. When she heard the lock scraping again, she didn't even look toward the door. She assumed it was another meal, but the bark of a voice startled her.

'Sit up. I've got someone who wants to talk to ya.'

Charlie scrambled to sit up straight, tucking her legs underneath her. She was surprised when a man sat on the bed beside her, openly revealing his face. He was in his forties, with a full head of black hair. He was dressed in a nice, dark suit with a white shirt and tie. He looked like a lawyer, making a stop on the way to his office. Yet, his face was far from that of an everyday lawyer. It was clean-shaven, making it easier to see the scar that ran from the corner of his mouth, over his jawline, and down his neck to disappear under his shirt collar.

His eyes were a cold blue-grey. They held no warmth and little of anything else. His gaze covered every inch of her face before trailing down her body. She suppressed a shiver.

'You're a very lucky woman.'

She didn't know how to respond to that statement. At the moment, she didn't feel lucky.

'Aidan is being very generous with you. I would not have been so lenient.' He paused and they exchanged stares for a few moments. 'You're going to leave Ireland. You're going to leave Aidan alone. You're going to forget he even exists. And in return for doing so, I'll let you walk out of here, instead of sending you home in a box.'

Charlie knew he was offering her a very good deal, and she should jump at the chance to accept it. She also sensed everyone did what he said without question.

'That's very nice of you, but I need two things.'

His eyebrows shot upward, and she heard a grunt of surprise from the man holding the lantern, but she kept her gaze locked on the man in front of her.

'I need Simm to leave with me unharmed, and I need to know how I'm connected to Mr. Connelly.'

'I don't bargain.'

'I know, but it's very important to me.'

'More important than your life?'

'It wouldn't be much of a life if I spent it looking over my shoulder all the time, wondering when someone will attack me. And it wouldn't be much of a life without Simm.'

She detected something in his eyes. It could be appreciation, or it could be sadistic humor. He stood and straightened the creases in his trousers. He left without another word.

CHAPTER 55:

Charlie lay on her back on the inflexible mattress. Tears ran down the side of her face onto the dirty pillow underneath her head. She made no effort to wipe them away. Her chest heaved with sobs. She was convinced she had signed her death warrant. Any moment now, someone would come and kill her. Simm was perhaps already dead. Maybe he would have had a chance if she hadn't made those last demands. Maybe they would both be headed for the airport. Maybe not.

Over the next few hours, Charlie agonized about her decision. She hoped it would be quick and painless. A gunshot would be best. She had no clue how the Irish criminal mind worked, or what was their most popular method of disposing of those who dared to question them.

She should have said, 'Thank you very much, and I'll be off now.'. Why had she thought she could negotiate with a man like that? His eyes told the story; she just hadn't read it properly.

Charlie eventually dozed off until something woke her. It was the scraping of the door, and once again, the same two men entered. She couldn't see any weapons in the hands of either of them. Again, she sat up and watched as the dark-suited man sat beside her.

'You're a twice-lucky woman. Now, I'm going to tell you straight out that after this conversation is over, there will be no more bargaining. None. You either accept the deal I'm offering, or you die. Is that clear to you?'

No sound would pass her throat, so she simply nodded. She was granted a reprieve, and this time she would accept it.

'First of all, Aidan is a personal friend of mine. I quite literally owe my life to him. And now, so do you. He insisted no harm come to you. Believe me, the boys were very eager to get their hands on you and have some fun, but because of Aidan, you were left in peace. Do you understand?'

Charlie found it hard to breathe. The picture he had painted in her head was terrifying, and she definitely felt grateful to Aidan Connelly at that moment.

'I can assure you no one in Ireland sent you those letters, or committed any acts against you, and I can also tell you we have no idea who did. Now, regarding your demands, we have decided to grant them to you, but there will be a price to pay in return.'

He paused, letting the words sink in before continuing.

'Your friend Simm will be brought to you, and I will count on you to keep a short leash on him. Because, if he decides not to respect the agreement, both of you will suffer the same consequence. That takes care of the first request. As for the second, I will grant you a little knowledge, and you will have to be satisfied with what you get. There will be no more. And you can do nothing with the knowledge I give you. If you try to go to the authorities, or the media, or anywhere with this, you will have broken our agreement. Are you still following me? Speak up now.'

'Yes. Yes, I understand,' she stammered.

'Good. Then listen well, because I won't be repeating it, or offering any other explanation. Many years ago, Aidan worked as a doctor. He helped women who found themselves in trouble. He helped get rid of their trouble, if you know what I mean. Do you now?'

'Yes. He performed abortions.'

'Shh, now. That's a nasty word. We prefer to say he helped women in trouble. Isn't that better?'

Charlie was impatient to hear what he had to say, but she wouldn't tell him so.

'Now, sometimes the form of help was different. Sometimes the babies were born, but they needed a better home. Aidan felt they wouldn't be properly cared for where they were, so he would help find a place for them to live.

Charlie felt an electric jolt of shock. Connelly had been a baby trafficker, something that had never occurred to her.

'I see you're surprised, but that's the kind of man he is. He even gave up his own flesh and blood children, because it was too dangerous for them to be around him. That's a true sacrifice. Don't bother asking me any other questions. You have your answer, and you will soon see your friend. Now, it's time for me to tell you what you have to do in return for what I've given you.'

Charlie made an effort to wrap her mind around the information he had just given her, and she tried to force herself to concentrate on his next words.

'You're going to take a message to your friend Marty Sullivan. There's no need to tell him who it's from. He'll know it's me.'

'What message? What do you want me to tell him?' She didn't try to deny she knew Marty Sullivan. It was too late for that.

'There's no need to 'tell' him anything. That's the nice part. You'll just leave him a little present. You're going to get an embryo. I don't care where, but it must be human, and you're going to leave it on his doorstep. He'll understand.'

CHAPTER 56:

Charlie was horrified. The thought of leaving a human embryo on the doorstep of the Irish Mafia leader in Montreal was spine-chilling. Not only did she have no idea how to find an embryo, the whole idea was revolting and unimaginable. She also knew Sullivan would know it was them who had left it there, and there would be hell to pay, conceivably with their lives.

When the man stood up and walked out of the room, leaving her with those images, she wondered whether she should call him back and have him finish her off right away instead of leaving her live in fear of Marty Sullivan.

The next time she heard the door open, an hour or so later, she hoped the man would respect the other condition of the bargain. She saw the outline of two men backlit with the light from the hallway. One was short, stocky, and upright. The other was tall, lean, and hunched over. The former shoved the other forward. He hit the floor with a clunk and a groan, and before Charlie even had time to stand, the room was cast in darkness again.

'Simm! Hold on, I'm coming.'

She got on her hands and knees, and crawled in what she hoped was the right direction. Her heart pounded in her throat, and she prayed she wouldn't be sick. Her fears had been right. Simm hadn't been treated as well as her.

She heard another groan and a shuffling sound. It helped to keep her moving in the right direction. When her hand touched him, she felt around carefully, not sure what she was touching and how severely hurt it was. When she felt his bicep, she oriented herself.

'Simm? Where does it hurt?'

'I'm okay,' he moaned.

'You're not okay. You can't even stand.'

'I can. Just give me a minute.'

'Where does it hurt?'

'Right now, everywhere, but if you give me a couple of minutes, I'll be fine.'

'Let me help you,' Charlie insisted.

'Are you alright? Did they hurt you?' he asked.

'I'm fine. They didn't touch me.'

'Are you sure?'

'Of course, I'm sure. I would know, wouldn't I?'

'Maybe you're just saying that.'

'Stop arguing. I'm fine. Apparently, Aidan gave orders I wasn't to be harmed. It seems they took out their frustrations on you instead.'

He groaned again as he tried to sit up. Charlie ran her hands up his shoulders to his neck. Her fingers touched something warm and sticky.

'You're bleeding!'

'Don't worry about it. It's superficial.'

'Come on. I'll help you up and get you to the bed.'

She gripped him under the arm and hoisted. With a lot of effort on both their parts, Simm stood, and she guided him to the bed.

'It should be over here. Yes, there it is,' she said, as her shin connected with the edge of the cot.

When Simm was sitting, Charlie tugged off her cardigan, felt around until she found the cut on his forehead, and used the piece of clothing to stem the flow of blood.

'Ouch!'

'I want to stop the bleeding. Hold still. This is hard enough to do in the dark.'

'It's okay. Foreheads always bleed a lot.'

'How badly did they beat you? Do you think anything's broken?'

'I don't think so. At first, they just shoved me around a little. I think this last bit was just for your benefit. Either that, or they knew it was their last chance, and they didn't want to miss out on the fun.'

'I feel awful for you. I was worried they'd do something like this.'

He put his arm around her and pulled her close.

'It's okay. I've been through worse.'

'Really?'

'No, not really.'

'I'm sorry, Simm. This is all my fault.'

'How could it be your fault? You didn't tell them to do it, did you? You didn't plan this whole thing.'

'I may have made them angry.'

There was total silence. If it wasn't for the warmth of his body beside her, she would believe she was alone in the dark again. Even that warmth seemed to turn cold to match the tone of his voice when he spoke.

'How did you make them angry?'

It was a simple question, but the way he deliberately enunciated each word made it sound ominous. Charlie knew there was no way to retreat.

'I asked for certain things. I asked for you to be set free,' she said, hoping to appease him. 'You were also supposed to be unharmed, but obviously they ignored that part.'

'You asked or you demanded?'

'Demand is a strong word.'

'Charlie, I told you to cooperate. I told you to do whatever it took to get your freedom. You were supposed to leave without me. You promised me you would.'

'But, it worked. The end result is what counts. You're here, and we're leaving.'

'How do you know we're leaving? How can you be sure they won't come in here and kill us both?'

'Because he promised.'

'He promised?' he said, his voice rising. 'Maybe his promises are as worthless as yours!'

'Calm down. I'm sure it'll work out.'

'Jesus Christ, Charlie. I can't trust you to listen to me. Ever.'

Their argument was cut short by the opening of the door. The man with the lantern was there, along with two others standing behind him.

Charlie's breath caught. Would she be proven wrong? She took advantage of the dim light to look at Simm. His face was bruised and swollen. The cut on his forehead was clotting, but he looked the worse for wear. Seeing the evidence of his abuse in the light upset her, but the look in his eyes made her want to cry. He looked at her as if it was his last chance to see her alive, and perhaps it was.

'Well now, ye've had yer little reunion, it's time to move on. Go ahead lads,' he said, gesturing to the men behind him. They moved around him and approached the couple on the bed. Charlie was relieved to see they didn't carry weapons, but they had the canvas bags in their hands. Neither Simm nor Charlie struggled, knowing it would be useless. Simm's hand closed around hers and gave it a squeeze as the bag closed over her head and the string was pulled taut.

Chapter 57:

'How do I know ya didn't do it to her? I should be callin' the peelers on ya. And ya lookin' like ya had a right desperate donnybrook. She put up a fight, did she? What kind of scum bastard are ya? I should slap ya inta the middle of next week.'

Charlie tried to tell the man to stop yelling, but no sound came out of her mouth. She concentrated on her vocal chords and tried again. This time a squeak escaped her lips.

'Charlie? Charlie, wake up.'

She opened her eyes, just to slam them shut again. The light was blinding, but she knew it was the sun this time and not a lantern. A wisp of fresh air on her cheeks helped her believe that she was outdoors.

'We're free?' she managed to say.

'Yes, I'm trying to get a ride back to the hotel. They took my wallet. I don't have any money for a cab, and this man thinks I hurt you.'

She turned her head a little to the right and saw a man with a deeply-lined face leaning over her, his thick brows touching above his concerned eyes.

'Are ye alright, lass? Ya looked like ya been dragged through a hedge backwards. Did this brute do this?'

'No, he fought for me. He saved my life, and look what they did to him.'

Charlie's exaggeration had the right effect. The old man clapped Simm solidly on the shoulder. Charlie saw Simm wince, and she presumed the shoulder had already seen enough action today.

'That's just what I be thinkin'. Ya look like a man who'd put the fear of God in the divil himself. Here now, help me with the little lass, and we'll get her into the car.'

Simm sat back with a sigh once they were settled in the back seat of the old jalopy, and it chugged toward Dublin.

'What happened?' Charlie whispered. She couldn't remember anything since sitting on the cot with Simm beside her.

'They drugged us, with ether, I'm sure. When I came out of it, we were lying on the side of the road in the middle of nowhere. I couldn't get you to wake up.'

'We're not the same size. It took longer for it to wear off.'

She held on to his hand, never wanting to let go. The ominous feeling of near-death from earlier still wafted through her mind, and she was sure Simm felt the same.

The rest of the drive was made in silence, partly because of the hair-raising driving skills of their savior. Charlie didn't know if he regularly drove so erratically, or if it was because he felt a sense of urgency on their behalf, but there were many times she wondered if they hadn't escaped the jaws of death after all. As they entered the city, the driver lessened his speed, but seemed confused by the abundance of cars and streets, and Simm had to help him find their way to the hotel.

'If you give me a minute, I'll go to the room and get some cash. We certainly appreciate your help,' Simm said as they pulled up to the hotel.

'Ah, there's no need for that. Fer sure, this story will be worth its weight in gold with the lads at the pub. They'll be right impressed,' the man responded.

Before going up to the hotel room, they said goodbye and gave him directions to get out of the city. Charlie felt absurdly grateful for the comfort and security of a room that had felt so ordinary a few days earlier. Her enjoyment was disturbed by the clearing of Simm's throat.

'Charlie, I have to insist that from now on you'll stay at the hotel while we're in Dublin. We can't risk something like that happening again.'

'It won't happen again. We're leaving.'

'What?'

'We have to leave. That was the deal.'

Simm lowered himself to the chair facing her. He frowned again, and Charlie knew the argument would pick up where it had left off, but there was no avoiding it.

'What deal?'

'I made a deal with that man.' She held up her hand when he started to ask another question. 'I don't know his name. He was a man in a suit. He spoke well. He was Irish. He was definitely the boss, although I think Aidan Connelly was calling the shots.'

'What deal?'

'We have to leave Connelly alone, and we have to leave Ireland. Right away.'

'In exchange for what?'

'A few things. Obviously, I had asked to see you.' She smiled at him, hoping to put him in a better humor. The scowl never left his face. 'And I asked for our freedom, which worked,' she said, spreading her arms, indicating the comfort of the hotel room.

'A few things. That means more than two. What are the others?'

'There's only one other. I don't know how we'll handle that one.'

'What is it?'

'We have to leave a human embryo on Sullivan's doorstep.'

'Oh, sweet Jesus,' Simm said, his head falling into his hands.

'I know. I know. We can't do it for all kinds of reasons. I realize that, but I couldn't say no. He would have killed us.'

'And if we don't do it, he'll make sure we die anyway. Obviously, this guy's connected to the Irish Mafia, and he's got a beef against Sullivan. We'll never be safe if we don't do it.'

'We'll never be safe if we do. Sullivan will know it was us.'

'I want you to tell me every word of the conversations you had with this guy. Every word. Don't leave anything out.'

Charlie had already spent hours analysing every word she had exchanged with the mysterious, suited man. The conversations were imprinted in her brain. She regurgitated it all for Simm's benefit. His expression turned black when she got to the part about not accepting the man's offer to set her free without conditions. She continued on, despite her fear the top would blow off of Simm's head.

When she explained about Connelly's other activity, she faltered. It was something she hadn't wanted to deal with.

'He was trafficking babies?'

She nodded. 'Yes, unwanted babies, I guess. Or perhaps stolen babies.'

'Good Lord.'

'Even his own.'

'What?'

'He said Connelly had given up his own babies. That he had made the ultimate sacrifice and sent his own children to be safe elsewhere.'

Simm stared into her eyes.

'No, it's inconceivable,' she said, shaking her head. 'I reject any of the possibilities.'

'This has been all about you from the beginning.'

'There has to be another explanation,' she said.

'Do you have a birth certificate?'

'Of course, I have a birth certificate.'

'And your parents are listed as Patrick and Patricia Butler?'

'Yes. They're my parents. I'm not one of those children. I'm not...'
She couldn't even say it. It was unimaginable.

Her trembling hands were taken between his.

'We agree you're connected somehow to all of this,' he said.

Charlie pressed her lips together. She was incapable of making a sound.

'We agree, don't we?' Simm insisted. 'That's why we're here, because of you.'

'It has to be something else. Connelly was involved in all kinds of things. It could be anything. We have to forget about it now. We're not going near Connelly again. We're going to leave Ireland and go home. That'll be the end of it.'

'Except for the little issue of an embryo and a Mafia boss.'

'Yes, except for that. What kind of message are they trying to send Marty Sullivan? I don't understand.'

'I don't know. Apparently, it has something to do with babies. And it must be a kind of threat. Probably Sullivan was involved in the trafficking somehow and they're threatening to expose him.'

'Sullivan is involved in all kinds of crime. Why would it make a difference to him if they start a rumor about baby trafficking?'

'You're right,' Simm said. 'At this point, I can't answer that question, but I hope someday I will.'

Chapter 58:

They were very obvious about their departure. Simm loudly announced their check-out intentions at the front desk. He asked the clerk to call a cab to take them to the airport. Anyone hanging around was left in no doubt they were leaving the country.

Before leaving their room, Simm had placed a much more discreet call to Inspector O'Reilly to let him know they were leaving, they wouldn't be back, and they were no longer interested in Aidan Connelly. The police officer didn't seem surprised by this information, and wished them a pleasant journey home.

At the airport, they didn't waste any time getting through the check-in process or security. The condition of Simm's face drew interested looks from the security guards, but it didn't stop him from passing through. They were at the gate a full hour before it was scheduled to board. Charlie stared at the monitor as if willing it to move up the planned time of departure. She felt watched, even though she knew it was improbable someone would have passed through security just to watch them. But she also knew the organization employed people everywhere, including the supposedly secure area of an airport.

Through unspoken agreement, all conversation was limited to banal observations without any mention of Aidan Connelly. Charlie was happy for the reprieve, and she was aware it was only a reprieve. Simm wouldn't let it go. His serious expression convinced her he was mulling over the whole case from start to finish, and trying to figure out how they would resolve their present dilemma.

Their flight boarded on schedule, and Charlie hurried to settle into her seat. She hastily put in her earphones to watch a movie, sensing

Simm wanted to talk to her, but she didn't want to get into it in a public place. It was better to wait until they were alone.

The takeoff was a little rough, but Charlie didn't pay any attention to it. She stayed focused on remaining in her bubble, and she rationalized that if they crashed it would at least save her the misery of discussing the dark-suited man's conditions.

Simm apparently decided to call a temporary truce. He relaxed and alternately dozed and watched movies during the flight home. He even generously allowed Charlie to rest her head on his shoulder as she slept for a few hours.

As soon as Charlie was on home turf, she was impatient to see Frank and Harley, but Simm insisted they drop off their bags at his apartment and freshen up before going to the pub. Charlie knew the real reason behind his suggestion, and she dreaded it.

'I want you to find your birth certificate for me,' he said, as the door shut behind them.

'I will,' Charlie said, turning her back to him while she opened her suitcase and sorted through the contents.

'Where is it? At the pub or at your apartment?'

'I'll find it for you. I know where it is.'

'I need it as soon as possible.'

She threw down the sweater she had been struggling to get on a hanger and turned on him.

'I told you I'd find it. Give me a chance. I just got home.'

Simm placed his hands on her shoulders.

'I know. I'm just telling you we can't delay. It's the key to everything. It may even help solve our problem with Sullivan.'

'I don't see how.'

'Neither do I at this point, but if I can move forward with this investigation, it may open up a possibility for me.'

'The investigation is over. We're not looking in to it anymore. We'll have to find another way to satisfy the guy in Ireland.'

'What if you keep getting letters? What if someone goes to your home again and threatens you? Is that something you want to live with?'

'Of course not, but…I can't…' She shook off his hands and turned away.

'We'll deal with it,' Simm said.

'It's not your parentage that's in question here. It's mine. You don't know what it's like to live your whole life believing something only to have it shot to hell in a few seconds.'

'You're right. It's not my life, but I'm willing to help you get through it, whatever it is.'

Charlie walked into his arms and rested her head on his chest.

CHAPTER 59:

Charlie threw open the door and scanned the crowd, a smile splitting her face. She weaved her way through the maze of people, excusing herself along the way. Somehow, he sensed her approach, because he turned and their eyes met. A replica of her smile appeared on his face. When she reached him, his arms were open and ready. He lifted her up in a bear hug that felt like it could crush her ribcage.

'God, I missed you,' she said.

'Me too. It's great to have you back. Holy Jesus, what happened to him?'

Charlie turned to look at Simm, who had followed her into the pub.

'Oh, he got out of line, so I smacked him upside the head.'

Frank grinned and raised his hand for a high five.

'Way to go, girl.'

Simm wasn't amused, but he had to admit, seeing Charlie happy was a balm to the soul. The gloom that had hung over them for most of the trip to Ireland, especially the last few days, was shed, at least temporarily.

Frank held Charlie at arm's length and looked her up and down.

'Are you alright? You didn't get hurt?'

'No, I'm fine. I'll tell you all about it in a bit. I want to see Harley first.'

Simm followed her to the office where they found an ecstatic Harley, his entire body wriggling and shaking with happiness. He whimpered and licked Charlie's face as she greeted him and reassured him she wouldn't be leaving again. Simm was also given a welcoming lick as he reached over to pet the pug.

'It's great to be back,' she said. 'I hadn't realized how much I missed this place until I walked in the door. It's home for me.'

Simm couldn't disagree. Charlie and the bar fit together like a picture in a frame.

'That's not to say I won't make changes. I'm thinking about hiring a real chef to prepare things other than finger foods. I'd like to have authentic Irish meals. If I could duplicate Harry's setup, I'd be thrilled.'

'If anyone can do it, you can.'

He relished the smile she gave him, because he knew it would soon disappear.

'Charlie, I need to see your birth certificate. Could you find it for me please?'

As expected, the smile vanished. With her lips pressed together, she took a key out of her desk drawer and unlocked a cabinet behind her. She grunted slightly as she lifted the fireproof box onto her desk. Papers rustled as she rifled through the box. She took out an envelope and peered inside. Wordlessly, with a smug smile, she handed it to Simm.

It was an original birth certificate from the Province of Quebec. It stated her full name, Charlene Iris Butler, and those of her parents Patrick and Patricia Butler.

'Great. Perfect. Can I make a copy please?'

Charlie gestured with her arm at the photocopy machine, inviting him to help himself.

'I told you,' she said, as he handed her back the original.

'You did.'

He wouldn't get into it any further tonight. He had already done enough to spoil her homecoming.

CHAPTER 60:

Charlie was exhausted by the end of the evening. Thankfully, it was Wednesday, and they closed early. But midnight was five o'clock in the morning, Dublin time, for her. When she went into the office to collect Harley and Simm, she found the man asleep in her office chair, his long legs sprawled out in front of him. The dog slept, curled up on Simm's stomach, but he lifted his head as she walked in, and his curly tail wagged in greeting.

The movement didn't wake Simm until Charlie came closer, and Harley stood up to stretch, his little nails digging into Simm's abdomen.

'Ow, what the hell?'

'Time to go,' she said.

'Is it? Already?'

'Are you being sarcastic?'

'Never. How did you last so long? You must be dead tired.'

'I am, but I'm a happy dead tired. It's good to be back to a normal life again.'

Neither of them mentioned the fact that her life was not necessarily normal yet. They still had a potential stalker out there somewhere, not to mention a promise made to one Mafia boss to send an inflammatory message to another Mafia boss.

Charlie collapsed in bed as soon as they arrived at Simm's apartment. She was asleep before her head hit the pillow, with Harley curled up on the comforter beside her feet. A few hours later, she woke and glanced at the clock as Simm climbed into bed beside her. She wondered for barely a second what had taken him so long to come to bed before she fell asleep again. She didn't even think for a moment about the fact that he was sleeping in the same bed as her without a barricade of pillows between them.

The following morning, he was still unconscious when she went to the kitchen to put on a pot of coffee. Happy to be home, she threw together a batch of pancakes, along with eggs and bacon.

'What's that smell? I don't think I've ever had anything smell so good in this place.'

Charlie smiled.

'I was in the mood to cook.'

Simm gratefully set the table, and they sat down to enjoy their breakfast.

'Why were you up so late? You couldn't sleep?'

'Uh no, I was doing research.'

'On what?'

He set down his fork and looked at her.

'I was validating your birth certificate.'

Charlie didn't like his tone. She moved her gaze to her plate. Her breakfast didn't seem so appetizing any longer.

'There's no record of your birth in Quebec,' he said.

She looked up at him.

'I have a birth certificate. You saw it. You have a copy of it.'

'It's fake. It's a very good one, but you weren't born here.'

Her heart plunged to settle in the vicinity of her stomach.

'They were my parents.'

'Of course, they were. Just because you may not be their biological child doesn't mean they weren't your parents. It's the same for all adopted children.'

'So, that's what this is all about? The fact that I was adopted from Ireland, and not necessarily through the proper channels?'

'I think so,' Simm said.

'I don't understand. If they wanted to adopt a child, why didn't they just do it legally?'

'Maybe the process was too long, or too difficult. Maybe they wanted an Irish-born child. I don't know. I can't speak for them, but the fact remains that you were seemingly brought here with the help of

Aidan Connelly and Jim O'Reilly.'

'Jim was his middle man,' she said, the truth of her parentage sinking in.

'I would guess so.'

'Do you think I was stolen from someone, or given up willingly?' Charlie's voice was almost inaudible.

Simm shook his head. 'I have no idea.'

'I don't know which is worse, knowing someone mourned a lost child, or knowing someone didn't want me.'

'We have a lot of unanswered questions.'

'Like what? What are you thinking?'

'Like were you stolen, were you given up but taken out of Ireland through illegal channels, or are you one of Connelly's own children?'

'Oh God, I hope not. This is all bad enough, but the thought that I could be the daughter of that monster...,' she said, pushing her plate aside.

'The probability is low. I'm thinking he trafficked hundreds of babies. And I'm thinking the guy in the dark suit was one of them.'

Charlie's eyes widened.

'Of course. You're right. He said he literally owed his life to Aidan. That's why he was doing whatever Aidan told him to do. He was adopted by someone.'

'And maybe he was Aidan's biological son,' Simm added.

Charlie's brain was sifting through all the possibilities.

'What about Sullivan? He's tied to this too. He told us to keep quiet about whatever we found.'

'Yes. He has a son. He's thirty years old. I saw his picture. He doesn't look anything like his father.'

'Another one. And another friend of Jim's,' Charlie said.

'But there's another question that hasn't been answered.'

'What?'

'Who is sending you the letters, and why?'

Chapter 61:

Every morning, Simm caught up on the news, getting the highlights of what was happening in the world. Most mornings it had little effect on him, but today one of the headlines was the announcement of the death of business and real estate magnate, Winston Simmons, the Second. It was accompanied by a picture of the man he hadn't seen in over ten years. It was a recent photo, showing the ravages of age, sickness, and a good dose of payment for his sins.

Simm had noticed a missed call from his brother the previous evening and he guessed Walt had either wanted to convince him to talk to his father one last time or to inform him of his death. Either way, he didn't regret missing the call.

Simm didn't want to feel anything, but he did. He felt the pain of loss. Not the loss of his father, because that was a pain he had suffered and gotten over long ago, but the pain of all he had lost because of this man. The picture revived all those memories. He knew he shouldn't, but he hoped the old man had suffered during his final days, as he had made others suffer during his lifetime.

Simm's cell phone rang beside his elbow. He recognized Charlie's name on the display and had a sense of foreboding.

'Simm, I'm so sorry.'

'There's nothing to be sorry about. You didn't kill him.'

'I know you're joking to cover up your pain.'

'Charlie, I don't want to talk about it.'

'I understand.'

He had at last found a way to get her to stop digging. Maybe he was onto something here.

'I know it's early yet, but when you know the details for the funeral,

I'd like to go.'

Simm wanted to groan out loud, but he suppressed it. She now had a new bone to chew on.

'Charlie, I've got to let you go. I have another call coming in,' he lied.

'Okay, I'll see you later. Keep your chin up.'

Simm set aside the phone and put his head in his hands. She wouldn't rest until she witnessed him bawling his eyes out at the funeral, proclaiming to everyone who would listen how much he loved his father.

He would have to be very creative to get out of this.

His phone rang again. This time, it was Walt.

'Did you hear?'

'Yes, I saw it on the news.'

'He died peacefully.'

Simm was tempted to say he died very differently than he had lived, but again he held his tongue.

'Why don't you come over to the house today?'

'Maybe later.'

This time, when he hung up, he knew he had appeased his brother more handily than he had Charlie. He had no desire to go to that house. When he left it ten years earlier, he had made a vow, and he intended to keep it.

Chapter 62:

Even though Simm had described the place to her, she was still taken aback. It was so luxurious Charlie had no idea how any ordinary person could afford it.

It had been Simm's idea to visit Sylvie O'Reilly this morning. Charlie thought there were better things he could be doing on the occasion of his father's death, despite his apparent hatred for the man, but Simm was insistent. So, she decided he probably needed the distraction.

As it had been for Simm, there was no problem being admitted to Mrs. O'Reilly's room. Charlie was shocked to see the woman looking so frail and helpless. She had been a bit of a princess, but a very healthy and vibrant princess. She remembered the contrast between her and Charlie's mother, who had seemed dowdy compared to the bejeweled and fashionably dressed Sylvie.

Was that what had led Jim to organized crime? Was that why he had helped Aidan Connelly traffic babies? To keep his beautiful wife in jewels and clothing? Charlie knew he had adored the woman, but she never thought he would sacrifice his principles for her sake. But, maybe he'd thought he was doing something good. Maybe he sincerely believed he was saving the lives of children. It's possible Jim had been brainwashed by Connelly.

It wasn't just Sylvie's appearance that was distressing. Her reaction to their arrival was extreme, at least from Charlie's point of view. The woman's eyes widened in something resembling fear, and her body pressed backward in the chair, as if she wanted to distance herself from them.

'Sylvie, it's me, Charlie. Do you remember me?'

'There's no need to introduce yourself. I think the fact that she recognizes you is the problem,' Simm said.

'Why?'

'That's what we need to find out.'

Simm pulled up a chair and sat facing the older woman, almost touching knees with her.

'Hello, Mrs. O'Reilly. I think you remember me also, don't you?'

Her gaze narrowed on him.

'I have a few more questions to ask you this time. I'm sure you don't mind.'

Charlie recognized the sarcasm in his voice, and was about to tell him to be gentler with the older women when she observed the expression on Sylvie's face. It was pure hatred, and it seemed to be directed at both of them.

'We've discovered a lot of things since my last visit. It seems your husband dabbled in other activities besides laundering money. He had another side business, didn't he?'

Sylvie O'Reilly turned her head to the window. A small amount of drool came out of the side of her mouth, and Charlie was tempted to wipe it off for her, but she didn't think her help would be appreciated.

'Did you know he was trafficking babies for adoption in Canada?'

Her trembling hand lifted to wipe away the drool with a tissue then moved toward the emergency button. Simm took the gadget and moved it out of her reach.

'I'll take that as a yes. Do you know where those babies went?'

The old woman wasn't a very good poker player. Her gaze jerked to Charlie and returned to the window almost instantly.

'Yes, the Butlers got one. Who else? Did Marty Sullivan get one also?'

This time, the look on her face could only be described as terror. She shook her head vehemently.

'I'll take that as another yes.'

Sylvie whimpered like a frightened dog.

'Simm, maybe you should let up on her.' Charlie was worried she would have another stroke, this one in front of them, but he ignored her and continued with his questioning.

'What are you worried about? Do you think Marty will hurt you? I doubt it. You're an old woman who's unable to talk. You wouldn't make much of a witness, or a victim. Are you worried about Terry?'

This created another reaction. Tears came to her eyes and ran down her papery cheeks.

'Mrs. O'Reilly, I'll make a deal with you. Sullivan will never know we were here if you help us trace those babies. I'm sure someone like Jim kept records. Where are they?'

CHAPTER 63:

'I had to do it.'

'You were too rough. You went too far,' Charlie insisted.

'She's fine.'

'For now. What if she dies today of a stroke, or a heart attack?'

'She's a little shook up, but at least we got something useful from the whole thing. It'll help to ease her conscience, and she'll rest easier.'

'Boy, you sure know how to rationalize your behavior.'

'I tell you what, why don't you go to work and let me do the investigating?'

'Ha. You're trying to get rid of me.'

'You're the one who's having a problem with this.'

He was right, but Charlie wouldn't admit it. She wanted to stay involved. And he was right about something else. They had received valuable information from Sylvie O'Reilly. Simm's hunch that Jim had kept a record of the adoptions was right. Through a series of yes-and-no-answer questions, they found out it was hidden somewhere at the pub. The exact location was still a mystery, but at least they had something with which they could work.

They had also pinpointed Sylvie's benefactor. Also going on a hunch, Simm had made her admit Sullivan was the person paying her way. She was living in extreme comfort because he had bought her silence. It wasn't just Terry she was worried for; she knew her luxurious surroundings were on the line.

Charlie had her work cut out for her. She wouldn't rest until she found that journal. Already, she was itching to get back to Butler's Pub, and the downtown traffic was frustrating in the extreme.

'You know, if you turned left here, and went down Sherbrooke

Street, we may get there faster.'

'Taking a detour won't get us there faster.'

'But there's construction ahead.'

'Take a deep breath and relax. That journal isn't going anywhere.'

Charlie huffed out a breath.

While Simm was looking for a parking spot, she gripped the door handle.

'Let me off here. I'll walk the rest of the way.' The door slammed behind her before he said a word.

'Where's your sidekick?' asked Frank, as she barrelled into the bar.

'Parking. I'll be in the office if you're looking for me.'

She noticed Frank's baffled face as she stalked by, but she wasn't in the mood to explain.

In her office, she picked up Harley to receive his enthusiastic welcome as she gazed around the room. When she had taken over the business, she hadn't made any changes to the layout. The furniture and cabinets were as they had been at the time of Jim's death. She tried to remember if she had ever done a cleanup of the files, but she couldn't recall, which likely meant she hadn't.

There were only two cabinets, but there were at least five large boxes filled with documents. Knowing Jim, he had kept every scrap of paper since he had started the business. Going through all of that paperwork wouldn't be a picnic, but it would surely be a challenge, and one that was long overdue. There was no time like the present to get started.

Twenty minutes later, when Simm joined her in the office, she was going through the first box.

'What took you so long?' she asked.

'I was chatting with Frank.'

'You filled him in?'

'I let him know you'll be preoccupied for the next little while.'

'You find this amusing?' she said, noticing the smirk.

'You're like a freight train. God forbid someone should step out in front of you.'

'You'd better heed your own warning.'

'I was going to give you a hand.'

'Then take that other box. Anything that's over six years old can go in the garbage.'

They worked side by side for hours without a break. Most of the boxes were deemed to be trash. Next, they tackled the filing cabinets with almost the same result. They contacted a company to come and shred all the old documents.

But they still hadn't found a journal.

Charlie dropped into a chair and ran her dusty hands through her hair.

'It would've been too easy.'

'It was a long shot that Jim would have left it someplace so obvious, but we had to look.'

The door opened and Frank came into the room.

'Any luck?'

'None,' Charlie said. 'He must have a secret hiding place somewhere.'

'It could be anywhere, maybe not even in this building,' Frank suggested.

'No, Sylvie told Simm it was here.'

'She could be lying.'

Charlie shrugged, hardly able to lift her shoulders.

'Anything's possible, but I think she was too scared to lie.'

'How about a break?' Simm suggested.

'You can take a break. I'm going to keep looking. Help me move these boxes away from the wall. I'll check for hiding spots.'

The walls were done in seventies-style dark wood paneling. Charlie easily imagined a secret panel lifting off to reveal a treasure trove.

Simm and Frank moved the boxes, and then pitched in to tap on the walls and search for traces of an opening. By the time that was done, to no avail, it was time to open the pub and get to work.

Simm saluted them and strolled to the door, assuring Charlie he would be back to get her later that night.

Chapter 64:

'I read the article about Simm's dad. That's really something, isn't it? I don't remember any of that,' Frank said.

'I remember something about a rich guy going to prison for fraud, but I didn't remember his name, and I never made the connection to Simm.'

Frank and Charlie were alone in the pub, setting up for the afternoon crowd. The previous day, Charlie had mentioned briefly to Frank that Simm's father had passed away, but she hadn't given him any further details.

'I guess that's why Simm hates him so much,' Frank said.

'I think there are quite a few reasons. At least, that's the impression I have.'

'I don't feel so bad about my father now,' he said, smiling sheepishly.

Charlie gave a short laugh.

'You and me both. I guess we can't choose our families, can we? We have to make do with what we have.'

Their conversation was interrupted by the sound of the door opening. Both heads swiveled toward the entrance. Frank and Charlie exchanged a guilty glance when Simm appeared. He narrowed his eyes in suspicion, and Charlie decided a distraction was in order.

'What do you think of the new look?'

'What new look?' he said, shifting his gaze around the bar.

'Not the pub. Me,' Charlie answered.

Simm stared at her, perplexed, for a moment before looking at Frank for help.

Charlie noticed Frank motioning to his head, making Simm take a good look at her.

'You changed your hair,' he said cautiously.

'What did I do to it?'

His gaze streaked to Frank again before returning to her triumphantly.

'You cut it.'

'Great. You've graduated from the Frank Hill School of Sign Language.'

'You should know better than to ask a guy a loaded question like that.'

Charlie didn't care if he had noticed her hair or not, she just wanted to change his mind, but Frank wasn't on the same track as her.

'Sorry to hear about your father, Simm.'

The animation dropped away from Simm's face. Charlie shot Frank a warning look and tried to salvage the situation.

'How about a beer? On the house.'

'No, it's a little early. I just stopped by to see if I could help you look for the journal.'

Charlie couldn't hold back.

'Simm, you shouldn't be working on that right now. Why don't you go see your family?'

'I don't need to see them, and they certainly don't need to see me. I won't be much of a comfort to them.'

Charlie couldn't help but agree with that statement. His hatred for his father was palpable. Anyone who was grief-stricken would not find any sympathy in Simm's presence.

'Alright, if you insist, we'll go to the office and look some more.'

Charlie and Simm worked for an hour, looking through both physical and computer files, in almost complete silence, but it was far from being a companionable silence. Even with an impassive expression and without saying a word, the tension rolled off Simm in waves. Charlie gave in to her inner demons.

'Simm, I read the newspaper article. I know about your father's past.'

He remained silent, but his jaw clenched rigidly.

230

'It must have been very difficult,' she continued. 'And, I understand how you could be bitter toward your father.'

'You don't understand anything, Charlie. Nothing at all. You don't know what he was like. You don't know what my life was like. You know nothing, and I don't want to talk about this right now.'

Simm stood and went to the door. Charlie was quick to follow, and caught up to him as his hand gripped the door knob. She grabbed his elbow and felt his arm jerk. For a split second, she thought he would take a swing at her. He seemed angry enough to do it.

'I'm sorry. I promise I won't talk about it anymore. I shouldn't have brought it up.'

He closed his eyes for a couple of beats, exhaled deeply, and turned to her.

'Give it a rest. Please.'

'I will. I'm sorry.'

'I gotta go.'

A few hours later, Charlie was in the office when Frank knocked on the door and came in without waiting for an answer.

'Simm's brother is here.'

Charlie jumped from her chair and headed for the door.

'Is Simm around?' she asked as she hurried past Frank.

'No, not yet.'

'Good.'

In the main bar, Charlie approached the man who looked so much like Simm, yet didn't look like him at all.

'Walt, it's so nice to see you again,' she said, taking his hand in hers. 'Please accept my sympathies on the passing of your father.'

'Thank you.' Charlie saw a flash of sadness on his face before being quickly replaced by concern. 'Have you seen Simm? I went by his place and he's not there. He's not answering his phone either. I'm getting a little worried about him.'

Charlie wasn't worried. She knew he was hiding away from his family.

'I'm sure he's fine. He'll undoubtedly drop by later. Is there a message I can give him?'

'I'd like to talk to him, but if not, could you please let him know the details for the funeral service?'

'Of course, I'll tell him.'

After Walt Simmons left, Charlie noted on a napkin the location and date of the funeral so she wouldn't forget. But, remembering the details would be easier than passing them along to Simm.

Chapter 65:

Charlene,

Where have you been? I missed you. I thought you didn't take vacations. Did the new man in your life make you change your ways?

My name is Nick. We've never met, but I know you very well. I would have liked to travel and see the world, especially Ireland. I feel I have an affinity with that country. Your roots are there also, aren't they? We should plan a trip together some time soon.

It was in the regular mail, as usual. Charlie set it aside after reading it, and continued opening her mail. She stopped, a half-opened envelope in her hand, and thought about what she had just done. Or rather, what she hadn't done. She hadn't panicked, gone running out to see Frank, or called Simm. And, she wasn't on the phone with the cops.

When had it become commonplace? When had it stopped scaring her? She thought about her experiences in Ireland, which had been truly terrifying. Receiving letters was easier to digest than having a bag thrown over your head and being kidnapped, not knowing if you would survive or not.

Also, she felt more in control now. They had found some answers, and she was confident it was simply a matter of time before they had all of them. And another little piece of the puzzle had just fallen into place. The letter-writer knew she had been to Ireland. She was certain that was what he was trying to tell her, and he thought the message would scare her. She refused to play into his hands.

Her cell phone chirped beside her elbow. It was Simm, texting her. Sometimes she thought he was psychic. He seemed to know when to show up or contact her.

She responded to his casual inquiry with a text saying she had received another letter. Before she set her phone on the desk, it was ringing. She smiled at his predictability.

'What did it say?'

She read the brief note to him, and shared her thoughts.

'You're right. It's someone close. I'll be right over.'

'There's no need. I'm okay.'

'Didn't you hear me? It's someone close enough to you to know what you're up to.'

'I'm not afraid.'

'Maybe you're not…'

He ended the call without finishing his sentence.

Charlie shrugged off Simm's pessimism. The person had always been close, right from the start, and she had never been bodily harmed. She was beginning to think it was a case of psychological harassment, pure and simple. While this was still unacceptable, she wouldn't give in to it. They would find this person, and they would discover the motivation behind the letters.

Meanwhile, she had a business to run. She had lost another morning looking for the mysterious journal. Now, she had finished the miserable task of bookkeeping, so she was free to work behind the bar. It was a Friday, and it would be busy.

It was, in fact, hopping. The weather was nice, people were in the summertime mood, and they wanted to socialize. The outside patio was overflowing onto the sidewalk, and when that was too much, the inside filled up also. Charlie didn't have any time to think about letters or journals. Around one o'clock in the morning, it slowed down. She grabbed a stool and sat for a minute with a cold glass of water.

The neighbouring stool scraped against the ceramic floor and she recognized Simm's boots from the corner of her eye.

'Lazing around again, Butler?'

'Funny guy.'

'Big night?'

'Very. Still is. I'm just grabbing a few minutes.'

'Even Frank has worked up a sweat,' he said, nodding in the direction of the bartender.

'He's the best. I'll get you a beer.'

Simm grasped her arm before she stood up.

'There's no rush. Sit for a bit. Did you look for the journal again today?'

'I did, with no luck, but I'm not giving up.'

'I didn't think you would.'

Charlie stood and headed for the bar. She couldn't let Frank handle it alone. She poured a beer for Simm and set it in front of him before heading outside to take orders from the customers enjoying the warm summer evening.

When she came back in and stood beside the bar to recite the drink orders to Frank, she glanced at the mirror behind one of the smaller shelves at the bar, but she didn't see her reflection. Instead a memory flashed before her eyes.

'What's the matter?' Frank asked.

Charlie shook her head to clear it.

'Nothing. Why?'

'You look like you saw a ghost.'

'I did.'

Suddenly, the night couldn't end soon enough. She looked around the room and gauged the crowd. There was another two hours before they had to legally close up shop. Was it possible they would clear out sooner? She could only hope.

'Hey, slow down. What's got into you?' Frank said, a concerned look on his face.

'I'm helping you. You should be grateful.'

Charlie knew of only one way to make time go faster and that was to keep busy.

'I'm glad to have the help, but you don't have to knock yourself out.'

'There's lots to do. People are thirsty.'

She turned to see Simm looking at her with a puzzled expression. She knew she was going overboard, but it was either that or go crazy.

When the last person left the pub, Charlie gratefully locked the door.

'Okay, what the hell's up with you? You turned into a mad woman,' Simm said.

'For once, I agree with him,' Frank added.

'I know where it is.'

'The journal?' Simm asked. 'How did you find it?'

'I remembered something from years ago. I recall walking in on Jim and surprising him.'

She went behind the bar and started removing bottles from one section of the bar. The wall behind the bar gave the appearance of being one huge mirror with shelves in front of it, holding the various liquor bottles, but it was literally the opposite. It was one huge set of shelves with small mirrors inset into each section. The section that interested her was about twelve inches in width and sixteen inches in height. When all the bottles were out of the way, she ran her hands over the mirror, pushing in various places. Finally, she heard a little popping noise and the mirror swung open, revealing a small cupboard.

Inside, was a leather journal.

Chapter 66:

'You're a genius,' Frank said.

'I feel stupid, very stupid. I can't believe I forgot about it. Jim had such a guilty look when I walked in, and he tried to brush it off as nothing. His ploy worked; I didn't think of it again until tonight.'

Charlie flipped through the journal, revealing pages and pages of Jim's neat precise writing, as Frank and Simm looked over her shoulder. She shut the book and hugged it to her chest.

'It's late. Frank, you need to get home. I'll take this back to the apartment with us, and I'll look at it tomorrow morning.'

'You'll tell me about it, won't you?' Frank asked.

Charlie smiled. He looked like a kid who'd been denied a piece of candy.

'Of course, I will. We're in this together. But, we all need our rest. Now that we've found it, it'll keep.'

They closed the pub and went their separate ways.

'You won't wait until tomorrow morning,' Simm commented when they were in the car.

'I might.'

'Liar.'

'Okay, maybe I'll have a peek tonight, but there's way too much stuff in here to absorb all in one night. And I'm tired. I still haven't gotten over the jet lag.'

'Why did you not want Frank to see it?'

'I didn't not want him to see it. It's late, and I didn't want to make him stay.'

'It seemed to be more than that,' Simm said.

'It wasn't. It's private. I need to look at it on my own.'

When they were in Simm's apartment, Charlie dragged herself

through the motions of getting ready for bed, her eyes burning. When she settled underneath the covers, she heard Simm in the bathroom. Picking up the precious journal from the bedside table, she opened it to the first page, deciding to read only that page.

Hours later, Simm grumbled, 'For God's sake, go to sleep. You keep muttering.'

'I will, right after this page.'

Simm lifted himself on to one elbow and looked across her at the clock.

'Jesus, it's five o'clock. The birds are singing outside. Don't you believe in sleep?'

'Shh. Quit complaining, and go back to sleep. I'll be quiet.'

Simm sat up in the bed and propped himself on the pillows, the sheet slipping to his waist.

'Okay, give. What's in it?'

'It's a diary. It starts in 1980, a few years after he bought the bar, when he started doing business with the West End Gang.'

'Really?' She had his attention.

'It's fascinating. I'm starting to understand his thinking behind the whole thing. I don't agree with it or condone it, but I can understand it.'

'What drove him?'

She set the book on her knee and leaned her head back against the headboard.

'When I saw Sylvie the other day, I wondered if she had been the motivation. She was a high-maintenance woman. I was right. Jim needed the extra money to keep her happy, so he helped out the Gang by laundering their money. And it was him that paid the price when he went to jail.'

'You do the crime you do the time. It was his choice.'

'I know, but still...I feel bad for him. He was like a father to me.'

'I get it. But what about the babies?'

'I haven't gotten to that part yet.'

'You're not curious enough to skip ahead?'

'I need to understand how he got to that point.'

Simm yawned, and lowered himself under the covers again.

'You're a strange one, Charlie.'

Chapter 67:

When Simm woke, Charlie was asleep with the journal open on her stomach, her arms spread out by her side, and the bedside light still lit. It was nine o'clock, and he had no idea how much sleep she had managed to get. He gently picked up the book, and took it with him to the kitchen. Sipping his coffee, he flipped through the pages, scanning most of the first section. He wasn't as methodical as Charlie when it came to this sort of thing. He wanted to skip ahead to the interesting part.

About mid-way through the journal, the style of writing changed from prose to note form. There were dates, names, and towns listed. In some cases, there were four or five names, in others three and some had just two with a question mark. Simm flipped rapidly through the pages. There had to be hundreds of entries.

He went back and looked at them one by one. It didn't take long to figure out the system. Jim had used acronyms like DOB, DOA, BP, BM, and AP. When there were five names it included the name of the child along with the birth parents and the adoptive parents. Often, only the birth mother's name was listed, with no father. Sometimes, the child's name would be written, and sometimes it was unknown. Dates would include date of birth, and date of adoption. Sometimes, just the date of adoption was known.

Simm saw Jim had tried his best to document the movement of children, but often the information wasn't available to him. Why had he done this? Had he intended to share it with the children at some point? If so, why hadn't he told Charlie, the one who was presumably closest to him?

Now that Simm was familiar with the system, he scanned for

familiar names like Butler and Sullivan.

'What are you doing?'

Simm dropped the book and looked up as Charlie hurried to his side. She snatched the journal away from him and looked at the open pages.

'You're reading ahead. I told you I didn't want to do that.'

'You can do whatever you want. I'm just trying to get to the important stuff.'

'It's all important.'

'No, it's all pertinent. What's most urgent, right now, is finding out about your past, what Sullivan's connection is, and who's sending you those letters.'

She hugged the journal to her chest.

'I know, it's just…'

'You want to know, but you're afraid to know.'

'I guess.'

'Then why don't you let me find it for you. I've figured out his system.'

'How many are there?'

'A lot. Hundreds, probably.'

'Hundreds? How can you smuggle hundreds of children from one country to another?'

'I guess, at that time, the security procedures were different. You didn't need a passport to travel by air between countries. The one trip your father made to Ireland was presumably to bring you back with him. Jim would've taken care of the fake identification, birth certificate, and whatnot.'

'It makes sense, but you'd think someone would get suspicious after a while.'

'Looking at the dates, this was done over a period of several years. With the number of travellers between the countries, no one would notice. It's not as if they booked an airplane and put a hundred kids on it.'

'You're right.' Charlie stared out the window, still clutching the journal like a life raft. 'How old was I?' she asked.

'About a month old.'

'Oh God. Was I…do you think…I was stolen?'

'It doesn't say. In your case, as in many others, the birth parents aren't precisely mentioned.'

'A month old. I was so young.'

'Yes, you were raised by your parents almost from the beginning.'

'I know they were my parents, but I can't help thinking about where I came from. Remember the letter I got talking about nature versus nurture? That's what I'm worried about now.'

'In other words, you're worried you may be Aidan Connelly's daughter.'

'Yes, or someone equally repugnant.'

'And I'm telling you, it doesn't matter. At least it doesn't matter from the point of view of how you were raised and who you are. It may matter for the case.'

'You think my parentage is the link to the letter-writer?'

'It may be.'

'What do you mean by 'not precisely mentioned'?'

'Your birth parents? There were no specific names, just initials.'

'What were they?'

'A and T.'

CHAPTER 68:

Charlie kept repeating the letters in her head. A and T. A and T. Could it be Aidan and someone? Of course, it could be any number of people, but her real fear was that it was Aidan. If she was his daughter, did she have his propensity for crime and selfishness? She would think those characteristics would have reared their ugly heads by now, but maybe they would skip a generation and be found in her children. That was a chilling thought.

How would she find the truth? Jim, for some reason, hadn't detailed it in his journal. He had to know who they were if he recorded their initials. Had he been trying to protect her from the worst? Or was he protecting the parents from discovery?

During the entire work day, she was distracted, alternating between being certain she was the spawn of the devil, or she was the product of two teenagers who had the choice to give up their child or be cast out of their family.

When Simm showed up, she gestured him into her office.

'So? What did you find?'

'Aidan's wife's name was Christine.'

'Oh, thank God. Why do you have that look on your face? Isn't that good news?'

'Aidan and Christine had two children whom they raised to adulthood.'

'They kept them? I thought he had given up his children.'

'Apparently, he was a prolific fellow. He had several mistresses, and he didn't believe in birth control.'

Charlie sagged into a chair and dragged her hands over her face.

'What the hell? He didn't believe in birth control, but he believed in, and performed, abortions?'

Simm held his hands out and shrugged.

'Go figure.'

'So, he could have had a mistress named Theresa or Tammy,' Charlie said.

'Perhaps. Or your parents could have been Alice and Tom.'

'Yes, I keep trying to remind myself of that possibility.'

'I made a couple of other interesting discoveries today.'

'What?' she asked anxiously. She hoped to hear at least a snippet of good news.

'Marty Sullivan got an Irish baby named Matthew.'

'As we suspected, he's the reason Marty didn't want us to reveal anything we discovered while in Ireland.'

'Precisely, he doesn't want anyone to know, especially Matthew.'

'Who are his parents?'

'Nothing was written in the journal.'

'I wonder what's worse, having nothing or having initials that mean nothing. And I wonder why Sullivan is so desperate to keep it a secret he will pay a small fortune to keep Sylvie in the lap of luxury.'

'I have a theory,' Simm said. 'I think he felt he owed something to Jim and helping Sylvie was his way of paying him back. I also think his son may have been one of the stolen babies. That's something he wouldn't want revealed. There's also, of course, a question of pride. He wants his son to think he's a true Sullivan in every sense of the word.'

'And the message they're trying to send with the embryo is that they'll tell Matthew about his roots,' Charlie said.

'That's what I think. There's definitely a strong connection between Connelly and the Mafia. It seems like the criminal underworld was one of the sources of Aidan's customers. And, through Jim, they made it overseas.'

'My father wasn't a criminal,' Charlie insisted.

'No, he was a friend of Jim O'Reilly, and that's how he made the cut. I suspect a lot of other people who weren't considered criminals also got babies through Aidan and Jim. Do you remember the connections to which Tom O'Brien referred? Connelly may have had customers like judges and police officers whom he could easily have blackmailed and used their influence to keep him out of jail.'

'Quite possibly, but what do we do with this information? How can it help us?'

'I have a theory. I think the letter-writer is one of these kids, or maybe he's one of the parents. Maybe something went wrong. Somehow, he knows you're one of them, and he's taking it out on you. He must know about Aidan, and the abortions, and the baby-smuggling operation.'

'How would he know he's one of the kids?'

'His adoptive parents, I would assume.'

'What could go wrong?'

'I don't know. That's what we must find out, but first I have to narrow down the list. I'll go through the families and see how many are living here in Montreal. Then I'll have to see if any of them have a connection to you.'

'That won't be easy. Like you said, there are hundreds of them.'

'That's part of my job.'

Chapter 69:

Job or no job, it wasn't fun. Simm didn't enjoy sitting in front of a computer all day long, but it was the only way to find the information he wanted, and even then, it took him several hours to narrow his search by merely a handful of people.

He checked his watch and stretched. There were definitely times he missed the more physical job of police work, even though it had its fair share of sitting at a desk, or in a car. Right now, he would head over to the pub and have a beer. He'd continue his work in Charlie's office. At least it would be a change of scenery.

It was a quiet Tuesday night at Butler's, and Charlie, being her ever-curious self, passed some time looking over his shoulder to see how he progressed. It was irritating at times, but it wasn't boring. Her incessant questions helped to pass the time. He managed to make it through a few other names. So far, he hadn't found any babies who were still living in the area.

The end of the evening came at last, and they headed for home a bit earlier than usual.

It was like déjà vu. The lock was visibly damaged. Simm wordlessly motioned for Charlie to stay behind in the corridor. She didn't say a word, but the expression on her face said it all. She knew it had happened again and it frightened her.

Simm cautiously opened the door. He wanted to swear. Loudly. But, he didn't know if the guy was still in the apartment, so he didn't make a sound. On his way in, he snagged a baseball bat that lived in the umbrella stand behind the door. He slung it over his shoulder, ready to go. Making his way from room to room, he stepped over broken furniture, overturned tables, and shredded paper. His laptop and all his electronics were smashed. Minutes later, he retrieved a worried Charlie from the hallway.

'Oh no, Simm. Look at what he did. It's a mess.'

'He was thorough,' he agreed, as he dialed 9-1-1.

Simm's second call was to Detective Ranfort. Since he had been in charge of the case from the beginning, he needed to know what had happened.

'I guess it's a good thing I took the journal to the bar with me,' Simm said.

'You think that's what he was looking for?'

'What else?'

'He would have to know we found it.'

'Unless he always thought so.'

'Right.'

Simm didn't have much faith the investigation by the cops would be of any use, but he knew they had to go through the motions. Ranfort arrived and sympathised with their situation, but couldn't offer any solutions, not that Simm expected any.

Again, they waited through the work by the police technicians and the questioning of the neighbours. The night watchman was called up and interviewed by Detective Ranfort. As he left the apartment, he smiled at Charlie.

'That's a cute little dog you have there.'

'Oh...um...thanks. It's just a temporary arrangement.'

'Hey, there's no problem. We don't mind when it's just small dogs and there aren't any complaints,' he said, scratching Harley behind the ears and winking at Charlie. 'Just keep sneaking him in and we'll keep looking the other way.'

It was the wee hours of the morning before they made the apartment more-or-less habitable. Simm took pictures for the insurance company. A lot of his furniture was ready for the trash heap and would have to be replaced. The rest they had salvaged.

'Now what?' Charlie asked.

'Now we go to bed. Tomorrow's another day.'

'No, I mean, now what do we do? I left my apartment after it was invaded, and we came here to be safe. Now he knows where we are, so where do we go?'

'Nowhere. We'll be safe here. I'll make sure of it.'

Simm had contained his emotions for the past few hours, but he was angry. He didn't like feeling violated, and he could tell the guy was escalating. He was more worried than ever for Charlie's safety, and he was more determined than ever to find the person responsible. This had gone on long enough.

The next morning, they continued the cleanup, filling large garbage bags with trashed papers and broken pottery. Luckily, Simm only had a few plants in the apartment and no knick-knacks, or it would have taken much longer to tidy.

His laptop and his television would have to be replaced. He had the habit of backing up his hard drive every day, so the information was safe, but he wasn't happy about having to go through all the bother of buying and configuring a new computer.

Charlie's cell phone rang mid-morning, and Simm could tell by the look on her face something was wrong. When she disconnected the call and looked at him, her face was white.

'He went to Butler's from here,' she said, her voice trembling.

'Oh, Jesus.'

'I'll kill him. If I ever get my hands on this guy, I'll kill him.'

'A lot of damage?'

'Yes. He was searching for the hiding place.'

They both turned and stared at the innocent-looking journal peeking out of her bag. Jim's need to document his misdeeds had caused havoc.

Chapter 70:

Charlie's blood simmered on low all the way to the pub, and she made an extra effort to keep it from boiling over. Police cars were parked in front of the property and she spotted Frank pacing on the sidewalk when they pulled up. When her friend heard the car, he swung around and rushed to open Charlie's door.

She wanted to get inside and see the damage as soon as possible, but getting past Frank was like walking through a steel beam. He grabbed her by the shoulders and bent his head to look her in the eye.

'Listen to me. It can all be fixed. The important thing is no one was hurt.'

His platitudes warned her the sight wouldn't be pretty, and she felt her blood heating up another notch.

'Let me by.'

'I just want you to stay calm.'

'I'm calm, but I won't be much longer if you don't let me by.'

Frank looked at Simm with an expression she found difficult to interpret. It could have been a cry for help.

Her anger turned to shock as she stepped through the door. There was no longer a mirror behind the bar. Actually, there was nothing behind the bar; no mirror, no shelves, no bottles. The floor, however was covered in broken glass and wood splinters. The place reeked of alcohol. The hole where the journal had rested for so many years was exposed and empty.

Whether the perpetrator had discovered this at the beginning or the end of his rampage, she didn't know, but he had covered all his bases. There were holes punched in many spots in the walls, and the furniture was overturned, most of it broken.

Her office was another matter. All the boxes Charlie and Simm had sorted through and put aside for shredding were upended. Every document was strewn over the floor and desktop. It was as if it had snowed papers overnight. There were many hours ahead of her to put everything back in place.

She clenched her hands and held back a scream. She kept telling herself Frank was right, to date no one had been hurt. But, someday, somehow, someone would be, if she ever got her hands on him.

'Frank?'

He appeared in her peripheral vision, but she didn't look at him.

'Did you forget to set the alarm last night?'

'No, it was set.'

Her head swiveled toward him.

'It was? How did he get in?'

One of the cops stepped into view. 'The alarm wasn't tampered with.'

'That's impossible,' she said. 'He'd have to know the code to get through.' Her gaze shifted from the cop to Frank. 'How could that be?'

'I don't know. Honestly, I don't,' Frank said. 'I've never given the code to anyone. As far as I know, just you and I know it.'

'A sophisticated burglar can bypass alarm systems,' the cop offered.

'I didn't think this guy was that sophisticated.'

She looked at Simm to see if he agreed with her statement.

'He's smart enough to cover his tracks, but he doesn't seem to be a whiz kid. To date, it's just been regular down-and-dirty break-ins and anonymous letters,' Simm said.

'Then, either it's not the same guy, or he got help from someone,' Charlie said.

'It's the same guy, I'm sure of it,' Simm answered.

Charlie threw herself into her office chair and ran her hands over her face. She felt like crying with anger and frustration, but she wouldn't give into it. She had never turned her back on a challenge before, and she wouldn't start now.

For obvious reasons, Charlie had to shut down the pub. From then on, she was inundated with insurance adjusters, police officers, and construction workers. She turned down offers from drop-by interior decorators trying to sell her a whole new look. She liked her old look, and so did her clients. Many of them stopped by and were dismayed to hear the news their favorite haunt had been vandalised.

Every day, Charlie was there from early morning until late at night, cleaning up after the vandal and cleaning up after the workers. She was like a bull dog, pushing everyone to work faster and harder. It was embarrassing for anyone else to stop and take a break, so the repairs and renovations progressed at top speed.

Frank was by her side most of the time. Simm did his part, but from time to time, he excused himself from the work detail with the excuse of having other business to take care of. She let him go without a fuss.

One evening, Simm showed up as Charlie was sweeping sawdust left behind by the workers. He settled onto a bar stool and watched her work.

'You could grab a broom and help me,' she suggested.

'I could, but I'm tired.'

Charlie stopped what she was doing and gave him a suspicious look.

'What's up?' she said.

'Nothing,' he replied, shrugging. 'I guess I'm just feeling a bit down these days. It doesn't happen often, but I guess I'm just impatient for things to return to normal.'

'Most people would feel that way after the loss of a family member.'

Simm scowled. 'It has nothing to do with my father's death.'

'It's me you're talking to. It's okay to admit it.'

'Charlie, stop it. I'm telling you it has nothing to do with my father. It's the case. I'd like it to be over and done with.'

Charlie didn't know what to think about that statement. Was he tired of dealing with her? She grasped the broom once again and concentrated on sweeping the floor.

'You and me both,' she muttered as a response.

'What do you see happening after all this is over?'

'What do you mean?'

'I mean us.'

'Us?' she said, stopping in her tracks and turning to him.

'Yes, us. Don't you think there could be an 'us'?'

Charlie was stunned. Simm had never given any indication he was interested in her as anything other than a client. She stood in the middle of the room, her broom propped in front of her, firmly gripped in her two hands.

'I guess I was wrong then,' he said, getting to his feet.

'Wait! Don't go. It's just that…you caught me off-guard…I didn't…I mean I never thought that you thought…' She relinquished the broom and went to sit on a stool beside him. 'Simm, I'm not throwing away the idea of an 'us', it's just that I didn't think you were the slightest bit interested, and with everything going on…'

He held up his hand.

'I know. With everything going on, the timing's far from right. You're dealing with a lot of stress and upset. That's why I'm anxious for things to return to normal, so we can start dealing with each other without all the other stuff hanging over our heads. It hasn't been easy, above all with the sleeping arrangement,' he said, rolling his eyes dramatically.

Charlie would have to get used to the idea that Simm wanted to have a relationship with her. The feelings inside her were growing hopeful, and she was also in a hurry to close the case, for several reasons now.

With a small smile, she leaned over and gave Simm a kiss.

CHAPTER 71:

She had done it again. Simm didn't know how it had happened, but he had started the day determined not to be anywhere near his father's funeral, and now he stood at the front of the church with the rest of his family, shaking hands with a steady stream of visitors expressing their sympathy at this difficult time. Yes, it was difficult, but not for the reasons they seemed to think. The vast majority of the people were complete strangers to him, and he suspected most of them were there more out of curiosity than anything else.

He glanced over to the fifth pew from the front. Charlie wore the same dress she had worn to visit Marty Sullivan. He suspected it was the only dress she owned. She looked so innocent, no one looking at her would suspect she was a witch capable of making a hard-headed man change his mind completely from one minute to the next. This was the last place on earth he wanted to be. But here he was, wearing his only suit, feeling so constricted he could hardly breathe.

Standing beside him was his brother, who had turned the stoic look in to a whole new style. He looked like he scarcely hung on to his emotions, but Simm knew his brother was probably just as happy as he was to see the old man dead, maybe even happier, since he stood to inherit quite a large amount of money. Simm didn't have to worry about that. He had been written out of his father's will many years ago.

His sister blubbered to his left. She was very good in that role also. He guessed she had spent the last few days alternating between practicing her crying technique to counting the ways she would spend her inheritance.

His stepmother was a cross between his brother and sister, discreetly wiping away the odd tear while appearing strong. She was a beautiful woman, twenty years younger than her late husband, and she had preserved herself well with his father's money.

Simm looked at his watch, not bothering to hide the fact that he was impatient for this to be over. He flicked another glance at Charlie and hoped she got the hint she owed him big time. Her begging and pleading had pushed him to come here solely to get her to leave him alone. One of these days, he would learn to say no to her.

The service began and was thankfully kept to a brief version. The priest had also been instructed to keep it brief at the graveside, and before the last rose was laid on the casket, Simm walked away with Charlie hurrying after him in her wobbly heels.

'Where are you going?'

'Home.'

'You can't go home. There's a reception at your family's house.'

'I'm not going.'

'You have to go. Your brother and sister need you.'

'They don't need me.'

'Okay, maybe they don't need you, but wouldn't it be nice to spend time with them. You can catch up on old times.'

'Yeah, we can reminisce about the prison visits to see our father.'

'You never visited him in prison.'

'You're right, I didn't. They did.'

She stumbled beside him, and he grabbed her elbow to steady her. He also slowed his pace. They didn't need to have a twisted ankle on top of everything else.

'If you go to see them today, maybe they'll leave you alone after that. You can get all the unpleasantness over with in one day, instead of spreading it out.'

Simm stopped walking, looked heavenward, and then shifted his gaze to Charlie.

'Why do you have to make sense?'

She smiled.

'It's just the way I am.'

CHAPTER 72:

Charlie had never been inside a house so huge. She had considered Jim and Sylvie O'Reilly's house a mansion, but it looked like the servant's quarters compared to this place. Winston Simmons had made serious money in printing and real estate, and hadn't lost any of it while he was in prison for fraud. He must have had very good lawyers and money managers.

The main living room of the house was crowded and people spilled into the hallways, the other sitting rooms, and outside into the gardens. Charlie stood by the buffet table looking over the astounding selection of food when she felt a presence beside her. She looked up to see Susan, Simm's sister, smiling at her.

'Charlie, I finally have a chance to speak to you. I'm so happy you could make it today.'

Charlie didn't want to mention she was the sole reason Simm had made it that day.

'You have such a lovely home, and this buffet is something else,' she said instead.

'Yes, well, my stepmother can take the credit for the buffet and the home.'

'This isn't where you grew up?'

'Oh no, that house was sold. My stepmother chose this one and had it remodeled. It's so big, we can all live here without getting in each other's way.'

'I guess,' she said wryly.

Charlie glanced around and noticed Simm on the far side of the room, deep in conversation with an older man. She couldn't pass up the opportunity.

'Susan, I was curious about something. I don't know anyone here of course, and I wondered if Simm's friend Helen was here.'

The color drained from Susan's face, and Charlie was afraid the woman would faint at her feet. Her eyes widened, and her mouth opened and closed a few times like a fish gasping on the deck of a boat.

'I'm sorry,' Charlie said, grabbing Susan's arm to steady her. 'I said something wrong, didn't I?'

Susan looked frantically around the room, and when her gaze fell on her brother, she turned to Charlie, her eyes still wide.

'He didn't tell you?'

'No, all I know is he had a girlfriend named Helen.'

'Yes, he did, but she's dead. She committed suicide.'

It was Charlie's turn to sway. That wasn't the answer she had expected. Her eyes automatically swung to Simm, standing tall above the crowd. He stared back at her, and when he saw the look on her face, his expression darkened, and his gaze swung to his sister accusingly. Susan excused herself and left the room like all the bats of hell were behind her.

CHAPTER 73:

The silence in the car was strained. A mere ten minutes had passed since Susan's revelation. Simm had stalked over to her and announced they were leaving. Charlie was too stunned to argue. They made their way out of the mansion, Simm grimly saying a few hurried words to people as he tried to leave the house un-assaulted by friends and acquaintances.

Charlie gripped her seat with white fingers as Simm drove away from his father's home and took the ramp to the highway leading back to downtown Montreal.

Suddenly, he slammed his palm against the steering wheel.

'Do you have to be so goddamned nosy?'

'I didn't think it was a big deal.'

'If I don't want to talk about it, it's because it's a big deal.'

'I understand some things are painful to talk about, but sometimes it helps.'

Simm veered right to take the next exit. Charlie had no idea where he was going, but she was smart enough not to comment. He drove into a donut shop parking lot, stopped the car, and shut the ignition. He released his seatbelt and turned to face her.

'Okay, ask away, Charlie. What else do you want to know?'

'Not like this. I want you to talk to me because you want to share things with me, share your life. And I don't want you to be angry.'

His hands ran through his hair and down over his face. He grasped his tie and wrenched it from around his neck. Next the top buttons of his shirt were undone.

'Okay, I'm better now,' he said, taking a deep breath. 'And I'm less angry. So, I'm going to tell you my story. All of it.'

'Simm…'

'No, I want to finish this. As I'm sure you've guessed, my father was a bastard, and that's the politest word I can think of. It was about money and status for him. We had to behave like rich kids, we had to be snobs, and we had to consider ourselves better than everyone else. That was drilled into us. Thankfully, our mother drilled it into us to be good people and to think of others. Somehow, that came to the forefront most of the time.'

'But you were young when she died.'

'Yes, we were, but we spent a lot of time with our grandparents who were truly good people, and they influenced us. It was through my grandparents that I met Helen. She was a girl who lived on the property next to them. She wasn't rich. Her parents were ordinary people with ordinary jobs, and she went to an ordinary school. She was like a breath of fresh air for me. She was lovely, down-to-earth, and the best thing that could've happened to me at that age.'

'How old were you?'

'Seventeen, and she was sixteen. We started as friends, just hanging out, but eventually we moved it up a notch.'

'Did your father know?'

'No. My grandparents did, but they didn't tell him. Anyway, Helen and I continued our romance for another year and were making plans to spend the rest of our lives together. Around the same time, I decided I wanted to be a cop. I knew this wouldn't go over well with good old dad. He wanted all of us, especially me, since I was the oldest, to work in the business. I had no interest in his business. I eventually confronted him and dropped both bombs on him -Helen and my career plans.'

After a short pause, Charlie couldn't help herself.

'What did he say?'

'He flipped his lid, said he would move heaven and earth to prevent both.'

'But you became a cop anyway.'

'I did.'

Charlie knew the most important part of the story was yet to come.

'And Helen?'

'He arranged for her parents to lose their jobs – he had powerful connections. He spread lies about her, terrible lies.' He shook his head at the memory. 'Then, he made sure she heard lies about me, about how I was cheating on her, and how I had always thought of her as trash.'

Charlie knew what was coming next, and she couldn't bear to hear it. She placed her hand on his arm, hoping to stop the words.

'Simm...'

'I found her...hanging from a tree...in a spot we liked to go to together.'

Charlie went into his arms. She held on tightly, wanting to pull the pain away from him. She was sorry she had made him go to the funeral. She was sorry she had ever mentioned his father in his presence. But Simm wasn't finished.

'Two years later, he was arrested and convicted of fraud. He went to jail for three years. I wish he had died in that prison cell. That's what he deserved. He didn't deserve the funeral he had today.'

'No, he didn't,' she agreed.

Chapter 74:

'What have you been up to these days? I haven't seen much of you.'

They were opening the pub again tonight, and Charlie was rechecking her inventory to make sure she was covered. It wouldn't do to disappoint customers on re-opening night. Simm had a list in his hand and was helping her out.

'I've been busy working on your case,' he said.

She looked at him in surprise.

'Oh? You never said anything.'

'That's because things just started to come together today.'

She had noticed him stepping outside to take calls rather often, but hadn't had time to question him about them.

'Do tell,' she said.

'First of all, I've been in touch with O'Reilly in Dublin and he came up with the identity of our dark-suited friend.'

Charlie set aside her papers and turned away from the boxes of booze. She waved her hand in an effort to make Simm speed up his story.

'His name is Colin McGrath and, as we suspected, he's head of a subgroup of the Irish Mafia in Dublin. He's not that big a fish in the pond, but he thinks he is, or at least he wants to give that impression.'

'In other words, he likes to push his weight around and look like the big boy on the block,' she said.

'Exactly.'

'So, what's the next step?'

Simm put his hand in his jacket pocket and removed an envelope. He handed it to Charlie smugly. She opened the envelope as she gave him a sideways glance. He seemed a little too proud of himself. But her suspicion soon turned to curiosity, and subsequently to shock when she read the newspaper clipping in her hand.

'What? I...when...you did it? Are you crazy?'

Charlie glanced around her to see how many people had overheard. A few workers were putting finishing touches on a few things, and her outburst had drawn their attention. She tugged on Simm's elbow and nodded her head toward the office. She wanted to strangle him and didn't want any witnesses.

She stepped aside to let him into the office and slammed the door behind them.

'You're crazy! You'll get the both of us killed. You know that, don't you? Why didn't you talk to me about this first?'

'Don't worry...'

'Don't worry? You've put us in the midst of a gang war, and I'm not supposed to worry? I'd kill you, but I think someone else will take care of that for me, except I'll be going down with you.'

'Charlie, if you'd stay calm and listen, you'll understand what I did.'

She folded her arms across her chest, but remained standing. She was too pumped up to sit and relax.

'Go on. Explain.'

'I didn't leave an embryo on Sullivan's doorstep.'

'But...'

Simm held up a hand. With an effort, she stopped.

'You're right. The newspaper story says it happened, but it's fake.'

'It was a fake embryo, or a fake story?'

'A fake story. I'm going to send this to McGrath so he'll be convinced it actually happened.'

'What reporter would print something fake? He could be sued.'

'The whole thing is fake. It isn't even a real newspaper clipping. It just looks like one.'

Charlie looked at the clipping she held in her hand. It looked and felt exactly like an article cut out of a newspaper.

'You made this? How? I didn't know you were that good with a computer.'

'Well...'

Charlie looked up and saw his sheepish expression.

'You had help,' she stated.

'I have a friend who can chop, slice, and dice with a computer. I told him what I wanted, and voila, that's what I got.'

'It's perfect. So, you'll send it to McGrath, he'll let us off the hook, and Sullivan will be none the wiser.'

'That's the plan.'

Charlie held up crossed fingers.

'Let's hope it works.'

Chapter 75:

Charlie felt like part of the weight was lifted from her shoulders. If Simm's plan worked – and it should – they wouldn't have to worry about any retaliation from Sullivan. But the large part of the load still weighing her down was her anonymous assailant. The level of harassment had escalated. There was a big difference between someone who sent relatively harmless letters, to someone who committed acts of breaking and entering, and vandalism.

They all agreed he was looking for something and the most logical item was the journal. How he had found out about it or why it was so important to him were still unanswered questions. Charlie knew the only way they would find the answers would be to ask the questions directly to the perpetrator, but they had to find him first.

Opening night served to make Charlie feel better. The pub was packed with happy regulars and enthusiastic newcomers. The weather was balmy, and the crowd spilled out onto the street. Simm was solicited to help behind the bar pouring beer and jotting down drink orders for Frank to prepare. Charlie had to hand it to him. He took to it like a fish to water.

By the time the last person staggered out of the building, the staff was exhausted. One by one, everyone shuffled out of the pub. Charlie went to the office to rouse a sleepy Harley, who yawned and stretched before cheerfully trotting out of the room.

She met Simm in the main room and saw him scrutinizing something in his hand. When she reached his side, he handed her a cell phone.

'Do you think this is Frank's?' Simm asked.

Charlie pressed the button to light up the screen. The screenshot

262

was of Frank standing on the lip of the Grand Canyon with his arm around a tall, slim, blond-haired man.

'Yep, it's his. That's Paul, his significant other. They went to Arizona last fall on vacation.'

'Should we drop it off?'

Charlie glanced at the time and hesitated. It was late, but Frank had just left ten minutes earlier. He'd still be up, and he might need his phone.

'Sure. It's on the way.'

It wasn't quite on the way. They had to make a small detour, but it only took a few minutes extra. They pulled into a parking spot down the street from Frank's apartment.

'You can wait here. I'll just be a minute.'

'Not a chance. It's late, and I'm not letting you wander around on your own.'

'I'm not wandering. It's right there. Oh, never mind. Come ahead if you want.'

There was no question of Harley staying alone in the car if the others were leaving, so the three of them made their way to Frank's apartment in the early hours of the morning.

Their arrival was announced through the intercom, and they were buzzed through. They climbed the two flights of stairs to find Frank at the door with a curious expression. He bent to pet Harley, who acted like he hadn't seen the man in weeks rather than a half hour earlier.

'What's up? Did something happen?'

'No. Everything's fine,' Charlie said. 'But you forgot your cell phone at the pub.'

Frank rolled his eyes.

'Sorry. You shouldn't have come out of your way for that. I could've waited until tomorrow.'

Charlie started to reassure Frank it was no trouble when she heard a noise coming from behind him, and she caught a glimpse of an uncombed blond head.

'What's going on?' Paul's sleepy voice asked.

Frank opened his mouth to answer when all eyes were drawn to

Harley. The little dog was growling, and the hair stood up on his back.

Charlie was the first to react.

'What's up, Harley? It's Paul. You remember Paul.'

The dog had known Paul ever since his arrival in Frank's life, and he had been a guest in their home several times. It was unlike her pet to growl at anyone, let alone someone he knew well.

Her knee-jerk reaction was to apologize to Paul on behalf of Harley, but when she looked his way, the words froze in her mouth.

Paul stared at Harley with wide, alarm-filled eyes. It wasn't the intensity of his alarm that surprised her, it was the other emotion she witnessed. Guilt.

She looked at her pug with new eyes. He was growling, but he was also cowering. He had positioned himself between her feet, looking for safety. Charlie glanced at Simm. He, along with Frank, stared at Paul. Simm's eyes were narrowed and calculating.

'Paul? What's going on?' Frank asked.

When Paul remained silent, looking at each of them in turn, his eyes still wide, Frank continued.

'Why is Harley afraid of you? What did you do?'

Charlie heard the tension and doubt in Frank's voice.

Paul swiveled his head left and right, looking for a point of escape, but they all blocked the doorway. When he turned and sprinted toward the other end of the apartment, Simm shoved past Frank and Charlie, and went after him.

Charlie lost sight of them, but she heard a grunt and a crash followed by the sound of scuffling. Frank, who had been frozen in place, ran toward the noise. Charlie looked down to see her pet, with his tail unfurled and tucked between his legs, shivering in fear. She bent, picked him up, and held him in her arms before stepping into the apartment. She understood the animal's fear. Things had moved in a direction she never would have considered.

When she rounded the corner of the hallway, Paul was facedown on the floor with Simm straddling him, and Frank standing beside them, his arms hanging loosely by his side, as if he didn't know what to do with them.

Paul's attempts to free himself gradually eased until he lay limply on the floor, whimpering and mumbling incoherently. Frank leaned back against the wall behind him, his chin on his chest. The full implication hit Charlie.

The blubbering man beneath Simm's weight was her tormentor. Yet, he was her best friend's lover. She didn't know what emotion to deal with first, her anger at Paul for the anguish and fear he had put her through, or the sympathy she felt for Frank and the pain of betrayal she knew he was dealing with.

CHAPTER 76:

Once again, and hopefully for the last time, they dealt with the police. By the time the authorities arrived, the last of Paul's resistance and efforts at denial were gone.

'It looks like it's finally over,' Simm said in a low voice to Charlie.

Charlie agreed, but was too flabbergasted to speak. The words tumbled out of Paul's mouth at a speed too fast for her to absorb. She suspected it would be days before it all sank in.

But she didn't seem to be the only one having trouble understanding. Simm and the police officer interrupted Paul several times to try to get him back on track. He spent most of his time apologizing to both Charlie and an almost catatonic Frank, and most of what he said didn't make sense.

It was decided Paul would be taken to police headquarters where his story would be recorded, documented, and legitimized. Then, hopefully, they would have a coherent explanation.

After Paul was removed from the apartment with a last look of apology at Frank, they sat motionless for several minutes. It was when Harley squirmed and whimpered that they were drawn back to the present.

Frank was the first to speak.

'I don't believe it. I don't know what to say, Charlie.'

'You don't have to say anything. It's not your fault,' she reassured him.

'But it is. He got the information through me. I told him about everything that was happening. The code...even the code for the alarm...he had to get it through me. He's gone with me a few times. He must have seen me enter it into the panel.'

He put his head in his hands and groaned. Charlie moved to sit beside him on the couch and put her arm across his back.

'Frank, you had no way of knowing. And, I know you didn't do anything intentionally.'

'He was using me.'

Charlie looked at Simm. What could she say? It certainly looked like Paul used her friendship with Frank to get to her, but was it the case? Had he fallen in love with Frank before discovering the connection to Charlie? Simm shrugged his shoulders noncommittally.

'He loved you. I could tell,' she said, hoping to give him reassurance.

'How could he do this? You're my friend. He knew that. He should never have hurt you.'

'I don't know. I don't understand what it's all about, but we will soon.'

Frank looked at her.

'You're very calm. I thought you'd be looking for blood,' he said.

'So did I. I think, right now, I'm dealing with the shock of it all. Maybe I'll look for blood another day. I'd rather have answers at this point.'

Simm stood.

'We'll get our answers tomorrow.'

'Will you be all right?' Charlie asked Frank.

Despite his nod of assent, she was worried about him.

'I'll see you tomorrow. We'll get through this,' she added, squeezing Frank's shoulder.

When they stepped outside, Charlie was surprised to see the sun shining brightly. She looked at her watch.

'What time is it? Five-thirty? Oh my God.'

'That's why I suggested we leave. The cops want us to be at the station around ten, so we should get some sleep beforehand.'

In the car, Harley didn't display his usual enthusiasm for the ride. Instead, he curled up on Charlie's lap, the same position he had held all the while they had been in Frank's apartment.

'Poor Harley. I'm sorry you had to relive the trauma with that man,'

Charlie said, scratching him behind his ears. He looked up at her soulfully, accepting her sympathies. 'But you're the hero today. You solved the case.'

'He did,' Simm conceded shaking his head. 'Who knew I'd be upstaged by a pug.'

'Don't feel too bad about it. He upstages everyone.'

Chapter 77:

Ten o'clock came too soon, especially since Charlie had a lot of trouble falling asleep in the first place. But she was at the police station with Simm at the appointed time. They were shown into a room where they were joined by an equally tired-looking Detective Ranfort.

Armed with coffee and doughnuts, they prepared to watch the videotaped recording of Paul's statement. He was much more coherent, and guided by the detective, he explained the motives behind his actions.

Charlie listened in fascination as Paul explained he was also a product of Ireland and the machinations of Aidan Connelly and Jim O'Reilly. The difference between him and Charlie was that his parents had shared the information with him when he turned eighteen years of age. They felt he deserved to know he was adopted. They also, rightly or wrongly, thought he should know he had been adopted outside of the legal system, and perhaps had even been stolen from his birth parents.

This led him to an obsession about his origins.

'I had to know. I desperately wanted to know who my birth parents were. My adopted parents only knew so much. They gave me the names of Jim and Aidan. At the time of my adoption they had asked where I came from, but no one would tell them, so the rest was all speculation.'

'Where did the connection with Charlene Butler come in?' asked the detective.

'I tracked down Jim O'Reilly. Unfortunately, he was dead, but I did my research. I knew about him leaving the bar to Charlie. I knew about his friendship with Pat Butler. And, when I found out Charlie was an only child, I started to wonder about her. I had been working with different websites for a few years. I knew where to look, and the more I looked the more I began to think she had been brought over from Ireland too.'

'Why would that make you target her?'

'My parents borrowed a lot of money to give to O'Reilly and Connelly so they could adopt me. We lived just slightly above the poverty line all my life. Yet, Charlie lived the good life. O'Reilly even left her a business, debt-free. It wasn't fair. Why should she have all the luck?'

Charlie glanced at Simm to see if he found this as strange as she did. Paul blamed her for being adopted by the Butlers?

'I started to think maybe if I poked the fire a little, I could get her to do the work for me,' Paul continued. 'And I was right. She hired that PI guy, and they went to Ireland. Then they talked about a journal, and I knew I had hit pay dirt.'

'You sent her anonymous letters, you damaged her apartment, you kidnapped her dog,' the detective said, counting off on his fingers. 'You broke and entered Mr. Simmons' apartment, and you vandalized the bar. You committed a lot of crimes in order to find your birth parents.'

'Nobody was ever hurt. I had to know. I needed to know my roots. Maybe if I found my birth parents my life would be better.'

Charlie felt sorry for the parents who had loved and raised this man. He didn't seem the least bit grateful for everything they had sacrificed for him.

'Why didn't you hire your own private investigator?' the detective asked.

'I can't afford it. She can. Look, I know it was wrong, but I needed to know, and I was sure if I planted the seed, she would do something about it. It worked. She found the journal. Now all she has to do is give me what I want. It's in there.'

Charlie was dumbfounded. He truly didn't get it. He had harassed her and endangered her life. The trip to Dublin hadn't been a barrel of monkeys. She still had nightmares about the abduction and had to sleep with a light on. Now, he expected her to give him everything he wanted, smile, and watch him walk away.

'It's not that simple, Paul. You've been arrested on a series of charges. You're going to jail. As for the information you're looking for, Ms. Butler would be quite within her rights not to give it to you, and I wouldn't blame her a bit for not wanting to share.'

'She'll do it for Frank's sake.'

'I don't think you're Frank's favorite person right now, so I wouldn't count on it.'

Charlie felt a shaft of pain for Frank. She could only imagine how he felt at this point. Thank God he wasn't here to listen to everything this clueless, self-centered person had to say.

'I've seen enough,' she said. She had to get away and try to come to terms with what had happened, and listening to Paul wasn't making her feel any better. Yes, she was thankful he was caught, and she knew the letters and harassment would come to a stop, but the bad memories and the pain would linger for her and Frank. All because of the journal and the information it contained. She looked at Simm.

'I think you were right. The names in that journal don't really matter. As a matter of fact, they're poisonous. It brought about all this,' she said, waving her hand in the direction of the television. 'I wish it had never existed.'

'You can't wish away something from the past. All you can do is put it aside and move on.'

Looking at the pain and understanding in his eyes, she knew he was not only talking about her situation.

Chapter 78:

Simm stared at his phone with his eyebrows drawn close together. It buzzed loudly, and Charlie wondered if he would answer or not.

He pushed the button, stood, and turned his back to her, walking to the other side of his living room.

'Hello.'

Several seconds of silence followed his greeting. Charlie saw the stiffening of his shoulders and she had a sense of foreboding. What could it possibly be now? Paul had pleaded guilty to all the charges and was sitting in a jail at the moment. The case was closed, the pub was back in order, and for all intents and purposes, her life was supposed be ordinary again. She was now in the process of packing up the few belongings she had at Simm's apartment to take back to her own home.

'I'll be there.'

Simm concentrated on the floor when he turned around, slowly pocketing his cell phone.

'Who was that?' Charlie said, surprised to find she held her breath as she asked the question.

'Uh...'

'Oh no, you don't. Don't even think of avoiding the question. I want the truth. What's going on?'

Charlie knew it was bad news and she wanted him to pull off the band-aid quickly.

'It was Sullivan.'

'Marty Sullivan?' Oh no.

'He wants to meet me.'

'You or us?'

He lifted his eyes to hers, and she had her answer.

'When do we go?'

'We have an hour to get there.'

A short argument followed as Simm tried to convince Charlie to stay behind and let him go alone. Simm lost that argument.

'He specifically asked for me to come with you. What would be the point in you going alone? He'll turn you away and tell you to go back and get me.'

'I can convince him you weren't available.'

'Let's go and finish this.'

Ten minutes later they were in the car, heading to the Port of Montreal and Marty Sullivan's favorite haunt.

It may have been the same two men who met them outside the door, or it could have been two other copies. It seemed Marty liked to employ the same generic tough-guy look. After the search for weapons, they were led into the private room occupied by their boss.

Charlie pasted on a smile and tried to make the atmosphere genial, but Marty wasn't having it. His expression was cold and stony. He nodded to the chairs at the table in front of him, and they got the message. They both sat stiffly and waited to hear the reason for the summons.

'How was your trip to Ireland?' Sullivan directed the harshly-spoken question to Simm.

'It was interesting. Very informative.'

'Did you find Connelly?'

'We did. He wasn't very helpful.'

Charlie saw a glimpse of a sardonic smile before it disappeared.

'I don't suppose he was. I have a feeling you met other people besides Connelly.'

'A few, yes.'

'I heard you got chummy with McGrath.'

'Chummy isn't a word I would use.'

Charlie jumped as Sullivan's fist shot out and hit the table with a resounding bang.

'Don't bullshit me. What the hell is your game?'

'How did you find out?' Simm asked.

'This is the twenty-first century. We don't have to wait for the boat to cross the ocean to get news from the other side. I know a lot of people on both sides.'

'We had a run-in with McGrath. We were both abducted and separated. I didn't know if Charlie was safe or not. He needed a promise that we would leave an embryo on your doorstep. I had to make him think it had been done.'

Charlie noticed how Simm had taken the blame for making the promise that she had, in fact, made. Simm reached into his pocket and took out an envelope that he tossed onto the table in front of them. Sullivan withdrew an identical copy of the fake newspaper article that had been sent to Colin McGrath. He read it attentively.

'Clever.'

Simm remained silent. It was hard to tell if he offered a compliment or sarcasm.

'But you forgot something. My honor demands I respond in kind.'

'This is what we were hoping to avoid, a war between the two of you,' Simm explained.

'There's always been bad feelings between us. We're forever at war.'

'We don't want anything to happen to you or your son.'

For several tense moments, Simm and Sullivan stared at each other. Charlie held her breath. She hoped Sullivan didn't take those words as a threat. Her gaze shifted quickly from one to the other, trying to evaluate Simm's expression and Sullivan's reaction.

'Neither do I.' Marty said, looking openly at Charlie. 'I assume you discovered everything you needed to know in Dublin.'

'Yes, we know everything. The person who was harassing me has been arrested. He was one of the children and he was very...misguided.' She didn't want to tell him they had also found a journal in Montreal. It had caused enough problems already.

Sullivan leaned back in his chair and joined his hands across his stomach.

'It's a very touchy situation, you understand. Some of those babies weren't removed from their homes legally. We wouldn't want people coming forward asking for their children back, would we?"

Charlie hadn't thought of that possibility, but it was a valid concern.

'Mr. Sullivan?' she asked. 'Do you know about my particular circumstances? I mean, do you know who my biological parents were?'

He stared at her for a long moment.

'No, I don't. All I know is that your mother desperately wanted a daughter, and your father asked Jim to help them. But your father had misgivings about the process. Jim said he carried a lot of guilt.'

Charlie thought about her mother's remarks and understood a little better what probably drove them apart. Her father hadn't been about to cope with what he had done to provide a child for his wife.

'So, what do we do now?' Marty asked, directing his question to Simm. 'I don't feel like getting into an all-out war with McGrath either, but I can't let him think I let something like that go by unnoticed.'

'You can pretend you don't know who did it,' Charlie suggested.

'Colin would know that I know.'

'I have a suggestion,' Simm said.

Chapter 79:

Simm had a bit of time to kill before things picked up at the pub. The bookkeeping was up to date, something he didn't mind doing, and he had organized Charlie's filing system. He smiled as he recalled how appreciative she had been when he told her he would take care of all those things for her from now on.

He turned to the computer again, thinking he hadn't checked the new Facebook page since yesterday. Signing in, he was intrigued to see two notifications. Reading them, his smile grew larger.

'Gotcha.'

'Got who?'

Simm looked up to see Charlie sauntering into the room. He loved to see her new attitude, or rather her old attitude that had come back home. Gone was the stressed out, looking-over-her-shoulder Charlie. This one was relaxed and happy. She had come to terms with the fact that she was adopted. Although she wanted to return to Ireland someday, she wanted to do it as a tourist, not to find her birth parents. If they had given her up voluntarily, that was their choice. If she had been stolen from them, she didn't want to dig up bad memories, or stir up the judicial system. Her adoptive parents had loved her, had possibly been driven apart because of the circumstances of her adoption, but she didn't regret the life she had lived.

Of course, her acceptance of the circumstances of her birth wasn't the only reason for her smile.

Charlie sat on Simm's lap, wrapped her arm around his neck, and tugged him in for a very appealing kiss.

'Who did you get?' she asked again.

'What? Oh. McGrath took the bait.'

'He did?' Charlie sat up straight and pinned her gaze on the computer. 'What did he say?'

Simm pulled up the comments posted on the page.

'He claims everything on the page is bullshit, and that it should be taken down by the authorities.'

'That's from someone named Donovan, not McGrath,' Charlie said.

'He's using a false identity, but I know it's him. He and Connelly are the only ones who have anything to lose.'

'You're sure they can't trace this page back to you?'

'Positive. My friend is an expert with this type of thing.'

'You're a genius,' she said, giving him another kiss.

'I'm glad it solved the problem. As long as McGrath thinks we can expose Aidan Connelly for what he is, and McGrath along with him, he won't threaten Marty Sullivan again. And we stay in Marty's good books.'

Simm was proud of his idea. Creating a Facebook page by the name of The Children of Ireland was his brainchild. The profile picture was a photo of a man with an eerie resemblance to Aidan Connelly, walking along a foggy street. Simm had enlisted the help of a computer geek friend to set it up. They had also posted false stories about children looking for their birth parents, using names and places only McGrath and Connelly would understand. Simm suspected the mafia member in Ireland was keeping the page a secret from Connelly, because the postings made it look like McGrath could be the instigator. He would let it play out for a while before taking the page down.

'I just had a chat with Frank,' Charlie said.

Simm directed his attention to her. He knew this was her last big worry.

'How's he doing?'

'Better. He's still hurting, and he has a lot of questions he'd like answers to, but I think I convinced him some questions are better left unanswered. He's happy we won't be pressing charges against Paul.'

'You're more generous than I would have been in your shoes.'

'Paul experienced the same beginnings as I did, but his growing-up years were not as fortunate. I can't forgive him, but I think I can understand. Besides, I want to do it for Frank. He may not want a future with Paul, but he doesn't want to think of him as being incarcerated.'

'Is he considering your other idea?' Simm asked, smiling.

'Yes, very seriously. I'm sure he'll go for it.'

'He's hesitating because he'll be separated from you.'

'We'll be separated physically, but regularly in touch. Besides, I know he'll love managing his own place, and you'll be running between the two.'

Simm looked forward to the partnership between the three of them, and the imminent purchase of another bar. Charlie would run Butler's, and Frank would take care of the new one. Simm would be available for whatever was needed at both of them, on top of taking care of all the paperwork.

He had also reconciled with his siblings, and accepted enough of his inheritance, the inheritance he thought had been withdrawn from the will, to finance the purchase of the new establishment. His days as a private investigator would soon come to an end, and his new life as the co-owner of a pair of Montreal Irish pubs would begin.

The last step in his plan was to marry his partner – the female one.

View other Black Rose Writing titles at <u>www.blackrosewriting.com/books</u> and use promo code **PRINT** to receive a **20% discount** when purchasing.

BLACK ROSE
writing™

CPSIA information can be obtained
at www.ICGtesting.com
Printed in the USA
FSHW04n2132100418
46530FS